CONFESS

Nicholas Rhea

Constable · London

First published in Great Britain 1997
by Constable & Company Ltd
3 The Lanchesters, 162 Fulham Palace Road
London W6 9ER
Copyright © 1997 by Peter N. Walker
The right of Peter N. Walker to be
identified as the author of this work
has been asserted by him in accordance
with the Copyright, Designs and Patents Act 1988
ISBN 0 09 477600 8
Set in Palatino 10 pt by
Pure Tech India Limited, Pondicherry
Printed and bound in Great Britain
by Hartnolls Ltd, Bodmin

A CIP catalogue record for this book
is available from the British Library

1

With a crackle of its exhaust, the bright red sports car raced past Detective Superintendent Pemberton's more leisurely Vauxhall. The action of overtaking seemed to produce a brief and louder reverberation, a throaty roar which sounded alien to this quiet road. It could have been a substitute for a two-fingered V sign, a display of contempt by the young against the mature, because the sports car surged past the Vauxhall as if the latter was moving at snail's pace.

Momentarily, Pemberton wondered if the lone driver was trying to impress Lorraine who was sitting in the rear seat of the Vauxhall but he was not tempted to compete. He was not going to challenge the youngster and he was content to watch the car pull away, the thick red hair of the driver vigorously rumpled in the quickening turbulence around his cockpit. It was a young man playing a young man's game as the gallant little vehicle, aged but lively, bounced and bounded ahead upon the country road.

On this stretch the carriageway was straight, bordered by neatly trimmed hawthorn hedges and wide verges now rich with the summer growth of meadow flowers. Behind them on either side were open fields with not a house in sight, but Mark Pemberton knew that a very sharp right-hand corner lay just ahead, announced only by a small roadside 'bend' sign and a couple of reflector posts.

There, the geography altered. A stream, running in a deep gulley, flowed beside the carriageway before abandoning its route beside the twists and turns of the road and meandering through the fields to join a distant river. The stream's path through the meadows was marked by a straggling line of heavily leafed alders and willows, but at this corner it flowed beneath a row of tall, sturdy oaks rooted at its far side, and the road swung sharp right beneath their overhanging branches. Pemberton knew the corner well; everyone had to slow down to safely negotiate such an acute right-hander.

Then the brake lights of the sports car showed red. The red-headed young man was braking yet the car continued to hurtle forward without any perceptible reduction of its speed. He'd never negotiate that bend. The driver seemed to be struggling with the controls. He should have slowed down long before now; at this late stage, he'd have to brake mightily and with great skill if he was to safely drive his speeding car around that corner.

Mark Pemberton, cruising at a steady forty-five miles an hour, found his heart pounding at the sight of the onward rushing sports car. An accident seemed inevitable – the overtaker must have been touching eighty when he'd passed Pemberton and now he was fighting for control of the vehicle.

'Look at him!' Pemberton called to the priest at his side. 'If I was on duty and in uniform, I'd have him for speeding! He'll never take that corner . . .'

'Typical of young people nowadays.' Father Flynn's strong Irish accent had a hint of music about it. 'Always rushing, never enjoying what's there to be seen around them. But if I had an old car as fit as that one I might be tempted –'

'He's going to crash!' cried Lorraine from the rear, as if reading Pemberton's mind.

What happened next appeared to be occurring in slow motion. The open-topped car roared ahead as if there was no corner. It sped across the verge and literally took off across the ditch. Upon leaving the road, its long bonnet collided head-on with the immovable trunk of an oak at the far side. There was a sickening thud accompanied by the rending of metal and the crashing of glass and then the car, with its driver slumped over the steering wheel and its engine ominously silent, sank towards the earth. It all seemed to be happening so slowly, like a film. For a moment, everything became very still and Pemberton continued to drive as if he was in a dream. As he approached the scene, he saw that immediately beneath the falling car was the open ditch – it was about ten feet deep and six feet wide with steep banks.

The wrecked car sank bonnet-first into the depths while its rear wheels, or perhaps the underside of the boot, settled on top of the near bank. As the bonnet disappeared, the car came to rest at a steep angle with its battered nose in the water and its rear end protruding above ground level.

Then they saw a cloud of something – steam or even smoke. Almost imperceptibly at first, it started to rise from the depths of the ditch. There was no indication of the driver's fate. From their position of approach, he was out of sight in the ditch but only seconds later, having driven as close as possible, Pemberton halted to assess the accident. He took one look, saw the driver strapped into his seat, made a rapid appraisal of the situation and its dangers, then snapped, 'Use my car phone, Father, it's between the seats. Call an ambulance, and the police. Tell them a doctor's needed, it's urgent. Lorraine, come with me.'

As the priest, a large and gentle man in his mid-fifties, began to punch out 999, Pemberton and Lorraine, trained police officers both, leapt from their car and raced to the hissing vintage MG Roadster. From the rim of the ditch, they could see the driver crumpled over the grossly distorted steering wheel and dashboard with his head among the shattered remains of the windscreen. His arms were dangling at each side of his inert body; he was like a rag doll which had been thrown into the wreckage of the fallen car. The impact must have been horrendous. The engine continued to produce ominous hissing noises; there was a smell of petrol, a leak somewhere, and it was all made more threatening by the steam or smoke which continued to issue from the engine cavity, emanating from somewhere beyond his sight. The vehicle had come to rest at an impossibly steep angle, its engine compartment shattered, its ignition system alive and shorting to cast rogue sparks, while its loose contents were strewn about the head and back of the man. Some of his belongings had been thrown out due to the impact and were floating in the shallow water or lying on the mud beside the stream. A black briefcase was amongst them and, somewhat incongruously, Pemberton noticed a heavy road atlas in the outer edge of the shallows of the stream.

'Let's get him out,' Pemberton snapped at Lorraine. 'Seat belt first . . .'

Working as a skilled and professional team, they leapt into the ditch, feet sinking into the water up to their calves as Pemberton released the seat belt. His first instinct had been to leave the man alone – with the injuries he had undoubtedly suffered, it would be best if he was not moved without skilled medical attention – and yet, mindful of the dangers from the car itself, there was no choice. The thing could burst into flames at any moment, so the man must be freed immediately; he'd have to be hoisted upwards from his seat. Carefully, Pemberton climbed on to the vehicle. It shifted beneath his weight but settled with him aboard. He had to do this to gain the leverage necessary to lift the unconscious driver. Standing behind and above him with his feet braced against the dashboard, Mark Pemberton put his hands beneath the armpits of the casualty as Lorraine managed to haul open the tiny door. The car began to rock with their movements.

'I hope it doesn't slide sideways and tipple over . . .' Pemberton muttered.

As he lifted the man free of the seat, Lorraine turned the casualty's legs to the right, towards the exterior of the car. Pemberton managed to rest the man's bulk momentarily on the side of the vehicle.

When he was supported in that position by Lorraine, Mark leapt back into the stream and then controlled the descent of the bloodstained man until he lay across his shoulder in the fireman's lift position. By this stage, the smell of petrol had intensified while the hissing continued. Petrol from the elevated tank was being thrust out of a fractured pipe; it was squirting out under the pressure. Fire was the real and imminent danger; Pemberton must not relax. With the casualty over his right shoulder, chest, head and arms dangling down his back, the detective clasped his right arm around the back of the man's knees. With his load securely aboard, Pemberton now hurried along the bed of the stream in water up to his calves seeking a place to clamber out. Lorraine, having found a route to the top of the bank, indicated the spot and Mark Pemberton aimed for it.

Meanwhile, Father Flynn had contacted the emergency services and was running along the top of the ditch, hands reaching out to help Pemberton clamber to the level of the road with his inert burden. He struggled out of the ditch some thirty yards from the wrecked sports car. Moments later, it made a whooshing sound; within seconds it was encased in flames and smothered with black smoke which rose into the air in a thick cloud. Meanwhile, other cars had halted behind Pemberton's and people were asking if they could help. There was noise and chatter now, the silence of those awful first moments had been broken as the rescue operation continued.

'I'll put him down here,' Pemberton said with relief, panting beneath the weight of the rescued man. Lowering himself to his knees, he gently allowed the man to be eased from his shoulders by the priest and Lorraine. Now free from danger, they laid him carefully on the grass verge, face upwards, and endeavoured to make him as comfortable as possible. They could see that his face was smashed and bloody, one arm appeared to be lying at an awkward angle, there was blood oozing from his chest, lots of it . . . his chest was a mess. A terrible mess. Pemberton also worried about the casualty's neck, mindful of the impact against the steering wheel. Where his broken body had rested against Mark's shoulders and back, the immaculate summer shirt and light trousers were soaked in rich red blood. Arterial blood.

'You told the emergency services where to come, Father?' asked Pemberton.

'I did, Mr Pemberton, sure I did.'

'He's breathing, thank God,' Mark whispered to Lorraine. 'I couldn't give him respiration of any kind, not with those injuries to his face and chest . . . I think his chest's caved in, his rib cage is smashed by the look of it.'

He shouldn't have been moved, Pemberton told himself yet again, but there had been no alternative. God knows what his heart and lungs must be like, or his spine, neck bones, internal organs.

'If we touch his chest,' he said to Lorraine, 'we could do terrible damage but we need to stem the blood, it's from an artery, or arteries . . .'

In the surrounding noise and commotion, Pemberton spoke so that the injured man would not hear his words or learn of his concern. You never told a casualty how serious their injuries were – you had to reassure them, make them believe they were going to survive and that they were being cared for by knowledgeable and attentive people. That was elementary first aid. But Mark Pemberton had seen this sort of injury before. The man was in a desperate state, and he needed urgent medical care. As Lorraine attended to the growing number of watchers and would-be helpers, trying to keep traffic moving and urging a small group of spectators to keep off the road and away from the casualty, Mark and the priest remained with him. Mark was trying to decide the best way to treat this man, wondering what he could do now to prevent his death or prolong his life until expert help was available.

He had to stem the flow of blood, that was vital. He knelt at the man's side to examine him at close range, the priest doing likewise at the opposite side. The expression on Pemberton's face revealed everything to the priest. Mark recalled a motor-cycle accident where the casualty had suffered similar appalling injuries – he had died soon afterwards in spite of intensive roadside care. First aid could not cope with such appalling damage to human bodies.

'We'd better not touch him, it's a hospital job.' Mark examined the man's mouth to make sure his tongue had not moved to obstruct the rear of his throat.

'His eyes flickered,' breathed the priest, continuing to squat at the man's side opposite Mark. 'He's alive, thank God.'

Then the young man opened his eyes. They looked bright against the bloodied skin of his face and the rich red colour of his hair, but for a few seconds did not appear to be focused upon any particular thing or person. Then they fixed not upon Pemberton but upon the dog collar of the priest. For a fleeting moment, a frown appeared on the injured man's brow and then his frightened eyes moved to look the priest in the eye. He had recognised the helper as a Catholic priest, he knew that beyond all doubt and it seemed to give him some relief. A smile appeared on his face and then there followed a long moment of silence before the casualty, apparently oblivious to Pemberton's presence, gasped, 'Father, I'm going to die . . . I know I am.' Then he blurted, 'Father, I committed murder . . . I haven't been to confession since then . . . God forgive me . . . she didn't deserve that . . .'

The man's words became fainter as the priest leaned nearer and then his eyes again closed as the confession dwindled into a mere whisper. Having heard the reference to murder, Pemberton automatically leaned closer to catch anything which might follow but he failed to distinguish anything further. The man was talking quickly and quietly, speaking at some length as the priest leaned very close to his face, hoping it would help him hear the man's urgent whispered outpourings. In spite of Pemberton's detective instincts and in spite of the reference to murder, his own good manners told him he should not eavesdrop.

10

He moved away because this was a dying man's confession, a moment of total honesty in the last seconds of his life, a vital link between him and a priest, the easing of a terrible burden as he went to meet his God. But in spite of his reservations, Pemberton could not ignore the fact that he had overheard a wholly voluntary admission of murder. For any detective, that was wonderful, a freely made statement of the finest kind, a firm and free admission of guilt. But to which murder was the red-haired man referring?

As Pemberton remained at his side, he ceased to whisper to the priest who then uttered the words of absolution as he made the sign of the cross. Then the youngster's battered head turned to one side as his tortured body visibly relaxed. It looked as if he had suddenly fallen asleep. While his little car burned like an inferno in the ditch, the man's life came to a quick and peaceful end. Quite suddenly, it was all over. With blue light flashing and siren sounding, an ambulance arrived and Lorraine guided the driver towards the casualty.

'He's gone,' said the priest. 'May the Lord have mercy on his soul.'

2

Because an ambulance should not be used to convey a dead body from the scene of a traffic accident, Pemberton produced his warrant card and told the driver, 'He's still alive, he needs a hospital immediately. Urgent.'

The driver did not argue with the bloodstained detective. Within a few moments, the mortal remains of the red-haired driver were being placed in the ambulance for a speedy journey to the hospital. He'd be declared DOA – dead on arrival – but it was a practical ploy to effect the removal of the body. As the ambulance sped smoothly away, a uniformed traffic constable approached Pemberton. He was one of a double-crewed patrol car.

'You witnessed the accident, I believe? The priest suggested I talk to you.' Clearly, he did not recognise the detective superintendent. An added factor was that Pemberton, considered the smartest man in the force and known for his immaculate appearance and polished image, was now covered in blood, his trouser legs were soaked in dirty muddy water, his shoes were caked with wet mud while his neat, beautifully cut fair hair was awry above his mud-stained features.

'Yes,' Pemberton said. 'Myself and my passengers, we saw what happened.'

'I'll need statements.'

'Now?'

'It helps if I can get them straight away,' said the constable. 'In my car?'

'Has the fire brigade been called?' Pemberton asked.

'No point,' responded the constable, a sturdy no-nonsense man in his forties. 'The car's burnt itself out, it's just smouldering now. There's not much left and no danger to the undergrowth, trees or hedges.'

'There was no body in the boot, was there?' Pemberton asked. 'It's hardly big enough to take an adult. A child perhaps?'

'Body? No, there was just the usual stuff – tool kit, tow rope, spare wheel, all burnt to cinders. Why do you ask if there might be a body?'

'I'll tell you in a moment, but it's important that I have that car preserved,' Pemberton told him. 'I want it exactly as it is now. And everything that's with it, including the charred contents of the boot and the items that were thrown out. I need to keep the man's clothing and all his personal belongings too, and anything he might have at his home, wherever that is. You can check the owner's name through its registration plates, the rear one's not been destroyed. That driver might not be the owner, of course.'

'And who might you be, sir, to want that sort of thing? Not a relation?'

'No, I'm Detective Superintendent Mark Pemberton, stationed at Rainesbury Divisional Headquarters,' and he produced his warrant card once again.

'Sorry, sir, I didn't recognise you. I'm Traffic Constable Broadbent. I've just been transferred to Rainesbury, only two days ago. I'm very much the new boy!'

'Well, you've got a nasty fatal to start your duties with us!

12

Now, my lady passenger is Detective Constable Lorraine Cashmore from my station, and my other passenger is Father Patrick Flynn, of Our Lady and St Hilda's Catholic Church, also in Rainesbury. We've been to a lecture by Father Flynn. At Ernedale Village Hall. We were following that car when it crashed, in fact, it overtook us at speed. There were brake lights as it went into that corner but it didn't seem to slow down . . .'

'A case of possible brake failure, sir? Or physical problems for the driver? Steering fault or even a tyre blow-out? There's lots of possibilities. We'll check the entire vehicle as you know – or what remains of it – so perhaps a verbal account now, and then I can call tomorrow for your written statements?'

'No, we'll do it now. But I must insist that everything's preserved, car, clothing, the lot. It's very important. I'll supervise the removal of the car. And I will need a sample of blood and saliva from the deceased. For DNA testing. You'll be attending the post-mortem?'

'Yes, sir, but that's unusual, sir, isn't it? For a traffic accident? Even if he was thought to be over the limit. It's a bit early for him to have been to the pub although he might have had a private tipple somewhere.'

'It's more than a traffic accident and I have no idea whether he's been drinking alcohol, or if he's over the limit. But the point is, PC Broadbent, that seconds before he died, he confessed to committing murder. For that reason, I need to know who he is and who he killed.'

'Murder, sir? Good God!'

'An unusual fatal for you, eh?' smiled Pemberton. 'But if I can match him to a victim, it'll clear up one major crime in somebody's files.'

'You know him, sir?'

'No, sorry, I don't. That's our next task – to get him identified as soon as possible. Can you radio Control and get them to put the registration number through the PNC? We'll have a name in seconds, and then I can get him identified and start to have his movements traced. Those are my problems – yours is to get the fatal RTA sorted out. You'd better keep in touch with me about your progress, we'll have to liaise on this one, PC Broadbent. I'll have to tell the coroner about the unusual background but not a word about that murder to the press. You'd better inform your senior officers, though. Ask them to contact me if there's any problems with your side of things.'

'I'll radio for the computer check now, sir, if you'd like to follow me to my car.'

It took but a few seconds for the Police National Computer to process the registration number of the wrecked MG: the vehicle's keeper was recorded as James Bowman Browning of Flat I, Highfield House, Hepworth Road, Bleagill, Harlow Spa, North Yorkshire.

The car, J registered, dated from 1971. Pemberton made a note in his private pocket diary and said, 'You'll be tracing relatives and arranging the formal identification? Before we start releasing names and jumping to conclusions, we must be sure that Browning is the man who's in our mortuary.'

'I understand, sir. I'll make the necessary checks. Now, I'll radio for a breakdown truck and my partner will measure the scene and ensure that the necessary photographs are taken.'

'Good, and you'll make sure the car is securely kept until my teams have examined it?' Pemberton instructed him. 'Now, while I'm waiting to supervise the breakdown vehicle's work, I'll take a closer look at the scene of the accident and the driver's briefcase and other belongings, then I'll make my statement. Meanwhile, you can talk to DC Cashmore and Father Flynn, they were witnesses too.'

A smartly dressed man carrying a small black bag approached them. 'Hello, I'm Dr Vernon. They said there was an accident.'

'Yes, the casualty's gone in the ambulance,' Broadbent told him. 'Perhaps if you rushed to the casualty department of Rainesbury District Hospital?'

As they drove from the deserted scene much later, Pemberton said to Father Flynn, 'I'll need to talk to you, Father, about James Browning's confession.'

'Mr Pemberton, with all due respect, there is nothing I can tell you. I am bound by the seal of confession. I cannot reveal anything that was told to me.'

'But I heard it too – well, to be honest, I heard part of it. It was the part where he said he had committed murder. He referred to someone, presumably the victim, as "she" – I heard that bit.'

'I do not know how your rules of evidence operate, Mr Pemberton, or anything about your responsibilities as a policeman, but I do know that I cannot reveal anything that I hear during confession, even if the person making the confession dies later. The seriousness of the crime is not relevant. I can say nothing, absolutely nothing. I'm sorry.'

'I may be able to give, in evidence, the few words which I heard, Father. Hearsay evidence is generally not allowed in criminal proceedings but in this case it might be accepted as a dying declaration. In this case we have a confession freely made by a guilty person at the moment of death and in the full knowledge that he was going to die. A statement of that kind does carry enormous weight. Few people would lie in such circumstances. And a coroner could accept my evidence to that effect, even if a criminal court refused.'

'There will not be a court case, Mark, he's dead,' Lorraine chipped in. 'The alleged murderer, I mean.'

'I know, but I intend to investigate this as if the guilty person was alive. I have to if I'm to establish his guilt. It could be an old crime he was talking about, on the other hand Browning might have killed his victim only minutes before he crashed. Maybe she's lying dead not far away at this very moment. Maybe she's in his flat, or at her own home. Or perhaps he only *thought* he'd killed someone. That can happen. His victim might still be alive for all we know, and in need of urgent medical aid. I've instructed PC Broadbent to have a uniformed constable search Browning's flat immediately, by breaking in if necessary. I hope he doesn't find a murder victim! I had a look in Browning's briefcase; he's in PR and it seems he'd been to see a client, a man. I'll have that checked, it'll help us trace his last movements. There's every chance we could have a murder to investigate before the night's out. You can understand why I need all the help I can get, Father!'

'Sure I understand, Mr Pemberton, but I'm afraid I cannot help you.'

'Suppose I issued a subpoena? Suppose I – or the coroner – ordered you to attend court and give evidence about the words, all the words, you heard Browning say? You'd have to obey. You are not above the law, Father.'

'I obey the laws of my country and the law of God, Mr Pemberton, and if there is a conflict, then the law of God must come first.

I would come to court but I could not and would not repeat what was said to me during confession. If I was sent to prison for contempt of court, then I should have to go to prison. I would have no alternative. To give you an idea of the inviolability of the seal of confession, if a man confessed to me that he had poisoned the communion wine which I was about to administer to myself and others at Mass, I could not withdraw the wine. I would have to trust in God as I drank it, and as I gave it to the communicants.'

'You can't be serious!'

'I give you those circumstances as an extreme example. It might help you understand why I cannot reveal to you or to anyone else what that motorist told me.'

'So if a man came to you in confession and said he'd poisoned the entire water supply to a major city, you could not alert the authorities?'

'No, I could not. But in those circumstances, any priest would attempt to persuade the poisoner to reveal his actions and warn the public. That same goes for the man who poisons the communion wine. He could – and should – warn the people but I, as his confessor, could not.'

'I don't wish to discredit your faith, Father, but surely, you'd be condoning multiple murders! Thousands might die! But I have no time for deep discussions and besides, all that is hypothetical – we're talking about a real case. You must understand that I am obliged to pursue the information which I overheard.'

'I can understand that you are bound to do your duty, Superintendent, but Mr Browning is now beyond human justice.'

'Maybe so but there is a victim to consider, and a victim's friends and family . . .'

'If you had not overheard that confession, Mr Pemberton, you would not have been faced with this problem. I ask you not to disclose what you overheard.'

'I am not bound by your restrictions. The public will never be told and I hope none of Mr Browning's family need to know about it, but I can't ignore it! I cannot pretend that I didn't hear a man admit murder!'

A heavy silence followed as they continued their drive home and after a few minutes, Lorraine asked, 'Mark, what are we going to do about this? We've no recent undetected murders on our books, we have no victim, no dead body, no scene of crime, no name for a deceased, nothing. You *could* ignore what you heard.'

'No I couldn't! If we don't find a victim on our patch, there's always the Muriel Brown case.' This was the force's only un-solved murder – an old crime, a rape and murder which had oc-curred about sixteen years ago. 'We can see if that's the one he was talking about. It would be wonderful to bring that to a satis-factory conclusion.'

'That was years ago, Mark, there's no hope of tracing the killer now. Besides, Browning is too young to have committed the Muriel Brown murder!'

'That remains to be seen. Kids in their teens are quite capable of rape and murder, but so far as your first point is concerned, there's always hope of solving murders, Lorraine. We've just witnessed an example of that!'

She smiled in acknowledgement of his argument, as he went on, 'So tomorrow – if there's no reported murder in the mean-time – we unearth all the files on Muriel Brown, but in any case, I want to find out all I can about tonight's accident victim. He's got to be investigated, Lorraine.'

They continued in a further silence, each with their own thoughts, and half an hour later, Mark eased his car to a halt outside the Presbytery. He waited for Father Flynn to leave the car.

'Thanks for the lift, Mr Pemberton. I do appreciate your kind-ness. It was, well, different from getting the bus home.'

'We did enjoy your lecture, Father,' Pemberton smiled. 'I learned more about the dissolution of the abbeys than I had pre-viously known throughout my life. It was a welcome break from police work and lectures on criminal law, I can assure you.'

'Mark and I are keen to learn more about our district,' Lorraine told him. 'We're anxious to have something to occupy us with interesting places to visit in our off-duty moments.'

'Goodnight, both of you, and God bless,' smiled the priest, closing the car door and waving his gratitude as he strode to-wards his home.

'I can't really believe a priest would let a maniac poison a whole town just because the seal of confession prevented him speaking about it . . .' commented Mark as he accelerated away.

'Forget it, Mark. We're supposed to be off duty and relaxing, not worrying about unsolved murders or problems of the confessional.'

'But –'

'Look at it another way, Mark. Browning might have already been prosecuted for murder, even as a juvenile. He might have served a period of detention or imprisonment for his crime, or even for manslaughter. He might have been in a secure hospital for killing someone; he might have done all that, and yet never confessed his crimes to a priest. Now, because he was dying, he wanted to unburden himself, to clean the slate, as it were. People do that. Perhaps we have no need to search for a victim? Perhaps that confession marked the end of Browning's worries?'

'But we'll never know unless I make enquiries,' Pemberton countered. 'If he has been convicted, his name will be on record. If that is the case, the matter can be concluded very swiftly.'

'You're too much of a policeman, Mark Pemberton. But get me home as soon as you can, and I'll make you a nice nightcap before I tuck you in.'

'After I've checked with Control Room to see if any murder victims have been found . . .'

Overnight, there had been no reported murders, no hit-and-run traffic accidents and no one reported missing, but Mark Pemberton had no intention of forgetting or ignoring that confession. As he settled into his office the following morning, Wednesday, his telephone rang. It was PC Broadbent from Traffic Division.

'Sir,' he said. 'The accident last night. As you know, the registered keeper of the car is a James Bowman Browning. The deceased had a driver's licence and other documents upon him, in that name. We're fairly sure it's one and the same person. Next, the duty inspector at Harlow Spa sent a constable to search the flat, but it was deserted. No corpses, no flat-mates, no relations. We got a spare key from the landlord, a man called Brooke, he lives above. We've sealed the flat, pending your inspection, sir. Enquiries from the landlord also suggest Browning is the deceased – he was described as about thirty years old, average build with distinctive red hair. He lived alone. And he had a red open-top sports car. We found some addresses in his flat, friends we think, and relations. I've had a quick look but maybe closer

18

examination is needed by your officers. His father's address was there, he lives in Staffordshire. We're trying to contact him this morning, sir, to ask him to come and make a positive identification. We'll ask him to notify his other relatives and be responsible for the funeral arrangements. We learned that young Browning's place of work is a public relations company called Greenwood's. It's in Harlow Spa, he was an account executive. I've told his boss about the accident, by the way, but obviously didn't refer to the murder aspects.'

'Thanks, PC Broadbent. At least we have a starting point even if we have no corpse. Now, where is the car? Can my teams have access to it?'

'It's in the Road Traffic garage, sir, here at Rainesbury DHQ. Sealed. I made sure all those bits and pieces which were thrown out on impact were retained with the remains of the car. Most of the stuff left inside was charred almost beyond recognition – no bodies though! I did a second check on that. His briefcase is there, it's intact. It was thrown out in the crash. You'll want to see it?'

'Yes, I will. I'll have a closer look for myself, then get Scenes of Crime to give everything a thorough going-over. Thanks for your help so far. Have the car's brakes been examined? And steering?'

'We thought we'd do that when your teams have finished, sir, we don't want to contaminate any evidence.'

'Good thinking. Right, thanks for that. I'll start digging into the life and times of James Bowman Browning.'

After explaining the events of last night to the sergeant in charge of the Scenes of Crime unit, he asked him to inspect the remains of the car as if it had been involved in a case of murder, then he buzzed for Lorraine. She entered his office moments later. Tall, slim, beautiful and not yet thirty-five, she was the finest detective on his section. She smiled as she settled on the chair beside his desk, showing a length of slender leg below the hem of her skirt.

'Sir?' She was formal now. At work, theirs was a boss and subordinate relationship. Pemberton gave Lorraine the name and address of James Bowman Browning, letting her know the result of the preliminary search of the flat, and said, 'Just so that no one's in any doubt of my intentions, Lorraine, I'm not going to

19

ignore the information which came my way last night. I can't. In fact, I mustn't. So, first, let's begin with the Muriel Brown file. We've no one working on the case at the moment but most of the data has been transferred to the computer, I believe.'

'It has.' She did not smile at him. Her case load was heavy and she had enough to do without worrying about an ancient murder case.

'Good. Run Browning's name through the index along with that red car of his and see if he entered the frame at all. If he's not in the frame for killing Muriel Brown, we'll look elsewhere.'

'But where, sir? Where can we start – we've nothing to go on.'

'We've a life of Browning to start us off,' he said. 'If he did commit murder, there's almost sure to be a report of a body being found somewhere, with some police force having an unsolved murder on their books. We can run a check on all outstanding murders of women in all UK police areas. I can't see that that would present any difficulties. Computers will throw up the data in no time.'

'Then let's hope his victim *was* Muriel Brown!' She sighed, smiled and left him.

When she'd gone, Pemberton rang Detective Inspector David Holroyd, the man in charge of Harlow Spa CID. After explaining last night's events, he asked if one of Holroyd's officers would undertake a little localised research into the background of James Bowman Browning, whose address he provided. What he needed were names of contacts, friends, colleagues at his place of work – in fact, anything about him would be welcome. Pemberton said he'd arrange his own CRO check to see whether Browning had a criminal record.

Holroyd promised he would oblige with the local angles, then asked, 'Sir, do you want me to search his flat or is it something you'd rather do?'

'I did arrange a preliminary search last night just to establish whether he'd left a corpse on the premises, but he hadn't. I am assured the place was deserted but yes, I would like to inspect it myself. You could come with me, just in case something does develop. It's on your patch after all. Meanwhile, it's been sealed, uniformed branch has the key, they got one from the landlord. If I decide to come this afternoon, would you be available?'

'Sure, no problem,' said Holroyd. 'Give me a call. And in the meantime, I'll begin some discreet enquiries about your James Bowman Browning.'

Feeling he had made a very positive start, Pemberton glanced at his morning post, buzzed for his secretary and began his morning's routine. Among the circulars received from other police forces was one about the Sandal Strangler series of murders. It was a reminder from Leicestershire police; their Detective Inspector Kirkdale was the co-ordinator for the long-running investigation. To date, ten prostitutes had been savagely raped and murdered in different parts of the country. All had been strangled, all had had their footwear – invariably sandals – removed. Furthermore, every murder had been committed very close to midsummer's day – 24th June – and the killer had struck every year since the first death in 1987.

As midsummer's day this year was approaching, all forces had been sent this reminder that somewhere within the next few days, a Sandal Strangler killing was likely to occur, and every police force was exhorted to put its officers on maximum alert for a possible suspect. Even at this stage, with ten deaths so far, no suspect had emerged. Pemberton read the circular, initialled it to indicate he had seen it, and then asked his secretary to arrange its circulation to all interested departments. Having despatched her with her pile of work, Pemberton thought how gratifying it would be if he could solve the Muriel Brown case before he retired. The force would then have a one hundred per cent detection record for murder, and Browning might be just the fellow to complete the file.

But, as he considered the logistics of that old case, he had to take into account that James Browning had been about thirty. It was true that his precise age had not been confirmed, but thirty was a fair estimate. Maybe a fraction less. Twenty-eight? Then he had to remember that Muriel Brown had been raped and murdered in her car on the moors some sixteen years ago. Give or take a year or two, Browning would have been fourteen or thereabouts, even as young as twelve. On the other hand, he could have been older. Fifteen perhaps? Fifteen-year-olds could commit rape, they could murder and they could set fire to motor cars, but had the very young Browning done all that? It was time to call his local Criminal Records Office.

'Run a CRO check on a James Bowman Browning, will you?' he

asked the girl who answered, giving her Browning's address and an approximate age. 'Local records first, then national. In particular, I want to know if he has a conviction for murder or any other form of violence.'

'Yes, Mr Pemberton,' she responded. 'Do you want me to run a check on variations of the name? He might have used his middle name as an alias. James Bowman? Or James as a surname. Bowman James. Lots do that.'

'Yes, good idea, give it the full works!'

Having set in motion the official procedures, Mark Pemberton decided to send a fax to every police force in Britain, asking for details of unsolved murders which had resulted in the death of women during the past fifteen years, adding that he already had the up-to-date details of the Sandal Strangler's crimes. There was no need to repeat those.

He called his secretary again and dictated the text; once he was happy with the wording, she would despatch it to the various CID headquarters around the country. Meanwhile he would await Lorraine's preliminary examination of the Muriel Brown file, and pop over to Traffic Division for a closer look at the burnt-out shell of the MG and the contents of James Browning's briefcase.

3

The blistered and burnt shell of the MG Roadster stood upon the concrete floor of the Road Traffic Division garage. A large tarpaulin had been spread beneath it and objects had been arranged around its outer edges. In the main, they were parts which had separated from the car during its recovery – lengths of chrome, a windscreen wiper, front number plate, headlamp rims and other bits and pieces of metal and glass. There were also some items which had been thrown out during the fatal impact.

Without touching any of them, Pemberton noted the road atlas he'd observed in the stream, a torch, some sweets, a mobile telephone, a small folding umbrella, some coins kept for parking meters, dusters, ballpoint pens bearing Greenwood's tree-shaped logo, a parking disc, a paperback book listing restaurants and hotels, and an MG owner's handbook.

Browning's briefcase was also on the tarpaulin with its lid open. Pemberton flicked through the contents. There were some PR leaflets produced by Greenwood's of Harlow Spa and a file which apparently related to Browning's meeting last night. It had been at Halton, a suburb of Rainesbury, and the client had been a Mr Joseph Phillips, the sales manager of Pomataste, the soft drinks manufacturer. There was a diary too; it contained Browning's business engagements and notes, along with some personal reminders of birthdays – his father's was shown there on 13th July, an uncle's on 16th May, while that of a friend called Hugh was on 24th June.

Virtually all the rubber, leather and plastic ware of the vehicle had been destroyed; some rusted wires were all that remained of the tyres while most of the metalwork was now rusted and blackened with the heat of the flames, the beautiful chromework ruined. The boot lid was standing open to reveal its contents – the remains of some tools, the spare wheel minus its tyre, a partially melted length of tow rope and what looked like a miniature fire extinguisher. Little had survived; the canvas hood and windscreen had gone altogether. The former car, such a beauty, was now a burnt-out wreck.

Pemberton did not know whether Scenes of Crime had concluded their examination and decided not to ferret among the relics yet. There was time for that – perhaps he'd need to re-examine the pieces in considerable detail when further information about Browning's murder victim came to light.

With the impression of the car in his mind, he returned to his office where searches in the various registries had produced no criminal record for James Bowman Browning, James Bowman or any other combination of his names. He did not appear in any of the 'Wanted' or 'Suspected' lists on the Police National Computer, nor had he been convicted of any crime. He was not even listed as having committed any serious motoring offences. Nonetheless, Pemberton made sure that PC Broadbent would take fingerprints from Browning's dead hands for eventual comparison with all the existing records, with due emphasis upon all unsolved murders and other serious crimes where identifiable prints had been found at the scene.

He also arranged for Browning's clothes to be collected and forensically examined for evidence of a killing. Along with a sample for DNA analysis, these steps would help enormously. Having set in motion these routines, Pemberton decided to visit Browning's flat. He could usefully do this while matters were moderately quiet, and so he rang Detective Inspector David Holroyd and agreed to meet him after lunch, suggesting two o'clock that afternoon at Harlow Spa police station.

Pemberton arrived on time. Holroyd was a sturdy man in his late thirties; thick, almost auburn hair with handsome curls graced his head with no sign of balding and he wore the clothes of a countryman – brown-shaded tweed jacket, cavalry twill trousers and brogue shoes. A native of West Yorkshire, he'd been in the police service since leaving school, and was known as a thorough and diligent detective, hence his rapid promotion.

He was universally liked, even by his subordinates, and was regarded as a good manager. As the two detectives drove to the flat in Holroyd's car, Holroyd explained that Browning had never come to the notice of the local police. This meant he was unable to provide any kind of character reference for the man and at this early stage had no details of his background. His officers were doing some discreet work on that, however. Pemberton told him that PC Broadbent of Rainesbury Traffic Department was tracing and contacting relatives and they might be able to assist. When the two senior detectives arrived at the flat, they saw it was on the ground floor of a detached Victorian house in Hepworth Road, Bleagill, once a village in its own right, but now a pleasant suburb of Harlow Spa.

Holroyd told Pemberton he'd spoken to the uniformed officer who had visited the flat last night and had obtained the key from him. The officer had left Browning's address book in the flat after copying out information about contacts and relatives, and had disturbed things as little as possible. Smiling, Holroyd inserted the key, eased open the door and said, 'It's all yours, sir.'

'You can help me search, David!' Pemberton told him. 'I need evidence of his involvement in a murder either recent or not so recent. As you know, we haven't found a corpse yet, but there could be something else – newspaper cuttings, maybe, names of women, address books, porn videos or books, regular contacts, evidence of odd interests, peculiar souvenirs like bits of hair or underwear, strange hobbies or weird pastimes, you know the sort of thing. Even a weapon – gun, knife, rope – or some means of disguise. Anything, really. The snag is we won't know what we're looking for until we find it.'

'I'll start in the bedroom,' Holroyd said.

'And I'll begin with the lounge.'

After two concentrated hours of searching, their endeavours revealed that Browning was a remarkably tidy man who kept his well-furnished flat in immaculate condition. Much of his furniture was antique or second-hand, but polished and well cared for. With one double bedroom and one single, plus a bathroom, lounge and kitchen, it was a typical bachelor's home, functional and tidy, but lacking a woman's touch. There were no flowers for example, no pretty curtains or floral wallpaper in the bedrooms.

Nonetheless, the crockery had been washed, dried and stored, the bed was made, all the surfaces had been dusted and the floors were clean. The kitchen was functional and tidy too, with a well-stocked fridge and deep freeze (without a body hidden therein). It was impossible to determine, from merely looking at the flat, whether or not he had ever entertained a woman friend although it did seem he used the double bed, albeit alone. Certainly, the bathroom did not contain any evidence of female presence – there was one toothbrush but no scented soaps, bath essences, body lotions, perfumes or powder. A man's bathroom.

Their visit confirmed that he worked as an account manager for Greenwood's, that he had a father living in Staffordshire, that his mother had died suddenly just over five years ago, that he was an only child and that his rent was up to date. They found his personal file, giving his date of birth and showing he was thirty-one years old; from the ages of eighteen to twenty-one, he had attended Swangate College of Media Studies in County Durham but had not attended university. The file contained certificates and a diploma, and a family snapshot on the back of which was written 'Mum, Dad and me, 1982'.

Another file contained a list of several local charities along with telephone numbers and the names of personal contacts. It seemed that Browning had worked for the charities in his spare time to raise funds and provide active and practical help. Apart from his MG Roadster, about which they found nothing among his belongings, his charity work appeared to be his only outside interest. Judging from some letters of appreciation, it was clear he'd been involved in very useful and welcome work.

There were no photographs of girlfriends, however, and no indication of any other interest or hobby. Pemberton found it strange that the flat did not contain anything relating to the MG: no registration document or MOT certificate, no photograph of Browning with his car, no papers or notices about forthcoming rallies or vintage car club membership. If he was an enthusiast, those were the sort of things Pemberton would have expected him to have.

Browning kept all his other personal and professional papers in a system of neat file jackets stored in a two-drawer filing cabinet in the spare bedroom, a wonderful aid to the detectives. But skilled as they were at locating concealed items, neither Pemberton nor Holroyd found anything remotely connected with a murder investigation nor did they find anything to suggest that Browning lived a seedy, criminal or secret life. There was nothing to indicate he was a homosexual other than the lack of photographs or other indications of a girlfriend. The clothes in his wardrobe and drawers were clean and neatly ordered; all the pockets were searched without revealing anything useful to the detectives.

'I'm coming to the conclusion he must have committed his murder just before he crashed,' mused Pemberton. 'There's absolutely nothing here to suggest he's a killer. Maybe it was a spontaneous killing? If so, there's a body awaiting discovery somewhere out there.'

'I agree there's nothing remotely suspicious among his belongings. He's as clean as the proverbial whistle.'

Pemberton pondered the lack of MG material, 'There's nothing of real interest at all. He seems to have lived a very quiet, ordinary and rather mundane life. Lonely, even. I wonder if he had another flat or house somewhere? A double life, in other words.'

'That's possible. Have we any idea where he'd been last night?'

'He'd been to see a business client, I'm having that confirmed at Greenwood's,' Pemberton said. 'I'd imagine a PR executive would operate across a wide area with considerable freedom so we might have difficulty tracing all his movements.'

'Sir, is all this really necessary?' Holroyd asked suddenly.

'There is absolutely nothing to suggest this man is a criminal, let alone a murderer.'

'I believe we must follow it through, David,' Pemberton said quietly. 'Remember he *did* confess to murder. And consider what we've just learned – there's nothing to indicate he killed anyone a long time ago and that makes me believe his crime is recent. It might even have contributed to his crash, a lack of concentration while brooding over what he'd done, perhaps. That's feasible if the murder was totally out of character . . .'

'You've no evidence of that either, sir.'

'No, but it might explain the car crash and his ready confession the moment he saw the priest.'

'Suicide, you mean?'

'No, I don't think so. I saw the brake lights come on. But I do wonder if his concentration was not one hundred per cent as he tore into that corner. If he had killed someone, even accidentally, I can imagine it would adversely affect his driving, it would be far from normal. You must agree it's a thought, David.'

'Yes, I'll go along with that. I can even imagine a sensitive person considering himself a murderer if the death he'd caused was accidental, say a fatal traffic accident. Such a person could let the guilt get to him. It happens to car drivers and train drivers who are innocently involved in fatalities. But in spite of all this conjecture, there's not much we can do unless a body turns up, is there?' Holroyd smiled.

'True. And there isn't one yet. Now for another question. How did his mother die, do we know that?'

'The obituary in that cutting from the local paper didn't say – it said she died suddenly, aged forty-five. Did he kill her? Is that what you're thinking?'

'We do need to know how she died, don't we,' said Pemberton. 'It might have some bearing on his confession. And I'd like Scenes of Crime to give this flat a going-over before the relatives arrive. They might find things we've missed such as cleared-up blood or semen stains, visitors' fingerprints perhaps. Other evidence.'

'I'll attend to that, it's on my patch,' said Holroyd. 'Shall I trace the people in his address book or are you going to do that, sir?'

'Leave that with me,' said Pemberton. 'It'll help me trace his recent movements. We mustn't overlook the possibility that he might have killed someone miles away from our force boundaries.'

'We're checking other force areas, are we?'

'We are. I've asked all UK police forces for lists of unsolved murders of women within the last fifteen years – other than the Sandal Strangler killings. They're the work of a serial killer – our man admitted just one. But a list of victims will be a starting point. Now, I think a chat with his landlord is called for.'

The landlord, a retired seaman called Samuel Brooke, said that James Browning was an ideal tenant. He had been in the ground-floor flat for about five years and Brooke had no criticism of him. Browning always paid his rent on time, he kept the place tidy and clean and never gave cause for complaint, such as playing loud music or having noisy parties. Brooke had never seen people visiting Browning and confirmed that his tenant led a very quiet and secluded life. There was no garage with the flat, Brooke explained upon being asked by Pemberton, but there was a hard-standing beside the building which all the tenants, including Browning, used for their cars. Everything that Browning rented could be reached from inside his flat – two bedrooms, a bathroom and toilet, kitchen and lounge. Brooke could add very little about his quiet tenant and expressed genuine sorrow at his death; Pemberton told Mr Brooke that his father was being contacted, adding that in due course he would be asked to take responsibility for the flat and its contents. The detectives left, Holroyd taking the key and deciding to leave the flat sealed until Scenes of Crime had conducted their more scientific examination.

While Pemberton was examining the flat near Harlow Spa, the investigation into last night's accident was proceeding in a normal manner. The post-mortem on Browning's body had been arranged for 2 p.m. and the coroner had been informed. The photographs taken at the scene of the fatality were being developed, sketch-plans were being compiled, an officer from Staffordshire police had located the father of the deceased to break the dreadful news of his son's death, and the little red MG Roadster, having been examined by Detective Superintendent Pemberton and the local Scenes of Crime officers, was next subjected to vehicular tests which concentrated upon its brakes and steering, its tyres having been destroyed in the blaze.

From enquiries at Greenwood's, it had been confirmed that Browning was visiting a client, Mr Joseph Phillips, at Halton shortly before the accident; in turn, Mr Phillips had confirmed that Browning had been with him at his office from 7 p.m. until shortly after 8 p.m. during which time he had behaved quite normally. The timing of his meeting and the route back to Harlow Spa coincided with the known facts of the accident. Browning had left his own office at 5.45 p.m. for the drive to Halton.

Lorraine Cashmore, meanwhile, was ploughing through the accumulated data of the Muriel Brown murder, first checking those portions which had been entered into the computer, and then examining the file index cards of the original enquiry, scanning records which had not yet been computerised. She sought anything that might point to the involvement of James Bowman Browning. But all her careful searches produced nothing to link him with the murder of Muriel Brown. Lorraine felt she had done a thorough job, her effort being very conscientious because Pemberton was relying upon her.

By the time Pemberton returned at 5 p.m., several new factors had been established. The post-mortem showed Browning had died from severe internal and head injuries, plus shock, consistent with being the driver of a car which had suffered a head-on impact at high speed. He had been fit and healthy, and there was no medical reason for him to have lost control. He had not suffered any kind of attack while driving and there was no evidence of an excess of alcohol, although further tests of his stomach contents would be necessary to confirm that.

Examination of the car, even in its severely charred condition, suggested that failure of the front brakes was the likely cause. There was a weak point in the couplings of the pipes at the front; it was known that these could chafe through and a sudden exertion upon the brakes could cause a burst – and that car had not been fitted with a dual braking system. Traffic experts said that they were satisfied he had crashed for that reason – a sudden and violent application of the brakes had probably produced the failure. The steering was in good condition for a car of that age and none of the tyres had suffered a blow-out. Examination of the wheel rims had confirmed that. Instead of trying to turn the corner, it was suggested Browning had panicked at the last moment due to his loss of control and while struggling to activate the non-existent brakes. This analysis helped to discount suicide as the reason for his death.

There was nothing to indicate the car had struck another vehicle or collided with a pedestrian before the accident, further proof that Browning had not killed anyone with his MG.

Mr Browning senior had rung to confirm he was leaving Stone in Staffordshire very early tomorrow morning for the drive to Rainesbury. He would come to the police station's Traffic Division offices, and he would stay in an hotel in Rainesbury rather than at his son's flat near Harlow Spa. Mr Browning – Frederick Joseph – added that he would inform the other relatives and close friends of his son's tragic death.

As Pemberton scanned the various notes, memoranda and reports, there was a knock on his door. 'Come,' he called.

It was Lorraine.

'Come in and sit down,' he smiled. She always made him want to smile. 'I won't be a minute.'

He signed some of the letters which had been left by his secretary and then said, 'Well, what have you to report, Detective Constable Cashmore?'

She raised her eyebrows at his fake formality, and said, 'I've had a really boring day ploughing through really boring old records, it's going-home time and I could do with cheering up!'

'Then let's eat out, shall we?'

'I thought you'd never ask!'

Lovers, partners at home and at work, they left the office together, she a tall, slender woman in her early thirties and he, at just over six feet in height, a taller man in his forties. He was renowned for his smartness and was now at peace with himself following the early death of his wife. Lorraine and Mark had a pact – they would never discuss work while they were off duty – and so, during the fifteen-minute drive home, Pemberton updated her on everything that had happened so far as Browning was concerned.

'So you're going to forget it, are you?' she challenged him before they reached their home.

'I am not!' he stressed. 'Once I'm satisfied there's no local murder which could have been committed by Browning, I shall

30

delve into the information I receive from other forces. If he did commit murder, Lorraine, we'll clear up somebody's crime for them – it'll be another detection recorded.'

'We're home, Mark,' she said, implying that he should stop talking about his work. 'Bags I the bath first!'

'I might jump in with you!' he grinned, parking the car.

'I wouldn't complain.' She kissed him on the cheek as she climbed from his Vauxhall.

Afterwards, they drove to a moorland inn which was popular with hikers and ramblers where they ate a snack from the bar while sitting outside in the warm evening sunshine. Pemberton was relaxed in smart but very casual clothes while Lorraine sported shorts and a sleeveless top. As they enjoyed their meal with a single glass of wine each, they were happy enough not to talk unnecessarily. They savoured the expansive views of the dale spread below them, the quiet of the evening with the sun setting on the moors and above all, their own company. After their meal, they went for a short walk through the heather, not yet in bloom. In August, this would become an immense sea of rich purple flowers, a stunning sight.

'That was really nice, Mark.' In the car after their stroll, she leaned over and kissed him on the cheek as they prepared for home.

It was the middle of summer and not yet nine thirty so darkness had not yet enveloped the moors, but the setting sun was casting long shadows across the undulating landscape.

'I was just thinking, out there with the moorland breeze touching my cheeks, that I could be very happy as a retired man,' he said. 'Just imagine having the time to do this sort of thing whenever we wanted, without the cares of office . . .'

'It's up to you,' she said. 'You're approaching your twenty-five years' service. You could soon retire . . .'

'I'm far too young to even think of retiring.' He fastened his seat belt and started the engine. 'Men – people – of my age shouldn't retire, they'd stagnate!'

'You don't retire, Mark, you leave the police service with a small pension and use that to finance whatever you want to do with the rest of your life. You'd find some interesting part-time work, you could become a consultant or take up watercolour painting or study wildlife. There's plenty of ways of making life interesting and even earning enough to top up a police pension!'

'Don't forget I'll not get my pension immediately, they keep it in cold storage until I'm fifty-five. But in any case, I think I'd miss the excitement, the uncertainty of police work.' He engaged first gear and began to move out of the car-park. 'Even retirement can become boring, like an everlasting holiday.'

'It doesn't have to be boring,' she countered. 'A happy retirement is what you make it and, let's face it, people who retire before they are fifty should seek some kind of active interest.'

'I do enjoy my work,' he said. 'I can't think of anything else I'd rather do. Being a private detective, snooping on adulterers and unearthing moles who sell industrial secrets, doesn't have the same appeal as solving a complicated murder or fraud case.'

'Well,' she said, 'one day you're going to have to make up your mind. You can either spend your days worrying about crime statistics and pressures from chief constables, or you can enjoy outings like this.'

'Or I can do both!' he laughed. 'Like tonight!'

And then, as he gathered speed out of the car-park, his car phone rang. Lorraine looked at him, and he looked at her, each thinking they should ignore it.

'I hope it's not work,' he said. 'Not tonight.'

'Shall I leave it?' She rather hoped he would say yes.

'No, you must answer it. You never know what it might be. Family wanting help . . .'

Lorraine lifted the handset and said, 'Pemberton.'

'Is Detective Superintendent Pemberton there?' asked a male voice.

'Who's calling?' she asked before giving an answer.

'It's Force Control Room. It's important.'

'I'll put him on,' she said as Pemberton brought the car to a standstill on the wide, sheep-shorn verge.

'Pemberton.' He picked up the receiver, a look of anxiety on his face.

'Control Room, sir, duty inspector speaking. I'm sorry to have to call you when you are off duty. I tried your home number, sir, and thought I'd try the car phone . . .'

'I'm on the moors, Inspector, above Rossetdale. What's the problem?'

'We've a report of a body, sir, a woman. Found by a man walking his dog. She's in a ruined building beside the River Raine,

32

quite off the beaten track, sir, just outside Crayton village. A beat man has been to carry out a preliminary investigation and confirms it's a suspicious death. Strangulation, by all accounts. I've called out Scenes of Crime, the scene has been secured, sir. I thought you should be told.'

'Of course. Any CID attending?'

'Detective Sergeant Linton from Rainesbury is on duty, sir, he's *en route* to the scene now.'

'Good. Tell him I will rendezvous with him there. Have you a map reference?'

The inspector provided the necessary reference and Pemberton said, 'I'll leave immediately. I should be there in three-quarters of an hour. I'll provide you with a sit. rep. once I have examined the scene.'

'Very good, sir.'

'Work?' asked Lorraine, who had not heard both sides of the conversation.

'A body,' Pemberton told her. 'A woman's body, near the river at Crayton, not far from Rainesbury. Found in suspicious circumstances, apparently strangled. I wonder if our deceased Mr Browning had anything to do with this?'

4

The young woman's body lay in the sparse ruins of a derelict mill which occupied a wooded corner overlooking the River Raine. Once a busy place producing flour by the power of the flowing water, it now lacked its ancient mill wheel and was roofless and windowless. It was little more than a haphazard pattern of broken stone walls, a secret venue for lovers and vandals and a refuge for wild creatures. Birds nested in the ivy, owls sought their prey among the ruins and bats slept their days away in crevices among the stones.

Pemberton, after identifying himself to the uniformed constable on duty, entered through a gap in the wall which had once contained a door. Teams of officers were waiting nearby, Detective Sergeant Linton having decided not to proceed until the boss had viewed the scene and the body. Pemberton saw the dead woman was lying on her side on the earthen floor in a corner of the ruin, almost as if she was asleep, except that her face was grossly swollen and highly discoloured and there was a sturdy and knotted white nylon rope around her neck. There were some flies around. A few nettles and weeds partially obscured her remains but she seemed to be fully clothed. At first sight, her plum-coloured dress had apparently not been interfered with, although Pemberton saw that she did not wear any shoes.

His heart stopped. This was no ordinary murder: it bore all the familiar hallmarks of the Sandal Strangler. From where he stood, he could not see her footwear lying anywhere within the ruin. A detailed search would be necessary and he hoped the shoes would be found but had a gut feeling they would not be recovered here. After a few minutes' silent contemplation, absorbing the details of the scene, he went outside to talk to DS Linton.

'Thanks, Ray, you can start now. No shoes, eh?'

The import was not lost on Linton. He had read the circulars too. 'There's no sign of them near the body, sir. If what I fear is true, this will be number ten or eleven. I'll check with Records. She's been certified dead, by the way. Dr Fairbrother.'

'So the Sandal Strangler has paid us a visit,' muttered Pemberton with a feeling of near despair. 'How long's she been here? Any ideas?'

'Not long, judging by the appearance of the body. Two days at the most, I'd say. Fairbrother couldn't be more precise, he says the pathologist might provide a more accurate estimate.'

'Let's hope so. Has she been been raped like his other victims? Reports said he'd used excessive violence on the others.'

'We won't know until the pathologist has examined her,' said Linton. 'We haven't touched her but her clothing doesn't look disturbed.'

'He always leaves his victims as if they're sleeping, all very neat and tidy,' Pemberton reminded him. 'Any clues to her identity?'

'Not yet, her handbag isn't with the body.'

'Any girls reported missing locally?'

'None's been reported, but she's no child. She's in her mid-twenties, I reckon, sir, probably from the locality – local people,

34

kids especially, know this place. And, if the killer is the Sandal Strangler, she'll be a prostitute. He always kills prostitutes.'

'You're saying *she* brought her killer here? It's usually the killer who brings his victims to their deaths, not the other way around. Is that a hallmark of the Strangler?'

'Local courting couples know about the old mill – they often come here for a bit of nookie, it's tucked nicely out of sight, well off the beaten track. It's unlikely that a stranger would find it. It's not the sort of place a casual visitor would come across or take a girl into – unless the Strangler's a local too, which I doubt. Although no one has any idea of his identity, we've never had reason to think he lives on our patch.'

Pemberton, with James Browning in mind, wondered whether Harlow Spa could be considered 'local' even though it was thirty miles away. 'Could a car get this far into the wood? Are there other ways of approach to the mill?'

'No, sir. There's only that lane from Crayton, it terminates in a small parking area, and then there's a stile over the railings. The path comes into this wood.'

'The place where I parked?'

'Yes, sir. Access is by foot only from that point, there's no other route into this place. In its heyday, there was a track from Crayton Hall – that's in the opposite direction from here – but that route ceased to be used years ago when the Hall was sold. It's fenced off now, the old path is totally overgrown. You'd never get a pedal cycle through there, let alone a car. This is the only way into the mill, a rather neglected footpath through the woods. We could consider a search of the car-parking area for tyre marks but it's surfaced with tarmac as you know. It's doubtful if we could isolate tyre marks on that, it's a busy place and the weather's been dry for a week or so. But of course we'll search it for dropped or cast-away objects.'

'House-to-house enquiries might produce descriptions of any cars seen there in the last few days. Or we might learn about people seen walking in the woods or towards the mill. And what about fishermen? Do they use this stretch of the river?'

'No, sir, it's private water. The open fishing ends a mile downstream. I'm having enquiries made at the estate office to see if anyone's been given specific right of access to the woods or the river in recent days.'

35

'OK, Ray, you know your job but don't overlook the value of quizzing poachers and water bailiffs. So it's full steam ahead. Will you set up the incident room in Rainesbury police station?'

'No problem, sir. There's available space and it's convenient for this scene. I'll radio Control to get things moving.'

'Has the pathologist been called?'

'Yes, he's on his way.'

'Good, then I'll wait,' said Pemberton. He started to walk away from the mill with Linton at his side. 'I'll liaise with Lincolnshire police on this one. They've a collator working on these Sandal Strangler killings, I'll call him first thing in the morning. His name is Kirkdale, Detective Inspector Kirkdale.'

'It couldn't be a copy-cat killing, could it?' suggested Linton.

'I don't think so. The business about the missing sandals has never been given to the press or the public. Only the killer and the other teams know about that trade mark. It means this is no copy-cat murder, it's the real thing, Ray.'

Pemberton glanced at his watch. Ten thirty on a midsummer night and the light was fading fast. He decided that the scene should be thoroughly investigated as far as possible tonight, even by floodlight if that was possible. If not, the wooded surrounds could be sealed by uniformed officers until daylight. A more detailed search of the woodlands would be conducted tomorrow. Tonight's work would include examinations by the pathologist, forensic scientists and Scenes of Crime officers while the incident room could be assembled for commencement of its work at nine tomorrow morning. Heading across to Lorraine, who was chatting to the recently arrived force photographer, Pemberton explained his plans, saying he'd remain here until the pathologist had conducted his examination and Scenes of Crime had concluded their search of the immediate surrounds of the old building. Once the body had been removed, Pemberton could go home. Lorraine said she would wait with him.

Examination of the scene took longer than anticipated, chiefly due to the lack of vehicular access and the difficulty in carrying equipment to the site. Daylight was almost exhausted and floodlights would be difficult to install. In the meantime, Dr Martin Swain had arrived.

After briefly explaining the situation, Pemberton watched as the forensic pathologist carried out his preliminary work, studying the ligature and its knot, taking the body temperature, looking for external signs of injury, insect infestation and the other basic requirements. It was a careful examination and then he lifted her dress and underslip so that he could peer underneath.

'It's rape,' he called across to Pemberton. 'Vicious by all accounts, there's some blood, her underslip is stained, it's protected the dress. Underclothing absent. No knickers, stockings or tights. Footwear gone, as you can see. Rape and murder is my provisional prognosis, Superintendent Pemberton, but I'll confirm my findings when I've examined the body in laboratory conditions.'

'You know about the Sandal Strangler?' Pemberton asked.

'I do, we've had all the circulars. For the moment I can confirm that you have definitely got a murder to be going on with. She didn't tie that knot around her own throat. See her face? And I shall liaise with my colleagues about links with the other so-called Sandal Strangler deaths. My provisional diagnosis is that this is his handiwork.'

When Dr Swain had concluded his examination, Pemberton instructed Scenes of Crime and the official photographer to commence their work around the body.

'I'll carry out my detailed post-mortem first thing tomorrow,' said Swain.

'Don't tell the press about the absent shoes,' Pemberton reminded the pathologist. 'We don't want the public or copy-cat killers to know about the footwear fetish.'

'I'll refer all media enquiries to your press office,' Swain assured him. That remark reminded Pemberton to compile a brief news release before he went home. It would be issued by Control Room during the night-time press calls and would confirm that detectives were investigating the discovery of a woman's body near Crayton. It would say that the circumstances of her death were suspicious and would stress that the woman had not yet been identified. The accompanying description would say that she appeared to be less than thirty years of age; it would add that the detectives would appreciate the names of any young women who were missing from their usual haunts, particularly those who had not been seen within the last couple of days or so. That would be sufficient for the media at this stage – from that brief statement, they would know that a murder enquiry was under way and that news conferences would be arranged tomorrow.

On his way home, Pemberton called at his office in Rainesbury police station to collect the CID file on the Sandal Strangler. It contained memoranda which had been circulated to all police forces over the years. He left a note in the office to say he had taken the papers. Sitting at home with a glass of The Macallan, he quickly scanned the contents, reading out the salient points to Lorraine. He was breaking their rule about not taking work home but on this occasion she did not remind him of their pledge.

To date, ten murders in the so-called Sandal Strangler series had occurred at widely differing locations, all in rural settings and all the work of the same killer. If the Crayton girl was his victim, it would bring the total to eleven. The MO of the Crayton killing did have the hallmarks of the earlier murders. All the victims were women in their mid-twenties, all were white women, all were prostitutes and all had been raped with accompanying violence and then strangled with a length of white nylon rope. After death, all had been left in a tidy state after having their underwear removed and taken away, and all had lost their footwear. In every case, the victims had worn sandals which had disappeared, an odd factor. Another odd factor was that the killings had occurred at the rate of only one a year, very close to midsummer's day. Currently, nine police forces were investigating the ten killings, two of them having occurred within the Lincolnshire force boundaries, and the co-ordinator for all the enquiries was Detective Inspector Gregory Kirkdale of that force. As in previous years, circulars had been sent to all police forces in England, Wales and Scotland asking that if a murder occurred with the distinctive hallmarks of the so-called Sandal Strangler, then Kirkdale had to be informed.

'We might be able to provide him with the name of the killer, eh?' Pemberton smiled at Lorraine. 'That would be a real breakthrough.'

'Do you really think James Browning was the Sandal Strangler, Mark?'

'I have no idea, Lorraine, but we couldn't have a more positive suspect for elimination, could we? Even the timing is right.'

'I've got to admit that!'

'And so I want to see all the detailed files on the entire series of murders – to see if his name or description crops up in any of them. With that red hair of his, he's not easily overlooked.'

'Come on, you've done enough work for one day,' she said. 'It's bedtime. It's after midnight and you need a good night's sleep before tomorrow, it's going to be a busy day.'

He drained his malt whisky, carried his glass to the sink and said, 'Browning's flat was very tidy, you know. He's obviously a tidy-minded person. That girl's body had been tidily arranged.'

'You're persuading yourself he's guilty even before we've established a link between him and the girl – or any of the girls!' she said. 'You're not behaving like a senior detective, Mark, you're like a keen young recruit, believing his own imagined thoughts instead of establishing all the facts and then basing a reasoned decision on them.'

'Muriel Brown was raped as well,' he reminded her, drying his glass.

'But she wasn't a prostitute,' Lorraine pointed out. 'And her sandals weren't missing, were they?'

'I don't know,' Pemberton confessed. 'That's something else to check!'

'Yes, but not now!' Gently, she took his hand and led him to the bedroom. 'For the rest of tonight, I want you to forget all thoughts of rape, Mark Pemberton!'

Pemberton was in his office at seven thirty the following morning, Thursday, keen to activate and supervise the investigation into the Crayton murder. Lorraine had accompanied him and was working in the background, preparing for a long, busy day. Already, she had examined the Muriel Brown file and had found a photograph of the body wearing shoes. It seemed Muriel had not been the victim of the Sandal Strangler.

Meanwhile, the incident room was taking shape. The room they had commandeered – the conference room – was being equipped with filing cabinets, desks, computer terminals, telephones, blackboards, photocopiers and all the paraphernalia of a busy office. Detective Inspector Paul Larkin had been put in charge of the day-to-day running of the incident room and was already directing operations and setting up the complex reference system by which modern murders were often solved. Pemberton chose a momentary lull to take him to one side; they adjourned to Pemberton's office where Lorraine produced some welcome coffee.

'Paul,' Pemberton began, 'there's an added dimension to this enquiry, it's something the teams will have to be told when I address them this morning. You should know in advance.'

He then explained about Browning's fatal traffic accident and the moment-of-death confession he had made, suggesting that Larkin liaise with the Road Traffic Division and the CID at Harlow Spa to familiarise himself with the background of the case.

One point of contact would be Browning's father who was expected to arrive today to complete the formal identification of the body.

'He'll have to be interviewed but I'll do it, Paul,' Pemberton decided. 'It could be tricky because I don't want him to know about his son's confession. It's not fair that we should inflict that upon a mourning parent without further proof that it is true, but I can justify my involvement by saying we need background information for the inquest. I want him to throw some light on his son's behaviour, pals and movements.'

'And I'll need to trace Browning's movements over the last ten or eleven years!' sighed Larkin. 'That's not going to be easy. I wonder if we can tie them in with the other killings. Or is that DI Kirkdale's job?'

'Both, I'd say. We've all got to work together on this one, Paul, no demarcation lines! We need to pool our knowledge. I'm going to ring Kirkdale soon, when he's had time to get his chair warmed up!' Pemberton smiled. 'I'll establish who does what, bearing in mind his rather special role! I would hope his information is readily accessible. The first thing is to see if Browning's name or description, or even that of his car, features in any of the earlier cases. I'll acquaint DI Kirkdale with the material we've already gathered if you can concentrate on Browning's movements – remember, this is as much an elimination exercise as one to prove he's guilty. I don't want Browning declared the Sandal Strangler if he couldn't have done those crimes. That would set up a whole trail of false leads and get the real villain off the hook.'

'Browning seems a long shot, sir, as the Sandal Strangler.'

'Yes, but he did say his victim was female. Unfortunately, I didn't hear everything Browning said to the priest, but he did use the singular. It's important to remember that – he confessed to one murder, not a series. I do realise he might have confessed to the others on previous occasions – but I think that's unlikely.'

'We'll bear all the factors in mind, sir.'

At eight thirty, Pemberton rang Lincolnshire CID Headquarters and asked for Detective Inspector Kirkdale. Kirkdale was already in his office and listened intently.

'I'll come immediately, sir,' he said after Pemberton had outlined the case. 'Rainesbury police station, eh? I know the town, we went there for holidays as kids. Give me two hours.'

'You'll bring your files?' asked Pemberton.

'The lot, sir, some on disc. And some original statements and files on paper; this enquiry goes back a long time, remember. I've been chasing the Sandal Strangler for five years, others have worked longer, so if your Mr Browning is our man, I'll buy champagne for all your teams!'

'That could be a costly visit,' chuckled Pemberton. 'But I look forward to our meeting. I'll delay my first conference of detectives until your arrival – perhaps you'd address them?'

'That will be my pleasure, sir,' replied Detective Inspector Kirkdale.

5

One of Pemberton's earliest incoming telephone calls was from the Road Traffic Division. It was the duty inspector saying that Mr Browning senior had arrived from Staffordshire to formally identify the body of his son and that it was understood Detective Superintendent Pemberton wished to talk to him. Pemberton spoke to him on the phone and learned that Mr Browning would be in Rainesbury all today and possibly longer. He explained he would be making the necessary arrangements for his son's funeral, visiting the registrar of births, deaths and marriages, and carrying out various other sad but necessary tasks. Today, the inquest would be opened on his son for the purposes of identification only, Mr Browning senior having to formalise the identification. Pemberton therefore arranged to meet Mr Browning at 2 p.m. in the Road Traffic inspector's office.

Having secured that appointment, Pemberton turned again to Inspector Larkin. 'Have Scenes of Crime finished with the flat?' he asked.

'Not yet, sir, the Harlow Spa team is there now. They were there first thing, the early turn team, sir. They started at six with a brief to determine whether or not anyone has been killed or raped there. Any clothing in the flat will be taken away and examined too. They should be finished by two this afternoon.'

'Good, well done,' said Pemberton. 'And clothing he was wearing when he crashed?'

'The night duty team examined it overnight, sir, they found nothing to suggest he's a killer. No blood, semen stains, earth from the Crayton Mill area on his shoes. Nothing in fact, but Forensic may need to make a more scientific examination.'

'Keep them at it, Paul. Now, Mr Frederick Browning has enough chores to keep him occupied but when it's convenient – certainly before he leaves – I want him to take possession of his son's belongings and the contents of his flat. That means we must finish our work before Mr Browning goes home.'

'He'll be here until the funeral service so it shouldn't be a problem. Are you going to tell him his son's in the frame as a serial killer?'

'Would you?'

'It's a tough question but if James is in the frame for all those killings, we can hardly keep it from his old man.'

'And if he's innocent, he's got to be eliminated,' Pemberton said. 'It's best the old man doesn't know. I'd like to keep it from him, if only for humanitarian reasons. In the end, there may be no reason for him to know about his son's confession or our suspicions, but if it becomes necessary to break the news to him, then I shall have to do it.'

Larkin left Pemberton to his thoughts, then shortly before ten thirty Detective Inspector Kirkdale arrived from Lincoln. He was shown into Pemberton's office where two coffees and some biscuits materialised. Kirkdale was a cheerful man in his mid-forties with an infectious smile, an untidy mop of light brown hair and ruddy features; he was dressed in a Lovat green suit and a somewhat gaudy tie. He seemed relaxed in Pemberton's presence.

'You've made good time,' commented Pemberton.

'The Humber Bridge makes a huge difference when we drive north,' smiled Kirkdale. 'And traffic was light. So you want me to talk to your opening conference?'

'Yes please, Mr Kirkdale. Can I call you Gregory?' Kirkdale nodded his assent. 'First, let me tell you about our victim, and our prime suspect.'

Over coffee, Mark Pemberton provided Kirkdale with details about Browning's confession and the subsequent discovery of the dead woman, whereupon Kirkdale confirmed that the Crayton murder bore every indication of being the work of the so-called Sandal Strangler. While he went through the relevant facts from the known Sandal Strangler killings, Pemberton listened carefully, his chief endeavour being to determine whether or not Browning might have killed them all. Kirkdale concentrated upon the similarities. The Crayton murder matched in several respects, the most obvious of which was the removal of the victim's footwear, a killer's trade mark if ever there was one. In all cases, none had been recovered. So far as suspects were concerned, Kirkdale produced a long list of known sex offenders, rapists and released murderers whose crimes, in various parts of Britain, had had a sexual connotation. He added that none could be considered a prime suspect for any of the killings – many had been interviewed and eliminated. Several had not been in the right place at the relevant time – some had been in prison, for example, and others had equally tight alibis. Only those sex offenders who were living in the vicinity of each killing had been considered. The nation had too many perverts for all to be considered and interviewed. This lack of suspicion of any known offender had led Kirkdale to believe that the killer had no criminal record, that he was not known to the police in any of the British forces, and that he had never appeared on a list of suspects for any crime, let alone murder or rape. A classic serial killer but, in Kirkdale's opinion, one much cleverer than most.

'So you've no sightings of a suspect? No photofit impressions or artists' drawings from witness statements?'

'No one has seen him, Mr Pemberton,' said Kirkdale. 'That is our primary problem. We have no idea what he looks like, how old he is or anything about him. It's almost as if he's invisible, he merges into the background to such an extent that no one has noticed him. He has never left any clues at the scene – other than the victims themselves of course, and what he's left with them. The only possible exception is a man who was observed near the scene of the first murder but that was two days after the body was discovered. And it was ten years ago, remember. Nothing was found to link that man to the killing – he just happened to be walking past the scene some time later – and there are no reports of him being seen at any more of the scenes, either before or after the event.'

'You refer to the suspect in the masculine. Could it be a woman? Using an instrument to imitate rape?'

'No, there's always been a discharge of semen. We've retained samples which we can submit for DNA analysis if a suspect is traced. There's no doubt a man is involved, although he does assault his victims' vaginal areas after intercourse. One pathologist thought he kicked them, others haven't expressed an opinion about the weapon or weapons used.'

'And motor vehicles? Do you have any evidence of a motor vehicle being used? Browning owned a red MG Roadster, an old model, quite distinctive.'

'All the murders have been in fairly remote wooded areas, often with thick cover and popular with hikers and ramblers. Some were beyond the range of four-wheel vehicles or even motor bikes, so we are confident that he did not use a vehicle to take his victims to the scene, or to escape afterwards. We think he walked to the scene of each crime with his victim, then walked away afterwards before using a car or other transport to get completely away. We do not know if he drove, with or without his victim, to within walking distance of the murder scene or whether he used public transport. We can't ignore the possibility that he was taken there, even by taxi or by a friend, but when he did arrive and leave, he managed to blend into the background without being noticed. All I can say is that we've had no reports of cars being observed at the scenes, and I think something as distinctive as a vintage MG, especially a red one, would have been noticed. We have lists of car registration numbers in each file. As you know, we check all garages and petrol stations for details of cars seen in the area or known to have bought petrol or oil around the material times – lots of garages and filling stations keep registration numbers and credit card details. There are literally hundreds on file – maybe the red MG's among them? A search task for somebody, sir! What we do know is that the victims were all killed where they were found, that has been well established. In all cases, the finders of the bodies were people who went into those quiet places for recreation – anglers, bird-watchers, dog walkers, ramblers and so on. As you know, Mr Pemberton, the finder of the body becomes Suspect No. 1, but in this series of deaths they have all been eliminated – except the first. In what is generally regarded as the first of the Sandal Strangler killings, an anonymous telephone call tipped off the police that a body was in woodland at Penthorne near Swangate in County Durham. The caller was never traced; he'd rung from a kiosk in Penthorne. We've had no anonymous tip-offs since that one.'

'Where were the other killings?' Pemberton asked.

'The first was in County Durham, then one in Northumberland, one in the Lake District, two in Lincolnshire in successive years, hence my role, one in Derbyshire, one in North Wales, one in Gloucestershire, one in Oxfordshire and one in Leicestershire. All in remote wooded areas. And now North Yorkshire in another wood. Details of the scenes are in my files. Next year, who knows?'

'So ours could be the last, or could it? It looks like someone with a roving job, eh? Salesman? Freelance worker of some kind? Lorry or bus driver? Someone with great freedom of movement – and available transport.'

'He's covered a lot of ground, he's certainly very mobile,' Kirkdale agreed.

'Is there a pattern to the killings? I know they all occurred during the summer, June in fact,' Pemberton commented.

'On or around midsummer day,' said Kirkdale. 'It happens when the girls are in their summer clothes, wearing sandals. It's always been a girl who's worn sandals, there's been witnesses in every case to confirm they were wearing sandals before they died. It's the business about sandals which is so odd. Not shoes or trainers, always sandals. In all cases, their sandals have been removed and taken away. Why, for God's sake? Has the killer kept them? If so, why? And where? That's what puzzles me, puzzles us all in fact.'

'You've had an offender profile drawn up, have you?'

'We have. The belief, based on the type of person who would commit murder of this kind, is that our killer is male, young – thirtyish perhaps – a loner, a vehicle driver or owner, very tidy and careful, and unimpressive in appearance because no one seems to have noticed him. He's in employment where he is efficient and dedicated, where his private life is kept totally separate from his work routine. We think he's someone who dislikes, hates or is even terrified of prostitutes, someone who has this odd sandal fetish, someone who uses post-intercourse violence against his victims – and someone who has used the same type of white nylon rope on every occasion. We think each length has been cut from the same piece of rope – the style is now old, but nylon ropes of the kind he uses were on sale ten or eleven years ago. In the past, motorists bought these ropes for towing, for example, and mountaineers and rock-climbers used them, they're used by sailmakers and can be found on yachts. Farmers bought reels of them, some were used to secure tarpaulins by having weights hung from them . . . but we have not traced the manufacturer of this particular rope. We can't ignore the possibility that he bought it overseas. He leaves that length behind, by the way, around the neck of the victim, and the knot is always the same – a round turn and two half hitches which he draws tight, and we know he places one foot on her chest as he does so. One victim had cracked ribs . . .'

'He might have learned his knots from the Boy Scouts,' Pemberton smiled.

'Or on a War Duties course, outward bound exercises . . . any course to do with the outdoors would teach knots. And, of course, you could – and still can – buy similar ropes from mountaineering shops, marinas and other outdoor suppliers.'

'In your circulars, you've stressed that you've never told the press about the sandal fetish. In fact, I can't say that I have seen any press report which would suggest there is a serial killer at large.'

'No. To date, the press hasn't linked the killings. This series has enjoyed a very low profile, probably because the crimes are widely separated both by area and time. We've never said a serial killer is responsible or even suspected. Locally reported, they have all the appearance of very localised crimes. One murder a year is hardly a crime wave to a national paper so, other than ourselves – and the killer – no one knows we've a serial killer at large.'

'I'm a believer in the power the press can exert to help us detect murders,' Pemberton stated. 'The sandals he's taken from his victims must be somewhere – and their underwear. Maybe wide publicity would help us trace them?'

'Or it could persuade the killer to dispose of them, sir! That question has often been raised but it's felt we should not let the killer know we're aware of his fetish. Our offender profiling expert thinks the sandals will have been kept somewhere, in a loft perhaps, in a special place, even in a suitcase or cupboard. If that is the case, they'll provide irrefutable evidence of his guilt when we find him. It's my view we should not let him know that we are aware of his souvenir taking.'

'Right, I won't try to change things. So,' Pemberton glanced at his watch, 'it's getting on for eleven o'clock, and my teams will be anxious to get on with their first conference. Shall we talk to them now?'

Forty detectives, working in teams of two, had been assigned to the investigation and were assembled in the conference room of Rainesbury police station. They had been supplied with the basic facts by Detective Inspector Larkin and now awaited more detailed information and guidance from Pemberton. Through his introduction, he made reference to Browning, asking that the red-haired man with the open-top sports car be considered a suspect. Their enquiries should produce others. Pemberton next asked Larkin to assign an experienced team to trace Browning's movements in close liaison with Detective Inspector Holroyd's officers at Harlow Spa. This was an important part of the investigation; it must be done not only in an attempt to place Browning at the scene of the present murder, but also to establish whether he had been at or near the scenes of any of the previous crimes about which they were soon to be informed. Pemberton stressed that this aspect of the investigation – the possibility that Browning was a serial killer – was top secret at this stage. It was vital that the press – and certainly Mr Browning senior who was in town and even in the police station at this moment – must not be told.

Upon completion of his address, Pemberton introduced Detective Inspector Kirkdale and invited him to speak to the assembly. Kirkdale summarised the earlier killings, highlighting aspects of all the murders so they could be borne in mind during the current investigation. Pemberton's officers quickly appreciated they were hunting a vicious and puzzling killer who would enter the annals of British criminal history. It might be Browning – but it might not. The latter possibility was stressed. After a series of questions, the detectives, having each been allocated specific tasks known as actions, were despatched to their duties. As they left the room, there was an air of excitement and anticipation, for each officer wanted to make the all-important arrest or find the clue which led to the identification of the killer.

Pemberton, with Kirkdale at his side, returned to his office.

'Our victim will be undergoing her post-mortem about now,' Pemberton reminded Kirkdale. 'We'll be told the result before lunch. Will you be staying the whole day, Gregory? You're more than welcome.'

'Yes, I'd like to. I could go through your files and make comparisons with my own.'

'Fine. Don't be frightened to ask for anything you want. I'll find you a desk, or even an office to work in! Now, can I see your early files? The Penthorne murder for starters?'

And so Pemberton's search for the truth about James Bowman Browning began in earnest. He was particularly interested in the man who had been noticed at the Penthorne murder scene even if the sighting had been two days after discovery of the body. That man must be a suspect and greater efforts should have been made to trace him. Pemberton knew his own officers would trace the movements of Browning and in the meantime, he could complete a solid session of fact-finding before facing Mr Browning senior.

He closed his office door and studied the old file. Much of it had been compiled a year before the inception of HOLMES, the computer used specifically for complex murder enquiries. Nonetheless, the data was recorded in considerable detail. Pemberton learned that on 27th June 1987, Durham police had received a telephone call to say there was the body of a woman in woods near Penthorne. Police had investigated and found the remains of Josephine Crawley, a prostitute aged twenty-four. A native of Sunderland, she was known as Josie and had died from strangulation after being violently raped. A white nylon rope, tied with a round turn and two half hitches, was around her neck and she was bare-footed. Her mother, who had identified the body, said she had worn sandals, a new pair of plastic white ones she'd bought only two days earlier, and they were missing. Pemberton studied the official photographs and could see the likeness to the circumstances of the Crayton death.

She was lying in a natural hollow beneath the shelter of a beech tree, some thirty yards from a narrow footpath, and at first glance it seemed she was asleep. Her light summer dress covered her legs. According to the file, long and detailed enquiries had been made, but no suspect had been traced or interviewed. No one had seen Josie enter the wood with anyone. Her friends knew of her work as a prostitute, although her mother thought she worked as a waitress in a night-club, but on the eve of her disappearance, none of her friends had seen her with a client. She had last been seen alive at 9 p.m. on 26th June. The post-mortem had revealed the rape and the subsequent assault upon her private parts; she had not been pregnant at the time of her death and had been in good health.

There was a thick file of statements, the results of investigations and searches in the area, house-to-house enquiries, expert witnesses, forensic specialists, Scenes of Crime officers, official photographers and others, and there was a list of all names that appeared in the file. The list of names featured in the statements was highlighted with notations saying that none was a suspect, although one name had been listed as a possible suspect. It was a man called Bowman. James Bowman.

The reference was statement No. W.107. Bowman? Was this the man who Kirkdale had said had been observed near the scene of the murder? Heart thumping, Pemberton turned up the paper. It was a statement from a police officer, PC John Mitford.

It said that PC Mitford had been patrolling past the scene of the crime two days after the body had been discovered, when he had encountered a young red-headed man on the path which ran through the wood. Although examination of the scene had been completed by that time, PC Mitford had stopped the man to ask his name. He said he was called James Bowman, and gave an address in Newcastle-on-Tyne. Upon being asked the reason for his presence in the wood, Bowman had said he was bird-watching. He had been told that a golden oriole had been seen in this wood, and had come to look for it, explaining that the bird was a rare summer visitor to this country. The constable had accepted the story but had later realised the youth was not carrying binoculars or a camera; somewhat suspicious, Mitford had instigated a check at the address in Newcastle. No one there knew a man called Bowman; it was, in fact, a bookshop.

An annotation on the file showed that a description of 'Bowman' had been circulated to all north-east police forces, but he had never been traced. He was described as about twenty years of age, five feet ten inches tall, thick very red hair worn long, a fresh complexion and round features. He was clean shaven and had not been wearing spectacles.

He had been dressed casually in blue jeans and a T-shirt of a lighter blue shade. He'd worn trainers on his feet. There was nothing to suggest he was responsible for the killing, although had he been traced, he would have been questioned if only for elimination purposes. Pemberton picked up his telephone and dialled the number of the office in which Kirkdale was working.

'Gregory, pop in, will you?'

After pointing out the reference to Bowman, Pemberton asked, 'Does this name crop up in any of the subsequent crimes?'

'No, I double-checked, sir, on all the names which appear, especially that one. I am aware of the old belief that a murderer always returns to the scene of his crime, but he was never traced. The file does show that great efforts were made to trace that youth at the time, but everything failed. But a youth who gives a false address to a policeman in a wood isn't necessarily a murderer.'

'I know, but the man who died in our motor crash, and who confessed to a priest that he was a murderer, was called James Bowman Browning. He would have been around twenty-one at the time of that first killing and he had red hair. I know, as well as you, that a simple way of creating a false name is to drop one's surname. James Bowman. If this is the same man, I'd say that it was a remarkable bloody coincidence to say the least! And I'd be interested to know why he gave a false address. Now, I wonder if PC Mitford is still in the force?'

'I'm sure we can trace him, sir, even if he has retired.'

'A job for you?'

'If you like, Mr Pemberton.'

'You'll need a photograph of James Bowman Browning – there's one of him in our Scenes of Crime office, in colour and showing his red hair. Dead, but recognisable. Can you trace PC Mitford and ask if that's the man he saw in the wood after the Penthorne killing?'

There was a knock on Pemberton's office door and he called, 'Come.' Lorraine opened it.

'Lunch time, sir,' she said. 'I thought you'd better eat before meeting your Mr Browning.'

'Thanks, Lorraine. Yes, I'll do that. How about you, Gregory? Care to join me?'

'No, thanks, sir, not when I've got a gem like this to work on,' and he hurried from the office with a huge smile on his face. 'I'm off to find PC Mitford.'

'He looks cheerful!' smiled Lorraine.

'I've just provided him with a suspect for the first of the Sandal Strangler killings,' smiled Pemberton. 'A red-headed youth who gave the name James Bowman, and a false address.'

'Mark! Brilliant! Tell me about it!'

He told her of his discovery and added, 'Now, I'd like to go through all those Strangler files, just to see if Bowman's name crops up in any more. Or Browning's of course.'

'I'll check the other files on our terminals this afternoon, that's the only one that isn't computerised.'

'Right, now come on. I could do with a long cool drink and a nice prawn salad.'

An hour later, suitably refreshed and with Lorraine at his side, Pemberton walked over to the duty inspector's office in Road Traffic Division for his chat with Mr Frederick Browning.

6

When Pemberton and Lorraine arrived at the Traffic Division offices, PC Broadbent was waiting at the entrance.

'Mr Browning's waiting for you, sir,' he announced.

'How much does he know about the accident?' asked Pemberton.

'Not a lot at this stage, sir. We've said we suspect brake failure, but have advised him the final assessment won't be known until just before the full inquest. He hasn't been told about his son's confession, by the way.'

'OK, thanks. Do you want to be present during this chat? It might help if you're there to answer questions.'

'Yes, sir, I'll join you. I can answer any of his questions about the forthcoming procedure so far as the accident is concerned. He's a nice man, by the way – an architect, he tells me – and he's most co-operative.'

As they entered the small office, Mr Browning stood to greet them. He was a stocky man in his mid-fifties with a bald head, half-moon glasses and a ready smile. Soberly dressed in a dark suit, black tie and a dark grey waistcoat, he extended his hand to Pemberton. 'Detective Superintendent Pemberton, I believe?'

'I'm pleased to meet you, Mr Browning,' Mark proffered his hand. 'I'm only sorry it's under these circumstances. Please accept our condolences for the loss of your son. This is my personal assistant, Detective Constable Lorraine Cashmore, and I believe you've met PC Broadbent of our Traffic Division?'

'Thank you, yes. I must say I have experienced nothing but courtesy and co-operation from your officers. I believe you want to talk to me about James?' It was a forthright approach which considerably eased Pemberton's task.

'Mr Browning, this is not easy,' he began. 'First, you should know that Lorraine and I witnessed the accident in which your son died. We did our best for him at the scene – as did the ambulancemen and everyone else – but his injuries were very severe. I am sure he died peacefully . . .'

'There was a priest there too, I am told.'

'Yes, Lorraine and I had been to a lecture given by the priest, Father Flynn from Rainesbury. We were giving him a lift home. I know your son spoke to him seconds before he died. He died very peacefully, at ease with himself, and without pain, I am sure of that.'

'He was brought up a good Catholic, Mr Pemberton, but had lapsed in his teenage years. I don't think he actively followed his faith or went to Mass, but I am glad the priest was there. You know what they say – once a Catholic! I like to think he made a good confession before he died, that's something all Catholics want before they leave this world. I have to see the priest later today, about the funeral arrangements. I want to have James buried at home in Staffordshire, among his ancestors, but I think it would be appropriate to have the Requiem Mass here, said by the priest who was with him when he died. Now, PC Broadbent tells me you suspect brake failure. You don't think the brakes of his car were deliberately sabotaged, do you, Mr Pemberton? I thought it rather odd that a detective superintendent would want to talk to me about my son. James hadn't got himself involved in anything illegal, had he?'

'Not to our knowledge, Mr Browning, but I did want to meet his family. I feel very involved in this tragedy and wanted to know more about James. I'm sure it would help PC Broadbent too, in preparing his paperwork for the inquest. Now, PC Broadbent, can you help with the latest on the testing of the car?'

'Yes, sir. James's car was burnt out after the accident, after your son had been released from it, Mr Browning – by Mr Pemberton, I ought to add. There was extensive damage. It meant our examiners had very little to work on; all we can say at this stage is that the brakes appear to have failed and we are making further tests to determine whether or not that was the case. It was an old car, as you know, and didn't have a dual braking system.'

'I suppose there's always a risk,' said Mr Browning.

'I ought to say that I have no reason to suspect sabotage.' Pemberton sought to reassure Mr Browning. 'It does seem to have been a straightforward mechanical failure. We have no evidence that he had enemies, Mr Browning – unless you know something to the contrary?' Pemberton seized this opportunity to begin a line of positive questioning, the sort expected from a detective.

'Not to my knowledge,' said Mr Browning. 'He was very involved with his PR work and was very highly regarded in that respect. Because he rarely came home, I wasn't fully aware of his activities in this area and don't think he had antagonised anyone, although I know very little about his friends and business contacts. Even so, I had no reason to think he'd got himself involved in anything unlawful, drugs, stolen cars, that sort of thing. He did come to see me occasionally, once every three months or so. He was a quiet lad, Mr Pemberton, although he'd been quite lively as a youngster and in his teens. He seemed to become quieter as he matured; in fact, there were times I'd say he was withdrawn, morose almost. But he never provided us, me, with an explanation, and never grumbled. He rarely mentioned his activities in this part of the world, except to tell me about some of the big accounts he'd won, or the vintage car rallies he attended. His car was his hobby, you see, he'd always wanted an old MG Roadster and leapt at the chance to buy that one.'

'He's had it a while?' asked Lorraine.

'A few years, I'm not sure how long. He bought it from a friend, Hugh Dawlish. Even at college, he used to attend rallies, with his friends. That's when his interest in the marque developed, although it was a long time before he could afford one of his own. Once he was earning enough money he bought his beloved vintage MG. I do know he was very proud of his little car.'

'Did he go to university?' asked Pemberton, knowing the answer but wanting to gain this man's confidence and get him talking.

'No, it was a college. The Swangate College of Media Studies near Durham. He did well, he had an aptitude for publicity and advertising and was good at copy writing. He made a lot of friends during his course. Afterwards, he kept in touch with most of his friends, that was one of his strengths.'

'Male and female friends?' asked Lorraine.

'Oh, yes. He had girlfriends and men friends. He was not a homosexual, Mr Pemberton, although he never married. He did some charitable work too, he took after his mother in that. That, his work and his car kept him occupied. He enjoyed his role in public relations and did work hard for his success, putting in some long hours. I think he was hoping he'd be made a partner, but that hasn't happened yet . . . maybe if he'd . . .'

He wiped a tear from his eye and smiled apologetically at the police officers, then continued, 'He kept out of trouble at college, Mr Pemberton. No drugs, political demonstrations, wildness of any kind. He just worked for his diploma. He wanted to please us, his mother especially. She died a few years ago – a heart attack. He was devastated but he did make her proud of him before she died. He was our only child, we couldn't have more . . . but he fulfilled all our hopes. He was a lovely son, a lovely lad, I just wish he'd lived to provide me with a grandson or grand-daughter . . .'

More tears came from Mr Browning as Lorraine looked at Pemberton, signalling that in her opinion it was time to end their discussion. Pemberton left his seat and placed a friendly hand on Mr Browning's shoulder.

'Thanks for talking to us,' he said. 'We feel we know James much better now. I wanted to say I'm sorry we were unable to save his life.'

'I know you did your best, PC Broadbent told me. Thank you for that.'

'Is there anything we can do for you now, Mr Browning? Anything you wish to know?'

'There's the inquest this afternoon, I believe?'

Broadbent answered. 'Not the full inquest, Mr Browning, that comes later. It will be in a few weeks' time. This afternoon, though, we – you and I, that is – will be attending the opening of the inquest at half-past three. It's a formality, Mr Browning, where you state to the coroner that you have identified the victim as your son. That's all you have to do today. The coroner will give you a certificate which you take to the undertaker and that allows the funeral to go ahead. He'll then adjourn the inquest until further notice, that gives us time to complete our investigations into the cause of the accident and make a full assessment of the tests on the car.'

'I see, thank you. And James's personal effects? The contents of his flat?'

'Do we need further access to the flat, sir?' asked Broadbent of Pemberton. 'Or can I give the key to Mr Browning?'

'I think we have just about finished with it, PC Broadbent. You can hand Mr Browning the key then he can decide what to do with the furniture, clothing and so on. We did visit the flat earlier, Mr Browning, in our efforts to trace yourself and James's friends. I felt you ought to know that.'

'I understand. I shall be staying in the area for a few days,' Browning told them. 'There will be a lot of things to do, the funeral arrangements and so on. You can contact me at my hotel,' and he scribbled the address and telephone number on a piece of paper.

'When you've finished your commitments,' PC Broadbent said, 'we have a few other personal belongings of your son's. They were in his car. We'd like you to collect them whenever it's convenient.'

'Thank you, I'll get in touch before I leave the area.'

And so the interview, such as it was, was over. Pemberton shook Mr Browning's hand before he was led away by PC Broadbent, and then, with Lorraine at his side, he returned to his own office.

'What did you make of that?' Mark asked Lorraine as they made their way through the corridors.

'It looks as though young Mr Browning has managed to keep one side of his life very secret from his parents. They think the sun shone out of him,' said Lorraine. 'But after what Mr Browning senior said, I still feel we do not really know his son.'

'He sounds like a bit of a cold fish,' Pemberton grimaced.

'Yes, very dutiful and not a lot of fun. Rather deep, I'd say. Morose almost.'

'The sort who would commit murder, or a series of murders?' Pemberton asked her as they arrived at his office.

'He's displayed some of the characteristics of a serial killer,' she agreed. 'So what happens next?'

He led her inside and continued, 'I need to find out what Scenes of Crime discovered in the flat and I want to have words with the boss of the firm he worked for. And it will be interesting to see what our teams turn up in their first foray in this murder investigation.'

'We don't know who our local victim is yet, do we?'

'We should know soon, the morning radio and television news will have featured the crime. If anyone's missing, their family or friends should have contacted front office.'

'So shall we go down to the incident room now to see if there's been any developments?' suggested Lorraine.

There had been a welcome development. Someone had called Rainesbury police about a missing woman. As a direct result of local media publicity, Linda Butterfield had called to say she hadn't seen her friend, Debbie Hall, for two or three days. Her call had been transferred to the incident room where Inspector Larkin had responded.

'Can you describe Debbie?' he had asked gently.

'Dark auburn hair, thick and always clean, she's not very tall and had a reddish dress on.'

'Age?' Larkin had asked.

'Same as me, twenty-five.'

'Colour of her eyes? Did she wear a lot of make-up? Stockings or tights?'

'Brown eyes, not much make-up, no. No stockings, not in summer . . .'

As he'd chatted, he'd known even from that brief description that she'd been describing the victim who was then lying in the mortuary. He'd said, 'Linda, we need someone to come and look at the girl we mentioned on the news. You know she's dead, she's in the mortuary at the hospital. I do hope it's not your friend but can you come and have a look at her? To tell us if it is her?'

'She has a mum and dad, but I don't know where they live. Leeds I think, or mebbe Bradford.'

'We need someone now, Linda. Just to look at her face and tell us if it's Debbie. It's very important. We can send a car to bring you, a plain car.'

There was a long pause before the caller said, 'Yeh, right. If it is her, she'd want me to do it. 15a, Daker Place.'

Half an hour later, Linda Butterfield was standing outside the mortuary at the District Hospital with two women detectives at her side. She was a short, fat young woman with dirty hair, hardly the sort who would appeal to the sexual appetite of most men. Nonetheless, she was one of the town's busy prostitutes. One of the detectives, Detective Constable Unwin, had told Linda what to expect, explaining how the facial features were distorted and that it would not be a pretty sight.

'Ready, Linda?' asked Detective Constable Unwin.

'Ready as I ever shall be,' was the response.

Inside, she was taken to a clinically white slab in the centre of a bare, tiled room which smelt of disinfectant. On top of the slab lay a figure beneath an all-embracing white sheet and beside it stood a sombre man in a green gown, the mortuary attendant.

'Right, George,' said DC Unwin.

Slowly, he peeled back the portion of sheet which covered the head and face of the dead woman; her features were grossly distorted but Linda did not flinch. She studied the face and the hair, and whispered, 'It's her . . . God, it is her. It's Debbie. Now let me out . . . God, I need some fresh air . . .' and she began to sob.

'Thanks, George,' said DC Gibson, the second detective, as the sheet was replaced and the body prepared for return to the refrigerated cabinet.

'I'll need a statement from you,' said DC Unwin, catching up with the hurrying Linda and putting a friendly arm around her shoulders.

'That's great news,' Pemberton said when he learned of the identification. 'So we need to trace all Debbie's recent movements and contacts. DC Unwin and DC Gibson – an action for you. Talk to Linda Butterfield and her other friends and colleagues. How much they'll tell you remains to be seen, but we need a comprehensive profile of the dead girl and details of her regular clients – the lot in fact. And the name and address of her parents if you can establish that. Have a word with West Yorkshire police, Leeds or Bradford areas. They'll try to find her parents, there's probably a lot of people over there called Hall.'

As the victim's name was written on the blackboard in the incident room, Pemberton knew it would provide the extra impetus required by any murder investigation.

Pemberton spoke to Inspector Larkin.

'Paul, it seems our victim could have parents living in West Yorkshire. I don't think we should publicise her name in the media until we've done everything to trace them and notify them. But tell the teams. If Debbie Hall was active around town, the uniformed branch might know her, some of their patrols might have seen her with her killer. I just hope the ladies of the night will speak to our teams. Sometimes a crime like this makes them all speechless.'

'I'll put three of our best teams on that task, sir. We'll check every detail of her life. I'm sure we'll get some feedback.'

'Good. It could lead to her killer. Things are moving nicely. Now, Paul, any other developments?'

7

'There's a Mr Greenwood to see you, sir,' responded Larkin. 'Gordon Greenwood.'

'What about?' asked Pemberton.

'The murder enquiry, he's most insistent.'

'Who is he?'

'He's James Browning's boss, owner of the PR company for which he worked. Greenwood's of Harlow Spa. By coincidence, he's in Rainesbury today on business. He's often here, he told me, he's got several clients in town. He rang on his mobile phone a few minutes ago, when you were with Mr Browning senior. He can come straight away, before he returns to Harlow Spa.'

'Well, I did want a word with him in due course, so I reckon he's saved me a drive to Harlow Spa. But I don't understand why he wants to see me, there's been no public link between Browning's death and the murder . . .'

'Yes, I appreciate that, sir, but he heard your name on the radio. He's very insistent . . .'

'But is he linking Browning with the murder enquiry? If so, why? That's what I want to know. We've never openly linked Browning's accident with the murder and we don't want any publicity about that. So what's he up to?'

'I don't know, sir, all I know is that he insists on talking to you in person.'

'All right, Paul, I'll do it on the grounds I want to see him any-way.' Pemberton sighed. 'Tell him to come as soon as he can. Let's get it over with.'

Greenwood arrived quarter of an hour later. A large man with a military bearing, he was dressed in grey flannels and a smart blazer with a badge on the pocket, a white shirt and dark striped tie. He strode purposefully into Pemberton's office and extended his hand.

'Good of you to see me without an appointment, Superintend-ent.' He plonked himself on a chair before Pemberton's desk. 'What a dreadful thing to happen. Poor James. A good man, you know, a very good operative and an asset to our company. Dreadful news. Every member of my staff – and most of my clients – are devastated, I can tell you.'

'Mr Greenwood, my colleague said you wished to talk to me about the murder enquiry which is currently under way. I ought to stress it has never been linked to your Mr Browning.'

'Exactly what I wanted to hear you say, Superintendent. That kind of thug, a murderer, working for my company – it could be ruinous. Imagine how it could affect my business if my clients thought I was the sort of chap who'd hired a killer or a rogue of any kind. I came to tell I want the rumours halted, you see –'

'Rumours?'

'Well, yes, in view of what you've just told me. Maybe you hadn't heard?'

'Heard what, Mr Greenwood? I must confess I have no idea what you are talking about.'

'Let me explain. I was to meet a client over lunch at the Raine-cliffe Hotel. I arrived in good time and was enjoying an aperitif in the bar when I overheard some people gossiping. And gossiping is exactly the right word to use. They said the body of a woman had been found in some local woods and that the driver who'd committed suicide in his sports car had done it. Now, I can't see how such a tale has got around, Mr Pemberton, but I assure you that our Mr Browning is no killer, nor is he the sort of man to commit suicide. I felt I had to come straight here to you and make my feelings known. Your name was mentioned, you see, as the officer in charge of the investigation. I have – I had – the greatest respect for Mr Browning and in fact he was well on the way to becoming a partner in my business. I can recognise quality, Mr Pemberton, I'm not the sort of man who would ap-point a wrong 'un to a senior post in my organisation. That's why I am here – to ask you to halt those wild rumours.'

'Mr Greenwood,' Pemberton interrupted him, 'Mr Browning did not commit suicide. I am convinced of that. I actually wit-nessed the accident and am fairly certain that his car suffered a catastrophic brake failure. Clearly, experts are testing the car and its components, and their report is awaited. I am confident they will reveal brake failure as the cause of the accident, not suicide.'

'But is he under consideration as a suspect for the murder of that woman? I did hear the local news, Mr Pemberton, on my car radio. I do know you have had a murder reported.'

'Yes, there is a murder investigation under way in the town.'

'Exactly. And the news report did refer to the inquest on James Browning at the same time as the latest on the murder –'

'The murder is that of a prostitute, Mr Greenwood. I can con-firm that and although there is no prime suspect, everyone is a suspect in a murder investigation. That means that if your Mr Browning was known to have been in the vicinity at the time of the woman's death, then we shall have to investigate him very thoroughly, for elimination purposes. I stress that point. We do know he was in town on Tuesday evening, prior to his accident. He was meeting a client. That means he is no different from many other people we have to eliminate from our enquiries and it does not imply he is under suspicion. I am sure you realise that most detection work in murder cases involves the elimination of suspects, dozens of them in some cases. If it's any consolation to you, I have to say that I have no evidence to link him to the murder nor is there anything to suggest he was at the scene of the woman's death. Most certainly I have not authorised any news release which would even hint that he was a suspect.'

'That is pleasing to hear, Mr Pemberton. But those people, the gossips, said they'd heard it on the news, on local radio.'

'Then I had better have words with the news editor. What is happening today is that the inquest opens on Mr Browning, for identification purposes only, and if that item was broadcast along with details of the murder, as you suggest, then those people could have mistakenly linked the two stories. People do that, they do get very confused . . .'

'Don't I know it, Mr Pemberton! In my business, you'd be amazed what widely differing interpretations people can put on a simple statement . . .'

'I'll get the news editor to be careful how the news is read, Mr Greenwood. Now that you're here, though, I did want to have a word with you about James Browning and you are on my list of forthcoming visits. I have spoken to his father, only very recently in fact, and I did witness the accident. It means I do have a rather special interest in his background, as you can imagine. Now, if you've time for a chat?'

'You witnessed his accident, you say?'

'I did,' and Pemberton gave a brief account of it.

'Then of course I have time. I am dreadfully sorry we've lost him. He was very good at his work, Mr Pemberton. The best. Unflappable, cool, consistent, persistent, imaginative, very careful in everything he did, great attention to detail, good with administration, got along with his colleagues and clients. He was a good worker for charities, a very nice young man in every way. I'd rate him at a hundred per cent, Mr Pemberton.'

'And away from work?'

'He wasn't a great socialiser, not the sort to go partying or to join a golf club. He spent a lot of time with that old car of his, polishing the thing and doing bits of maintenance, going off to rallies and gatherings of vintage car enthusiasts, all over the country, in fact. A few years ago, his colleagues teased him because a woman's body had been found in the very village where he'd gone off to a vintage car rally for the weekend, but he would never get involved in anything like that. Much too decent a chap, Mr Pemberton.'

'Which village was that, Mr Greenwood? Can you remember?'

'Good God no! It was the year he bought that MG, the first time he'd taken it on a long run, so far as I remember. Everybody expected his car to break down, but he got there and back, and won a rosette of some sort. It's funny, I suppose, uncanny even, him being in the area on the occasion of *two* murders, eh?'

Probably three, said Pemberton to himself. There was another, the one where he'd surely been seen walking past the scene two days after discovery of the body, but he had no intention of telling Greenwood about that.

'Coincidence is a funny thing,' agreed Pemberton. 'It's something we've got to contend with during our investigations.'

'I can understand how careful you must be, Mr Pemberton. Now, what happens about James's belongings? I expect his family will take care of his personal effects but I'm thinking of his official car, for example. We shall need that back, of course, and there would be some client files in his briefcase. We need to recover those too.'

'I didn't realise he had an official car,' said Pemberton. 'I thought he used his MG all the time. He was using it for work when the accident happened.'

'We never objected to him using the MG for business trips so long as the right image was imparted, but he did have an official car, a Rover, which he used for the majority of his business engagements.'

'Did he really? And where did he keep it, any idea?'

'At his flat, Mr Pemberton. There's hard-standing beside the flat, all the tenants have their own space.'

'I see. We had no idea, but there again, the fatality did not involve that car.' Pemberton realised that the Rover would now have to be forensically examined. 'His father will be given the keys to the flat in the very near future and he will accept responsibility for his son's personal effects, except for the MG, of course. That is still undergoing tests in our care. When we have finished, all his belongings will be handed to Mr Browning senior, so I'll make sure he contacts you about the contents of the briefcase. He's here for a few days and I expect him to attend the Requiem Mass. I have his hotel address and phone number if you need it.'

'Thank you, yes, that would be useful. And the Rover? When can I have access to that?'

Pemberton spoke with some caution. 'I shall need to have it examined, Mr Greenwood, by our forensic experts.'

'Good God, what for? I thought you said James was in the clear!'

'We do need to check everything, Mr Greenwood, and my officers did not realise James ran a second car. I will have the task completed as soon as possible, the vehicle will be returned to you at the first opportunity – having been eliminated from our enquiries, I trust.'

'Then you *do* suspect him?'

'No more than any other young man who was in the area at the time, Mr Greenwood. I do stress that. It would be nice to eliminate him completely – and to finally dispel any rumours.'

'The way you chaps operate is sometimes a mystery to me!' Greenwood spoke softly.

'Mr Greenwood,' Pemberton continued, 'in our efforts to eliminate James completely, it would be most useful if we could trace his movements in recent years. Especially during the summer months, June in particular.'

'Well, he usually took his holidays in June. He wasn't restricted to school holidays like our staff who have children. June was when a lot of his motor car rallies took place, he saved up his holiday allocation and took three weeks or even a month sometimes.'

'But not this year? He was working. He'd been to see a client when he had his accident.'

'Yes, he changed his routine this year. The wife of a member of staff was due to have a child this week and James said he would swap his holiday so that his colleague could have time off to be with his wife during the birth. It was nice of him. He's that kind

63

of man, er, was that kind of man, Mr Pemberton, very thoughtful, most kind and considerate.'

'But if one of my officers calls on you, you could supply him
with details of Mr Browning's holidays or business movements
in recent years?'

'Years, you say? How far back, for God's sake?'

'As far as possible, Mr Greenwood. We have enquiries to complete which date from several years ago, probably before James
joined your company. All I can say is that I need to eliminate
James Browning. I can't be more specific at this stage.'

'Yes, of course, anything to have him absolved from any
possible suspicion.'

'I'll ask one of my colleagues from Harlow Spa to contact you
in person. We shall, of course, exercise the utmost discretion
with our enquiries, and I trust you will not reveal the reason for
our visits to you.'

'I'm not quite sure what you are implying, Mr Pemberton, but
I will gladly co-operate. And be assured that confidentiality
is our hallmark. I shall be pleased to assist and I must say you
treat murder investigations with far more care than I ever imagined.'

'We pay great attention to detail, Mr Greenwood. That is *our*
hallmark. That's how murderers are traced – and suspects eliminated – from our enquiries. Now, with your consent, we
will examine James's Rover and return it to you the moment we
have finished. Can you describe it? And give me the registration
number?'

Pemberton was told it was a bottle green colour and was provided with the registration details, Greenwood adding that he
had no objection to the car being inspected. But from the expression on Greenwood's face, Mark Pemberton knew that he
suspected his former employee was *not* in the clear, a fact which
might explain his arrival this morning. He had not fully accepted
Pemberton's assurances that these enquiries were purely for
elimination purposes.

'I would appreciate a call to say that James – and his car – have
been totally eliminated from your enquiries, Mr Pemberton, as
soon as that is feasible, and in the meantime, you can count on
my complete co-operation and discretion.'

'And we shall respect that, Mr Greenwood.'

Greenwood stood up to leave and laid his business card on Pemberton's desk. 'Goodbye, Mr Pemberton. I do hope I have not been a nuisance.'

'Not at all,' Pemberton said with feeling. 'You have been of great assistance.'

The moment Greenwood left, Mark Pemberton rang Detective Inspector Holroyd at Harlow Spa and asked him to arrange for the examination of Browning's Rover and the contents of his desk at work, as well as to enquire about his holiday periods. He also wanted to check the story of Browning's visit to a village where a murder had occurred. The investigation into James Browning's life had now assumed a new importance.

Pemberton's next job was to telephone the newsrooms of the two local radio stations and question the wording of their news bulletins; after discussions with the respective news editors, both of whom were very co-operative, he realised the media had not linked Browning's death with the prostitute's murder. But the news of Debbie Hall's death had been broadcast immediately preceding the item about the inquest on Browning. Pemberton was aware of a ploy adopted by some newspapers and radio stations – they would broadcast or publish two apparently unassociated items next to each other so that readers and listeners might unwittingly link them. He was assured that this had not been the case this morning and that they would separate the items in future bulletins.

As Pemberton debated his next course of action, his telephone rang. It was Detective Sergeant Meadows from the Scenes of Crime Department at Harlow Spa.

'Sir,' he began, 'Browning's flat. We gave it a thorough examination this morning. The only fingerprints in the place are his own – it seems he's never had visitors, or if he had, they've not touched anything. We couldn't even find a coffee mug or cup with anyone else's prints on. There's no sign of violence, no bloodstains washed or otherwise on the carpets or walls, and nothing that might suggest a murder or rape has happened here, no semen stains to indicate rape, no rope of the kind used for the stranglings, nothing in the waste bins, nothing to even suggest he had criminal links or tendencies. The clothes in his wardrobe

65

and drawers are not contaminated either, there's nothing incriminating in the pockets or on the fabric. Nothing at all in fact. The place is clean, sir. Totally and utterly clean. Bare, almost. Hardly a speck of dust or a dead fly.'

'Thanks for all that. Now, you know we've discovered he had another car?'

'Yes, sir, Mr Holroyd told me. It's being collected shortly.'

'I'm beginning to think this chap leads a double life, Sergeant. There's a good deal of circumstantial evidence to link him to the crimes, and yet we can find nothing positive and nothing about his rallying or trips in the MG. But thanks for all you've done. I'll await the results of the Rover's examination.'

Pemberton replaced the handset but in his heart of hearts he knew that the official Rover would not produce any evidence. If there had been any, he was sure it would have been in the MG – and that had been almost totally destroyed by fire. If this man went on rallies around the country, then that freedom of movement could have provided him with the opportunity to commit the Sandal Strangler murders. The precise dates of the rallies were important, so when had they been held? And where? It was important that Pemberton spoke to Detective Sergeant Meadows again. He rang back. The sergeant was still in his office.

'Sarge, something's just occurred to me. When you searched Browning's flat, did you come across any papers about rallies of vintage cars? Programmes? Club membership files? Documents relating to the MG in particular? Or anything at all to do with his car? Registration document, insurance, MOT certificate?'

'No, sir. We made a careful check for that sort of thing. Mr Holroyd reminded us about the chap's interest in the MG marque and asked us to look for those especially. But there was nothing, no leaflets, no correspondence – nothing.'

'That's mighty odd!' Pemberton sighed. 'Here we have an enthusiast and yet he kept nothing at home. I wonder if he kept those things at work?'

'It's possible. We haven't been through his office desk or files yet. But at home, there was no private diary. His work diary was in his briefcase, as you know, containing his appointments and things like his father's birthday.'

'Yes. You know, Sarge, it seems this fellow has always been hiding something, keeping things in the dark. . . .'

'If his flat was anything to go by, sir, he led a very lonely and quiet life. It was sparse, even by bachelor standards.'

'But did he really lead that kind of life, Sergeant? That's what I want to find out. Let's hope Greenwood's can help us. But thanks for your efforts.'

Pemberton realised there was a lot of work to complete before he could produce a comprehensive profile of James Bowman Browning; it would be necessary to have further interviews with those who knew him – Gordon Greenwood and his landlord included. Then the phone rang. It was Detective Inspector Kirkdale.

'Sir,' he said, 'I'm ringing from Darlington police station in County Durham. I've traced PC Mitford – he's now Inspector Mitford and is stationed here. He remembers the red-haired man at the scene of the Penthorne murder.'

'That's great!' Pemberton felt the tremors of excitement in his veins.

'From the photo of Browning's body, he's sure it is the man he saw all those years ago.'

'To be certain, ask him to come and view Browning's body, will you, Gregory? It's in Rainesbury mortuary. I need to be absolutely sure about this – an opinion based on the body will be far better than one based on a photo. Can you fix that?'

'Hang on, sir, Inspector Mitford's here. I'll ask him.'

There was a momentary pause then Kirkdale returned to the phone and said, 'No problem, sir. He'll come this evening.'

'Excellent,' and Pemberton replaced the handset. The proverbial net was now closing upon his suspect. It seemed that a serial killer was soon to be unmasked.

In the brief lull that followed, Pemberton checked his watch. It was four thirty, not quite knocking-off time. But it was time for a walk and time for a long, quiet period of contemplation.

'I'm taking a thinking break, a walk along the cliffs,' he buzzed his secretary on the intercom. 'I'll be back in about an hour or so. Tell Lorraine where I've gone, but don't wait for me. You go home when you've finished.'

8

Constructed upon the cliff top at Rainesbury was an intrigu-
ing network of paths and gardens. At regular intervals were
wooden seats donated by the families of those who had once enjoyed the panoramic sea views and salt-laced fresh air. The
names of donors and loved ones adorned the plaques which
had been fixed to the backrests. Pemberton chose one of those
seats. Here he could be alone, if only for half an hour or so, and
consider the problem which was beginning to dominate his
mind.

In the bright sunshine of that warm Thursday afternoon, he
relaxed and gazed across the ocean. Today, the North Sea was
blue and calm, almost Mediterranean in appearance, a welcome
change from its usual greyness. In the distance, ships were
steaming sedately along the horizon; in silent convoy, they were
cruising past this town with its ancient harbour and castle and
its ice-cream parlours. But soon his eyes began to ignore the
tranquil scene before him. Instead, he was concentrating upon
the dreadful crimes which presently lay unsolved; he was wondering about James Bowman Browning, an enigma, a man re-
spected by all yet scarcely known to anyone, not even his own
father. The man was a self-confessed murderer – but was he the
Sandal Strangler? If he wasn't, who was? That was the question
that Pemberton must answer, and it seemed to be increasingly
difficult as the hours slipped by. He did wonder whether he was
concentrating too much attention upon Browning, but there
were no further suspects, either for the Crayton killing or the
other Sandal Strangler murders.

It was vital that he determined the Browning question because
even at this very early stage, there were factors to suggest he was
the serial killer. Because Browning was not alive to answer questions, however, it would be extremely difficult, although not impossible, to establish that guilt. From experience, Pemberton
knew that if you talked face to face with a killer, your instincts
alerted you to his guilt in spite of denials and good acting on his

part. A personal interview was therefore a vital part of the detection process, but that luxury was denied him in Browning's case.

It seemed that Browning had already left several cold trails – was that a deliberate ploy to avoid detection? His only leisure passion – if passion was the right word – was his little red MG. Work had clearly been another major part of his life and it seemed he had been utterly absorbed in his chosen career. And, according to Mr Browning senior, he had loved his mother. But a lot of killers loved their mothers and a lot of mothers loved their killer sons. In spite of that two-way love, Browning's family life seemed very empty. His father knew very little about his adult son. There was some contact between them, but it seemed more dutiful than desired, probably little more than cards for birthdays and at Christmas, plus an occasional telephone call or visit.

As Pemberton sat with the sea breezes ruffling his hair and brushing his cheeks, he began to see that outside the office any passion – interest was perhaps a better word – of Browning's had been channelled into his car and his rallies. Any clues to his personality – and his movements – lay in the charred remains of that little red car. But how much had been lost in the blaze? When Pemberton had looked at the remains, it seemed the vehicle had been totally destroyed, but he knew that detailed forensic examination could produce a surprising amount of information from such a wreck. He hoped it would in this instance. It was in this car that Browning had toured the country; it was in this vehicle that he had attended rallies, met friends, called at new places . . . and travelled to kill prostitutes?

For the umpteenth time, Pemberton pictured the scene of that fatal traffic accident. It was like the rerun of a video film. The speeding car, the noise as it roared past Pemberton and his friends, the headlong dash into that corner, the brake lights, the crash. The car tumbling into the stream, the hissing noises, the smell of petrol, the blood upon the driver and that whispered confession to the priest . . . he could see it all now, so clearly. Most good detectives possessed the ability to recall scenes of murders in astonishing and almost photographic detail, and now Pemberton was doing exactly that. In this case it was not the scene of a murder but the scene of another death, a fatal road traffic accident. Nonetheless, his mind began to replay the scene

69

which had presented itself . . . he went over it time and time again, seeking a clue, any clue which would unlock the mystery of the lifestyle of James Bowman Browning. He saw the battered and limp remains of the driver slumped over the steering wheel, the contents of the car tossed out like confetti – and the heavy book of road maps lying in the shallows of the stream.

He'd seen it in the bay at the Road Traffic garage, part of the contents of the devastated little car. It was a thick red-backed atlas with a black spine, the *Reader's Digest Driver's Atlas of the British Isles*. It had been recovered, damp but not entirely ruined, and it was now among Browning's belongings in the Road Traffic offices, awaiting collection by Mr Browning senior. And although Pemberton had examined other things, such as the briefcase, he had not looked into or even opened the atlas. There had been no reason – until now. That atlas was part of the MG's life. It had probably travelled everywhere with the car; it had become part of the car's life and equipment. And what about the car's own life? How long had Browning owned it, for example?

What was its history? Browning senior said he'd bought it from a friend called Hugh Dawlish. Had it always been red? Had it been restored? Was it in its original state? Where had it been during its long life? Had there been other owners? The car began to assume a higher degree of importance in Pemberton's opinion and he decided to research it as well as its owner. A car could reveal a lot.

There must be car documents somewhere. The Scenes of Crime teams had confirmed they were not at Browning's flat, so where could they be? Had they been kept in the car and destroyed in the fire? There should be a registration document, certificate of insurance, MOT certificate, repair bills, manuals . . . Could they perhaps have been inside the book of maps? People quite often kept pieces of paper between the pages of their atlas in the appropriate places – hotel brochures, programmes of events, directions to places, marks on the maps showing places they'd either visited or intended to visit. It was quite sensible and it wouldn't surprise Pemberton to find the MOT certificate or certificate of insurance there either. Pemberton's dear departed wife, June, had done that sort of thing – his own road atlas had always been full of scribbled notes and bits of paper, although he had kept his official documents in a much safer place!

70

His mind turned to June, his lost wife. If she and Mark had gone off to find a National Trust property or a viewpoint or some other place in the countryside, she would read the maps and guide him there, and to aid her map-reading she would pencil a circle around the intended destination in the road atlas. Sometimes she remembered to erase the mark afterwards and sometimes she forgot. It was these thoughts that made him realise he must have another look at the salvaged atlas before Mr Browning senior removed it. In a trice, he was on his feet and hurrying back to the Road Traffic Department. PC Broadbent was on the point of leaving.

'Ah, just caught you,' said Pemberton. 'Has Mr Browning been for his son's belongings yet?'

'No, sir, he's gone to the registrar's office. There's usually queues of bereaved or those wanting to register births or get married. He said if he wasn't here by five o'clock, he'd call tomorrow. Is there something you want, sir?'

'I need to examine that road atlas we recovered.'

'I'll get it, I know where it is,' and PC Broadbent returned to the store with Pemberton. Having been examined by Scenes of Crime, the contents of the car were now in a large carton for eventual collection by Mr Browning, and there was a receipt for him to sign.

Pemberton found the atlas and said, 'I'll pop a note in here to say I've got this; if it doesn't give me what I want, it'll be back here first thing in the morning for Mr Browning.'

'I'm on days tomorrow, sir, like today. I'll be here.'

'There are no documents relating to the car among these belongings, are there?' Pemberton sought confirmation. 'Registration document, MOT, history of the car, that sort of thing. I wondered if Browning had carried them with him.'

'No, sir, nothing of that sort. He had a driving licence in his wallet, and a certificate of insurance for the MG. The Rover is insured by Greenwood's company. But there were no papers in the MG itself.'

'They couldn't have been lost in the fire, could they?'

'Nothing's impossible, sir, but in this instance, I doubt it. We found no pieces of charred paper of that kind. I reckon we recovered almost everything. Most of it was thrown out of the car on impact.'

71

'That's easily done with an open top, especially when coming to that kind of sudden halt.' Pemberton had another vision of the crash.

'Bits of the contents of the boot survived, sir – tool kit, spare wheel, bits of the tow rope. But there were no papers there.'

'OK. So what I need now is the history of the MG, previous owners and dates of transfer. I'll get Inspector Larkin to do that.'

'DVLC would help, sir, if we can't find the documents.'

'I'd like to find the papers if they are around, but that's nothing for you to worry about. Sorry I've detained you.'

'No problem, sir. See you tomorrow?'

'More than likely,' said Pemberton, walking up to his office with the road atlas beneath his arm. Moments later he was settled at his desk to examine it, first flicking through it to ascertain that none of the documents he sought were tucked between the pages. Then he turned to the pages marked with the red ribbon. They displayed maps of this locality – probably Browning had identified the pages because of the meeting he'd arranged just before his death. The pages showed Rainesbury – they also contained Crayton, he noticed – without any pencil marks around the areas in question.

On the first page of the atlas was a dedication from James's mother: 'To James with love, Christmas 1988. Mum. XXX', so the book would now be slightly out of date. He turned the pages one by one, scanning each in turn for signs of markings. The first few pages were lists of contents, followed by advice on coping with a breakdown, then first aid, and after that came the gazetteer. He flicked through the long list of towns and villages and was tempted to give it a mere cursory examination when he noticed a pencilled cross. It was against the name of Kingsleadon, in Gloucestershire, with the map reference alongside. He turned to the map. It was a tiny village on the River Leadon between High Leadon and Upleadon – and it had a pencil ring around it. His heart began to pound. He looked at his watch – six o'clock. His secretary would have gone home, so he buzzed Kirkdale on the intercom, and was moderately surprised when he got a response.

'Ah, Gregory, it's Pemberton. I wasn't sure you were there.'

'I've decided to stay on, sir, probably until tomorrow. I've got digs in a local hotel. I've just returned from Darlington. Can I help?'

'Pop in, will you? Bring your files. I want to check something.'

While awaiting Kirkdale, Pemberton checked the list and found two more marked villages, each with a cross beside the name, but hadn't time to examine the relevant maps before Kirkdale arrived. When he walked in, Pemberton indicated a chair. 'So your witness is coming to look at Browning this evening?' he said.

'Inspector Mitford, sir. I'm expecting him at half-seven. I want to chat with him about the Penthorne killing. I'll look after him, sir, I'll take him out for a pint and a snack. He's pretty confident that Browning was the man he saw all those years ago. So, what have you for me to check, sir?'

Pemberton opened the atlas and indicated the marked village of Kingsleadon.

'Does this village mean anything to you?'

'Kingsleadon? Yes, it's not far from the scene of one of the deaths, sir, well, to be precise, not far from where the body was found, although we think the victim died there too. That was Kempley Woods, near the boundary with Hereford and Worcester, that's in West Mercia force area. Are you drawing a chart of the killings? You needn't, you know, I've already done that – with your Crayton murder included.'

'No, I'm not. I've just been glancing through this atlas, it's from Browning's car. It seems he's marked that village for some reason . . .'

'Has he, by God?' Kirkdale exclaimed.

'How far do you think it is from the scene of the Kempley Woods murder?'

'Six or seven miles, sir.'

'So it's not where the body was found?'

'No, sir, but close enough to be of interest. Why's he marked it?'

'I was hoping you might tell me! How about motor rallies? Rallies of vintage cars? MGs in particular.'

'In each case, the investigating force was asked to note every public event in the area around the time of the murder, hoping to get lists of participants, especially if they were club gatherings. I'll check my files.'

It didn't take long for Kirkdale to turn up details of a vintage car rally which had been held at Kingsleadon the weekend before the Kempley Wood body had been discovered. The rally had concluded on the Sunday afternoon, the body of the murdered prostitute being found the following Tuesday; she had probably died on either the preceding Friday or Saturday.

The snag was that the rally organisers – the Kingsleadon Vintage Car Club – had had no idea who had attended, or who was expected to attend. They had advertised the event in the local papers in addition to club circulars, thus it had been open to the public. The police had obtained a list of club members, all of whom had been interviewed and eliminated from the enquiry, but nothing of use had come to light. It had been impossible to trace members of the public who had visited; indeed, they'd all dispersed and gone home on the Sunday afternoon.

'Is Browning on the members' list?' Pemberton asked.

Kirkdale checked. Neither Browning's name nor that of Bowman was on the list. 'How about the other villages, sir? Have you checked any more?'

'Not properly, so let's look at them together.'

They found eight further villages ringed and marked, and all eight were less than ten miles from the scene of each of the Sandal Strangler killings. They could not check back beyond 1988 because that was the year of publication of the atlas, but there had been only one Sandal Strangler killing before that date. That had been in 1987, the Penthorne murder in County Durham.

'It's very good circumstantial evidence, sir, but it doesn't put Browning at the scene of the crimes,' Kirkdale pointed out. 'If this was a living suspect, a good defence counsel would say it didn't prove anything. They'd dismiss it as nothing more than an atlas with rings around the names of some villages, rings that could have been put around those names *after* the murders.'

'But it is a very good lead!' Pemberton was compelled to say.

'A lead, sir, yes, but it doesn't give us the *proof* we need. But I agree it's the best clue we've had in years!'

'I accept what you say about it not being proof, but I reckon it would have been strong enough evidence to justify an arrest on suspicion if he'd been alive. And the atlas has his name inside, with an inscription from his mother. We can link the atlas to him, and him to villages very close to all the killings since 1988. From my point of view, it brings him one step nearer to being the Sandal Strangler. I'll get Paul Larkin to compare your files against Browning's movements when they're fully known.'

'It does strengthen the case against Browning, sir, but what about a DNA test? Did you say you'd arranged for a DNA sample to be taken from his body? We do have samples of semen found in the women, sir, although many of the early samples were not taken with DNA in mind. The procedure didn't exist at that time, so some of the samples might not be suitable for analysis. But it's a thought; it could prove our case conclusively.'

'Looking at it through the eyes of a defence counsel, it might prove he had had intercourse with the women, Gregory, but not that he had either raped or murdered them. They were prostitutes, remember. Browning could have used them before the killer struck – that's the line a good defence counsel would use.'

'I realise that, but I still think most courts would accept positive DNA samples as very strong evidence. Rapists don't often use condoms, but prostitutes normally make sure their clients wear them. That's an argument for saying any semen found in the women was put there without their consent, possibly by rape.'

'True. Now, if there was a public event nearby which was attended by Browning, the prostitutes might have been working the area. If we did find his semen, it would be more circumstantial evidence, Gregory, even though it might not be totally conclusive.'

'So shall I arrange the necessary tests?'

'I've got to think of my budget, tests cost money, but yes. Do that. The snag is that DNA tests can take up to a week to get a result – and that's rushing things quite a lot. They can take several weeks otherwise. I can't see them rushing ours through if the suspect is dead! But even with that as a back-up, I'd like to continue my routine enquiries.'

There was a knock on Pemberton's office door and Lorraine entered to his response. 'Sit down, Lorraine,' he said. 'We're just finishing.'

He outlined his recent success to Lorraine who smiled and then said, 'While I had a quiet moment or two, I ploughed through some older sections of the Muriel Brown file, but I can't connect her death with Browning, sir. Not in any way.'

'Fair enough, let's set aside that case for a while. She wasn't a prostitute for one thing, and wasn't killed in a wood for another.'

Pemberton then acquainted Kirkdale with the Muriel Brown murder.

There followed a discussion about the red MG and how Browning might have used gatherings of enthusiasts or rallies of MG drivers to cover his tracks while committing the murders. They bore in mind that the killings had all occurred around midsummer day or on the weekend closest to that date. And that was the time the rallies were held – except there'd been no rally near the scene of the Penthorne killing and none close to the Rainesbury area this weekend. So where was this year's rally being held?

It was while they were talking that the telephone rang; it was Detective Sergeant Meadows from Harlow Spa Scenes of Crime Department.

'Yes, Sergeant?'

'A quick call, sir, just to say we've examined Browning's official car, the Rover. It's clean, sir. No sign of involvement with the Crayton death or with any killing or rape. It's a new car, sir, less than a year old, so that rules it out of being linked to any of the other crimes.'

'Thanks, Sergeant, I'll give the good news to Mr Greenwood.'

'I can do that, sir, his office is just around the corner from here.'

'Right, Sergeant, that would be a great help. You'll return the car to him now? Another job done, thanks,' and he replaced the handset.

'Sir,' Lorraine used Pemberton's official form of address as another officer was present, 'I had no idea Browning had a second car.'

'Neither did I until very recently,' he admitted. 'I only learned about it today. It's his official car, issued as part of his job.'

'Where did he keep it?' she asked.

'On a hard-standing beside his flat, each tenant is allocated a parking space. Why do you ask?'

'Well, if he parked his Rover there, where did he park his MG, sir? And surely, if he was such an enthusiast, he'd make sure his MG was in a garage or some secure accommodation. I know I would, if I had a lovely vintage car. I'd want somewhere to polish it, gloat over it and look after it.'

'God, I'd overlooked that . . . yes, he wouldn't leave that car on the street, would he?' His mind was racing now. If Browning

76

had a garage, there would be a key for it – and the key would be on a key ring, probably with the MG's ignition key. And that was still in the Traffic Department's offices.

He rang the duty sergeant, announcing his name.

'Sarge,' he said, 'the fatal RTA, Browning. You know of our interest?'

'Yes, sir.'

'Any idea where the keys to the MG Roadster are?'

'They're with the car, sir, pending its release when all the teams have finished their examination. They survived the fire.'

'They're not with Browning's other belongings, in the store?'

'No, sir, I checked myself. I saw the keys on the key ring, they were still in the ignition when we recovered the vehicle. There was one for the ignition and one for the boot, then a third key, sir. A Yale. I guessed it was for his garage. It's not the same as the one for his flat.'

'And the garage itself? Has it been traced?'

'Not by our officers, sir, no. We had no cause to visit the garage.'

'And has the key an identification on it? Address, door number, name?'

'No, sir, it's blank. There's nothing to indicate what it fits.'

'Make sure it is not taken from those keys, Sergeant. Thanks. I want that key – and a door to fit it! I'll collect it later.'

'Very good, sir.'

When he had replaced the handset, he said to Kirkdale, 'Somewhere in Harlow Spa, which has a population of around 120,000 people and mile after mile of streets, there is a lock-up garage which Browning used for his MG. How do we find that?'

'If it's very important, sir, you make copies of the key and send beat men around to try every lock-up garage – or you ask his landlord or you ask at his place of work, or his friends . . .'

'He doesn't seem to have any friends,' said Pemberton. 'But I think that is a very good job for Detective Inspector Holroyd's crew!'

'What are you expecting to find there?' asked Lorraine.

'We won't know until we look, will we?'

9

Detectives on the Crayton murder investigation worked from eight o'clock in the morning until eight in the evening. The four hours in excess of the eight-hour day were paid overtime in spite of constraints on expenditure. As a consequence, teams were still at work in the incident room with others on external enquiries as Pemberton went to find Inspector Paul Larkin. It was about an hour before knocking-off time that detectives began to return to base after their day's enquiries. Before booking off duty, they returned to process their findings, complete their records and indulge in informal discussions. This somewhat casual gathering was important in the progress of a murder enquiry and Pemberton encouraged his officers to chat over a welcome mug of tea before going home. It was during such moments that breakthroughs and new lines of enquiry could emerge.

Detective Inspector Kirkdale was not in the incident room at this time; he was awaiting the arrival of Inspector Mitford. Lorraine had also disappeared. She'd gone to ring Detective Inspector Holroyd with Pemberton's request to trace the MG's garage in Harlow Spa. With the road atlas under his arm, Pemberton entered the busy incident room and located Inspector Larkin, but before telling him of their latest discovery, he asked about local progress.

'There's not a lot to report at this stage, sir,' Larkin told him. 'But the teams are starting to come in, maybe they've learned something.'

'No more suspects in the frame then? Browning's the only one so far?'

'That's right. No more names yet, sir, but the teams are still digging into the underbelly of the area.'

'Anything more on Debbie Hall?'

'We're still trying to trace her last movements; I've two teams on house-to-house enquiries in the Crayton area, and the task force is checking the woodland around the old mill. But nothing's been fed into the system yet. It's early days, though.'

Pemberton smiled and told Larkin, 'I'm arranging DNA comparison of samples from Browning and the earlier Sandal Strangler victims. It takes time to get results even though they claim the six-week wait has been reduced to about one in emergencies. I know it's expensive and time-consuming, but it could determine whether Browning had unprotected sex with any of the victims.'

'Even that doesn't prove he killed them, sir.'

'I realise that, but are you suggesting he was present while someone else did the killings? What's Gregory Kirkdale think about that?'

'I've not asked him, sir, but I don't think we should overlook the possibility, bearing in mind that each victim had had forced intercourse and that their genitals had suffered further violence. That could suggest two participants, one who could perform sexually and one who couldn't.'

'Kirkdale's never hinted at that theory for the Sandal Strangler's crimes, but I agree it's a consideration.'

'I'll put it to him when he comes in.'

'You know he's got an inspector coming from County Durham to see Browning's body? He'll be committed for most of this evening.'

'Yes, I'll catch him when I can.'

'Right. Now, this atlas,' and Pemberton plonked it on Larkin's desk. 'I want you to examine it, Paul. Go through it with the proverbial fine-tooth comb. It's from Browning's car and there's evidence it belonged to him. If you check the gazetteer, you'll see someone – Browning more than likely – has marked certain villages. They're also ringed on the relevant maps. Those villages, Paul, are all within striking distance of the Sandal Strangler murder scenes going back to 1988. It seems there were vintage car rallies there. I'm not saying it puts Browning at the actual scenes of the murders, but it looks as though he's been pretty damned close. What I want you to do is check Kirkdale's files of the Sandal Stranglings, then produce a list of all those rallies, with dates, times, duration and location. I want to show how the rallies relate to the places where the bodies were discovered, and then I want those times and places checked against Browning's movements.'

'I understand, sir. No problem. But I understood Browning's flat revealed no record of his car or his rallying?'

'It didn't and I regard that as very odd. If he was so keen on his old car and attending rallies, you'd think he'd keep papers or records somewhere. So far as his movements are concerned, I'm having DI Holroyd check his holiday periods over the years. He'll contact you when he's done that. And another thing. We've just realised that Browning must have had a garage somewhere, where he kept his MG. Holroyd's men are looking for it. And I want you to trace the history of the MG, Paul. Previous owners' names and addresses, and dates of sales especially – I want to know when and where Browning acquired the vehicle. His father said he bought it from a friend called Hugh Dawlish. Then trace Dawlish, we need to talk to him.'

'We're checking the names we got from an address book in the flat. I've two teams on that, I expect them back any time. They should have Dawlish's home address.'

'Good. And we want to know if Browning had any close friends in Harlow Spa. It seems he was a cold fish, Paul, a loner. Holroyd's looking into that too, trying to get some background from his work place and his landlord.'

Larkin was making notes of these instructions. 'Sir,' he said after a moment, 'running a murder investigation is expensive, but I wonder if we need to spend a lot more time and money on this one? The more we discover about Browning, the more he fits the frame. He's almost certainly our man, it's just a question of tying up the loose ends. There's no other suspect for Debbie Hall's murder and from what you say, it does look as if Browning's a key suspect for the other Sandal Stranglings. It would save money if we concentrated on him instead of looking for others.'

'I'm aware of that, Paul. Certainly we should do all within our power to prove, beyond all reasonable doubt, that Browning is Debbie Hall's killer.'

'There's no doubt in my mind, sir.'

'Maybe, but I'm not so sure,' Pemberton admitted. 'I do have some reservations but, with a bit of luck, we should clear things up within the week. If we *can* prove he's the Sandal Strangler, we'll have done a great service to society and to other police forces across Britain. But, and I emphasise that, he might *not* be our man, Paul. After all, he did only confess to one murder. We must be careful about this – Browning can't answer back, remember – and so I'm prepared to hunt other suspects even if it does eat into my limited budget. If we can positively match Browning's movements with the rallies and the scenes of the Sandal murders, including ours at Crayton, we should be able to scale down our activities. Whatever we discover, or fail to discover, the DNA tests should clinch it – but it's a long wait for results and they're not conclusive; we still need good supporting evidence.'

'OK, sure, message understood. But if he is guilty, the public will never know?'

'True, but they will draw their own conclusions when we announce that the killer is dead, even without naming him – and so will Greenwood and, sadly, Browning's father.'

During their discussion, small groups of detectives continued to drift into the incident room before completing their shift and it was while Pemberton was pondering whether to remain or return to his own office that DCs Unwin and Gibson entered. They looked pleased with themselves.

'It looks as though you've had a successful day?' Pemberton greeted them.

'Yes, sir.' Sarah Unwin spoke for both. 'We've got a description of a suspect!'

'Not a red-headed man with a red sports car?' he smiled.

'No, that's what's so interesting, sir. We've been talking to contacts of Debbie and other local prostitutes. On Sunday evening, Debbie was in the bar of the Lobster Hotel, around half-past seven. It's on the sea-front, as you know, sir, popular with holidaymakers and trippers. The barman knows her – he's called Eddie Brodie – and says she often went in for a snack and a drink but she never entertained her clients there or used it as a meeting place. The landlord had made it known there were to be no pick-ups by prostitutes on his premises. Anyway, on Sunday she chatted to Eddie and bought a drink. She told him she was meeting a friend outside and they were going for a drive into the country. She had a soft drink, he said, then went outside just before eight. Eddie saw her through the windows. She met a man near the pillar box at the other side of the road, opposite the pub, and walked away with him. It was a fine, warm night, they went towards the town centre, walking towards the car-park.'

'And?' Pemberton smiled.

'Eddie doesn't know the man, sir, he'd never seen him before and has no idea if he is a local. Some of those sea-front prostitutes serve visitors, but a lot stick to local punters. Now, his description. He was tall, sir, about six feet, maybe even taller by a couple of inches. In his thirties, slim build with dark hair, clean shaven, not wearing specs or sun-glasses. He wore light tan cotton trousers, a short-sleeved T-shirt, a dark green one, and brown sandals, they looked like leather.'

'Sandals?'

'Yes, sir. And Debbie wore sandals too, we've established that from her friends, a pair of red ones with low heels. They've not been found, as you know.'

'And was this the last sighting of Debbie?'

'So far as we know, sir. None of her friends saw her after that time – eight o'clock last Sunday night.'

'The timing's about right . . . If he took her to the old mill and killed her, he'd be able to return to his haunts the same evening and not be missed by his friends or family. So, who is this joker?'

DC Gillian Gibson spoke now. 'We have asked around the town, sir, especially among the prostitutes and her friends, but no one can suggest a name. One thing did emerge – it wasn't a pick-up on the street or in one of the clubs or pubs the prostitutes use. It was a pre-arranged meeting, her comments to Eddie confirm that. She'd popped into his bar to while away the time until he turned up – she could see the pillar box from the stool at the bar. And when the man arrived, as near eight o'clock as dammit, she went straight out to meet him.'

'She didn't take him back to her place?'

'No, sir, we checked with her flat-mate. She didn't come back to the flat on Sunday night at all.'

'What was she wearing, apart from sandals?' Pemberton asked.

'The dress she was found in, sir, the reddish summer dress. No headgear of any kind, just the dress and sandals. A summer outfit.'

'Handbag? Did she have a handbag?'

'The barman wasn't sure, sir, but there's no bag in her flat. I think she would take her bag, that's not been found either.'

'And how long does it take to drive from that sea-front car-park to Crayton? Any ideas? That's assuming chummy did have a car.'

'Twenty minutes, twenty-five maybe if the town's busy.'

'Paul, detail an action for tomorrow. Check the car-park – security cameras, attendant's records, regular users – to see if anyone saw the tall guy or Debbie, with or without each other. Regulars might know Debbie by sight.'

'Right, sir.'

'Now, the timing of that sighting by Eddie fits the assessment given by the pathologist. So either that man took her into the woods and killed her at the old mill, or he was a punter who used her somewhere else, after which Browning took her to the woods. But Debbie did say she was going for a drive in the countryside, so that was planned too. Clearly, she knew the man. Was he one of her regulars? Do we know where she was during the earlier part of the day?'

Sarah explained. 'She was at home during the morning, sir, till about eleven, and then she went to the supermarket and did some shopping. She had a light lunch at home – some cooked ham, lettuce and a tomato, and then she went to the antiques fair at the Belvedere Hotel, on the edge of town. It was in the grounds of the hotel, in marquees.'

'Was she into antiques?'

'She collected thimbles, sir. She had a very big collection in her bedroom and was always looking for more. She'd told her flat-mate it was a form of insurance for her old age, something she could sell at a profit if she was desperate. She had a knack of finding the best. Anyway, she returned about five thirty, had a bath and washed her hair, then got a bit of supper and went out to meet the man we've described.'

'I wonder if the tall guy was someone she met at the antiques fair?' Pemberton mused. 'So that's your next job, Sarah and Gillian. Check with the hotel, see if they can put you in touch with the organisers or anyone who might have attended the event, and see if they remember either Debbie Hall or her tall, slim friend. Maybe she kept a diary with names in? Find out. And Paul . . .' He turned to Inspector Larkin. 'We need to find out if Browning attended that antiques fair. His flat didn't reveal any particular interest in antiques, did it?'

'Some of his furniture was antique, sir. He had one or two good pieces but there's no indication he was a keen collector.'

'But that's another thing to check while we're looking into his

83

movements. And I wonder if there were antiques fairs anywhere near those motor rallies? And there was no motor rally or vintage car event in Rainesbury over the weekend, was there?'

'No, sir, we checked,' Larkin assured him.

'This is fine.' Pemberton turned to the two detectives. 'Enter a description of that man in the files, put him in the frame as a suspect. We won't release this to the press just yet, the publicity might scare him away, especially if he's a visitor who's still in town. We'll keep it to ourselves for the time being but make sure all our teams have his description – and the local uniformed branch. If we can't flush him out or find him, then we can release a description to the press and radio. After all, his rendezvous with Debbie might have been totally innocent but we need to prove that. Well done, both of you. Two suspects will keep the enquiry alive.'

As the two women detectives began to program their information into the system, Detective Inspector Kirkdale entered the incident room, closely followed by a man who looked every inch a police officer. Tall, moustached, smart and confident, he approached Pemberton with Kirkdale.

'Sir, this is Inspector Mitford. We've just been to look at Browning's body.'

Pemberton shook Mitford's hand. 'Thanks for coming. And your verdict, Mr Mitford?'

'It was him, sir, the man I saw at the murder scene at Penthorne. No doubt about that.' Mitford spoke with a lilting Durham accent. 'I'd know him anywhere, even after all this time. I'd swear to that in a court of law. In hindsight I should have had him then, for interrogation.'

'If you had, I'm sure he would have had some glib answer, some alibi, so don't get a complex about it! Besides, you've got your chance to rectify things now, eh? We'll need a statement from you now, DI Kirkdale will see to that.'

'Yes, sir, it'll be a pleasure to help nail the bastard. A great pleasure, believe me.'

'Don't get too excited,' Pemberton smiled. 'We've got another suspect.'

'Another? That is different!' Kirkdale grinned. 'I thought we'd nearly got this job tied up!'

'Let's not make too many assumptions about Browning,' Pemberton cautioned them, and then explained about the tall, slim man seen with Debbie prior to her death.

Kirkdale listened and said, 'Apart from your man Browning, this is the first time we've had a description of any suspect. You'll be circulating it, sir, for elimination?'

'Only to our own staff, not to the press or public at this stage,' and Pemberton gave his reasons. 'Now, Inspector Mitford, while you are here, we might as well pick your brains about other aspects of the Penthorne murder. Before you go, let's sit down over a coffee and see if there's anything we can learn from you.'

'Sure, sir, it'll be a pleasure.'

During the forty-five minutes which followed, they learned only one other fact of any relevance – that there had been no motor rally or event with vintage cars anywhere near Penthorne at the time of that first murder. Kirkdale checked his old files and agreed with Mitford. The deceased prostitute had last been seen on the Friday night, her body being found on Saturday. It had been Monday when Browning had been noticed near the scene. Pemberton thanked Mitford for his time and told Kirkdale to provide him with a meal and a drink, at the expense of the investigation, before he returned to his own station.

The next call was of equal interest. It was from Detective Inspector Holroyd at Harlow Spa.

'Sir,' he said, 'we've traced Browning's garage. We have no key, so shall we break in to search it?'

'No, the key's here. I'll be there with it, within the hour. I want to see this for myself.'

10

Pemberton's car drew to a halt outside a row of ten lock-up garages at the end of a cul-de-sac in Harlow Spa. He was accompanied by Detective Inspector Kirkdale who regarded this as a breakthrough, Inspector Mitford who had come along for the outing, and Lorraine who'd acted as driver. Detective Inspector Holroyd in another car had guided them from Harlow Spa police station with one of his detective sergeants acting as driver.

As they stood in a group to examine the exterior, Holroyd spoke. 'Browning's landlord told us where it was, sir. He knew the location, he once gave Browning a lift here when it was pouring down. You've got a key?'

'I have, David, it was with the MG. Now, listen, everybody, this is a murder suspect's premises so don't touch anything! Hands off! Look with your eyes only!'

Painted dark green, the door was the up-and-over type; Pemberton inserted the key and unlocked it, raising it with the minimum of effort. It revealed a large interior fitted with lots of shelves on all three walls. They bore a mass of items, all neatly stored. There was everything necessary for maintaining a car, from spare parts to chrome cleaner, and also some DIY materials including several tins of paint. On the right at the far end was a work bench with a light above it; fitted to the wall behind was a tool rack and an array of smaller shelves. Nearby were two electrical sockets and the work bench boasted a solid metal vice. Like Browning's flat, the work bench was extremely tidy with no stray items cluttering its surface. As if to balance the work bench there was a desk at the other side of the garage, to the left of the rear wall. Old and somewhat battered but very serviceable, the desk was tidily adorned with a blotter, two letter trays and little else; it had a knee hole in the centre with drawers at each side, and there was an office chair before it. The space between the desk and the work bench was sufficient to accommodate the nose or tail of a small parked car. The wall space near the desk was fitted with several cork noticeboards and each was full of colourful posters, notices, letters and photographs. On the floor beside it was an electric fire whose lead connected with a nearby plug. Above the posters and notices there were further shelves and upon them Pemberton could see various trophies in the shape of shields and cups. A rosette was pinned to the front of the shelf and over it was a polished piece from a car engine, part of a valve he'd kept as a souvenir from a major repair.

With the other detectives, Pemberton moved to examine the display on the walls. It was almost a shrine to the MG – the only thing missing was the car itself.

'So this is where he kept his memorabilia,' Pemberton said to no one in particular before turning to Holroyd. 'We need to give this place a thorough going-over, David. We might find dates and venues of his MG rallies, bits about the friends he met there and so on.'

'There's a picture of him getting an award.' Lorraine pointed to a black and white photograph pinned to one of the noticeboards. Clipped from a local newspaper, it showed the MG with James Browning standing before it while being presented with a plaque by an official in a smart blazer and flannels.

The caption said, 'James Browning of Harlow Spa receives his award for the best turned out Roadster at the Market Rasen rally. It is being presented by the Chairman, Charles Barlow.'

Pemberton turned to Holroyd. 'David, before we start examining things, I think we'd better have the place checked over by Scenes of Crime, don't you? For fingerprints, Browning's and those of anyone else, and for anything that might be related to murder or rape. Lengths of rope especially, or blunt instruments. You know the score. Then we'll come back and look through his papers.'

'There's quite a lot of photos on those noticeboards,' Kirkdale pointed out. 'If we can trace the people on them, we'll be a long way to checking his movements and contacts.' He was staring at a photograph on the noticeboard. It showed a man who was clearly James Browning with a friend, a tall, dark-haired young man about his own age. There were MG cars in the background but not the red Roadster. Written on a piece of card pinned beneath it were the words, 'Me and Hugh, 1994, Kingsleadon.'

'A tall, dark young man . . .' Pemberton spoke very quietly, almost to himself, as he studied the colour photo. He was thinking of Larkin's earlier comments that two people might have been involved in the Sandal Stranglings, and simultaneously thinking of the suspect seen with Debbie Hall. 'David, this picture could be important. When your teams have done their stuff, can you have some copies made by the Photographic Department? In colour. I want a witness to have a look at this one.'

He told Holroyd, who did not work in the incident room, about this latest development and of the barman's sighting. Although this man's mode of dress – a pair of light slacks with a blazer and tie – was different from that of the man seen in Rainesbury last Sunday, his physical description was similar – but there again, such a description would fit hundreds of thousands of young men. However, the photo was a lead which could not be ignored, particularly as it portrayed two suspects.

Kirkdale spoke next. 'Bearing in mind we've never had a description of a suspect for the Sandal Stranglings, I'd appreciate copies of that picture, Mr Pemberton. I can circulate it to all the forces who've experienced one of the Sandal Stranglings. I'll get them to show it to the organisers of local motor shows or rallies. Someone might recall that pair of young men, especially if they were together.'

'We need to identify everyone in all these photos. If Browning's captioned them all, as I'm sure such a neat-minded person would do, then we're half-way there. But before we do anything else, David, it's down to your Scenes of Crime officers to give this place a thorough going-over.'

As the men had been talking, Lorraine had been exploring the garage to look at other objects. Walking with her hands tucked behind her back, the tall detective had mentally noted most things, including the remarkably tidy state of the place, and then she'd noticed a high shelf. It was above the work bench, much higher than the others and clearly there to accommodate all those things not immediately required. It was not easy to see what was on that shelf, partially due to its height from the floor, and partially due to the shadows which engulfed it.

Lorraine stood back to peer at it, finding that if she stood on tiptoe in the centre of the floor, she had a better view. Then she hurried to Pemberton.

'Sir.' She tugged at his sleeve, a sign of her request for immediate attention. 'Up there, on that shelf.'

'What is it, Lorraine?'

'A pair of woman's sandals, I'm sure of it!'

'Oh, my God!' he muttered. 'Show me.' The others had heard her urgent entreaty and everyone stopped to look in the direction she was pointing.

'I've a torch in the car,' said Pemberton, hurrying out to find it. 'Is there anything we can stand on for a closer look?'

While Pemberton went for a torch, the others realised there was nothing that could be used as a stool or ladder, and so they adopted the simple tactic of lifting the lightest man so that he could examine the shelf without touching anything. Mitford was deemed the smallest of the trio and so, when Pemberton returned with his torch, Holroyd and Kirkdale moved to a position best suited to examine the contents of the shelf. Mitford stood between them with his arms rigid by his sides; each of the others placed one of Mitford's fists in their cupped hands and at the command 'Lift', hoisted him off the ground. This schoolboy technique gave him about three feet of extra height as Pemberton shone the torch on to the heels of the sandals.

'Hold it . . .' called Mitford. 'Yes, a pair of woman's sandals. Blue plastic by the look of them. There's only the one pair. The other stuff up here is old bits of car engine, by the look of it.'

'Just the one pair?' Pemberton called. 'Are you sure?'

'Yes, sir, just the one.'

Mitford was lowered to the ground with some hilarity as Pemberton asked Kirkdale, 'Blue sandals? Does the colour mean anything? Are they from one of our victims?'

'Yes, one of them had blue sandals, cheap ones. Offhand, I can't remember which, but I can check with the files. It was one of those girls killed about five or six years ago, so far as I recall.'

'If these belonged to one of the victims, is there any way of proving it?'

'We've probably got a photo of the victim with her sandals on, sir, we could look at that, or show them to whoever took the photo. Their name would be on file.'

'It would appear we have found the den of a serial killer – or one of his dens,' Pemberton said to his colleagues. 'Right, David. Seal this place, tell Scenes of Crime what's required then we'll let our Forensic friends give it a thorough examination. After that we can get down to reading his documents. And now, I'd better take repossession of all the belongings from his car, and from his flat. We can't restore them to his father after all. All we have to do is put Browning at the scene of one murder – and those sandals might just do that!'

'Unless they belong to someone else, sir,' said Lorraine. 'There's no proof they have come from any of the victims.'

'They're another piece of circumstantial evidence against Browning, Lorraine, but let's wait and see what our scientific friends can tell us about them.'

Kirkdale spoke. 'Sir, we're looking for eleven pairs of sandals . . . not just one.'

'I know,' Pemberton acknowledged. 'I know very well indeed.

But this entire thing is a puzzle, is it not? Like a jigsaw – and we are assembling it very very slowly, piece by piece. Those sandals might be one of the missing pieces, or they might not.'

Holroyd said, 'Sir, do you want my men to start on the garage now? I've some officers working a late shift.'

'The sooner the better!'

'I'd like to stay and see how things go,' Kirkdale suggested. 'This is the biggest development I've had in years . . . any objections, anyone?'

'Your day of champagne for all is getting much closer!' Pemberton laughed. 'But I have no objections – I want to get back to the incident room before my teams knock off for the day, to update them on this development. It'll spur them on tomorrow. How about you, Inspector Mitford? Coming back with us? We'll be having fish and chips or a bar snack or something before we go home.'

'I'll get someone to run DI Kirkdale back to Rainesbury,' said Holroyd.

'OK, I'll come with you, sir. I ought to be getting back to base really, but thanks for including me in this.' Mitford was happy to have had such an interesting if temporary diversion from his current duties as a uniformed inspector. Pemberton and Lorraine, with Mitford as their passenger, would return to the incident room as quickly as they could, and in the meantime radioed ahead to alert them to this important development.

As Lorraine drove away from the garage, Pemberton said, 'I'm dreading this. Now I'll have to tell Mr Browning that his beloved son is our prime suspect.'

'And don't forget Mr Greenwood,' she reminded him.

'I might let David Holroyd deal with Greenwood,' Pemberton chuckled. 'That's the art of delegation! But come on, Lorraine, foot down! We've a lot to do tonight.'

Thanks to Lorraine's swift and expert driving, Pemberton returned to the incident room a few minutes before his teams officially went off duty. He was able to inform them about the latest development and everyone agreed it was one more pointer towards Browning's guilt. And in those final moments of Thursday's work, Pemberton learned more positive news. Enquiries at

Greenwood's had shown that Browning was on holiday at the time of the last ten killings. He had not been employed by Greenwood's when the first murder had taken place however – he'd been at Swangate College in Durham. Greenwood's employees had all been interviewed; none of them claimed to be a close friend of James Browning and none had socialised with him.

These new facts consolidated Pemberton's belief that Browning was a cool, distant and rather remote character, always pleasant, always efficient, but never allowing a close friendship to develop. None of the staff had been to his flat, for example, although from time to time he had joined them for a celebration after work, perhaps after winning a good contract or succeeding in some joint high profile PR success.

The staff confirmed he had always taken his holidays in the middle of June and had been away from the office on the dates of the ten most recent killings. On at least one occasion, according to Greenwood's staff, he had been within a few miles of one of the murders, a fact which had not escaped the notice of the office staff. By chance, one of the girls had read the story in a paper she'd seen while visiting relations in that area – they'd all made fun of the coincidence, but now they were wondering whether their joking had been grossly misplaced.

Detailed checks with Kirkdale's comprehensive files confirmed that vintage car rallies had taken place at around the times of nine of the murders – no such rally was recorded when the Penthorne death had occurred, and none was in the vicinity of the most recent one at Crayton. But, in the Crayton case, there had been an antiques show attended by lots of people, and, as one officer pointed out, in the case of the Penthorne death, there had been the presentation of diplomas and awards at the college on the weekend prior to the discovery of the body – and Browning had attended that with many others. So had Browning gone to the antiques fair at Rainesbury? No one could answer that but further enquiries would be made.

The team charged with tracing Browning's movements over the last ten years had had some success too. From addresses discovered in his flat and through his credit card spending on petrol, food and clothes, they had produced an itinerary for the past two years – and in June each time, he had been within ten miles of the relevant murder scene, in each case purchasing petrol with a credit card.

Checks against the records of the two garages concerned had confirmed his presence, because they had recorded his registration number. So both car and owner had been in the vicinity of those two murders – but still that did not place him at the exact scene, nor was it proof of his culpability. Further evidence – yes. Positive proof – no!

Enquiries at the addresses given in Browning's contact book had shown most were those of former college colleagues who received nothing more than an annual Christmas card from him. There had been talk of a reunion after ten years, but no one had bothered to arrange it and consequently it had never happened. Not all his former colleagues had been contacted – several houses were empty, probably through people being at work or away on holiday. They would be revisited. Some of the listed names were family members, they discovered – cousins, aunts and uncles – and it had been decided not to interview them until Pemberton had given the all-clear. This meant informing Mr Browning senior of the mounting evidence against his son.

Pemberton was fully aware, however, that nothing had yet placed Browning at the actual scene of any of the killings, and it was crucial that this be achieved. Still, the day's enquiries had ended on an upbeat note. To celebrate, Pemberton took Lorraine out for a meal and a drink before they went home but it was clear he was not completely happy with the developments.

In the car, he said to Lorraine, 'I shouldn't have any reservations about telling Mr Browning of our suspicions, should I? Really, I can't delay it any longer!'

'You still feel Browning might not be our man?'

'It's a gut feeling, Lorraine. As I said earlier, I do have some doubts although I can't ignore the damning evidence that's gathering by the day. The point is that if Mr Browning senior is to know of our suspicions – and I emphasise that last word – he must learn from us. From me, that is. And soon.'

'I can understand you not wishing to tell him yet,' she sympathised.

'I hope he never has to know our darkest suspicions. I'm increasingly uneasy about James being a serial killer, but I'm still puzzled about the murder to which he confessed. I know the circumstantial evidence points to him, it's enough to justify an arrest on suspicion of the Sandal Stranglings had he been alive. But I can't ignore the fact that he admitted just one murder. I do appreciate that he could have confessed to each killing as he'd done them, perhaps to different priests over a number of years, but that does seem unlikely. A man would hardly confess to murder, receive absolution and then go out and kill again, would he?'

'He might. There was a year between each and remember, we can't fathom the mind of someone who might have been mentally sick.'

'It's a valid observation,' he admitted. 'But in spite of everything, we've nothing to place Browning at any of the scenes, not even our latest one at Crayton. He's been very close to all of them, but being nearby doesn't make him guilty.'

'So if he didn't kill those girls, who did?'

'How about the tall thin man in the photo? The man I believe is called Hugh Dawlish?'

11

With a glass of The Macallan ten-year-old malt whisky in his hand, Pemberton relaxed in his armchair with Lorraine at his feet. She was sitting on the floor with her back against his legs, sipping from a small glass of brandy. For a few moments, neither spoke. It was nice to do nothing for it had been a long, busy day and they were tired but content. However, Lorraine knew that Pemberton was still pondering the life of James Browning and fretting about the significance of his whispered confession. In spite of their pledge not to talk about work when they were at home, she would not insist on this occasion; clearly he needed someone sympathetic with whom to discuss it.

'Browning is a murderer.' She sipped from her glass and played the Devil's advocate. 'We can't ignore that, we know he killed someone. But who?'

'Our efforts have been concentrated upon proving he is a serial killer when in fact he might not be,' he mused. 'However closely we examine our files, we can't escape the fact that he confessed to *one* murder, and one only, not a series. We can't even pin him down to our murder at Crayton.'

'Are you sure you heard him correctly?' she was compelled to ask for the umpteenth time. 'What did he say, exactly?'

'He said he knew he was going to die, and then he said, "Father I committed murder . . . I haven't been to confession since then . . . God forgive me, she didn't deserve that . . ." and I couldn't hear the rest because he was whispering and there was a good deal of background noise.'

'And that's all?'

'Well, he spoke to the priest for some time afterwards, whispering a fairly lengthy confession. I don't know what else he said. Those are the words I heard, Lorraine, they're beyond dispute. He would never lie under such circumstances.'

'But even so, Mark, there could have been other murders,' she suggested. 'He said, "I committed murder . . ." not "I have committed *a* murder". He didn't restrict it to one murder when he used that expression.'

'Yes, I know that part's open to interpretation, but the reference to his victim was definitely in the singular. Surely that suggests only one killing, a single murder.'

'You must admit there's an element of doubt.' She sipped from her glass. 'I don't think we can rule him out as a serial killer simply on the basis of his reference to one victim. That particular woman or girl might have meant something to him, we don't know what was going through his mind when he said she didn't deserve that – whatever "that" is. And what about the priest? Would another chat with him establish just what Browning confessed to? He might have admitted some earlier crimes to him, after the stage where you couldn't hear what he was saying?'

'If he did, there's no way we can get Father Flynn to tell us. If there had been any chance of Browning going to court, then we could have summoned the priest to appear as a witness but even then he'd never reveal what was said to him. He made that abundantly clear to me. But all that is academic – Browning is beyond human justice and there will be no court case which means Father Flynn will never be a witness. And I do know what I heard.'

'But you didn't hear everything he said to the priest, Mark, you admit that.'

'I know I didn't,' he sighed. 'And that's what's so frustrating. I wish I had heard the lot.'

'And you mustn't overlook the fact he might have confessed to other murders on previous occasions,' she reminded him. 'You've admitted that likelihood already, even though it's something you will never know.'

'You could be right,' he had to admit.

'And like Father Flynn, that other priest or priests would not be able to alert the authorities. They couldn't even discuss it among themselves. Imagine being told by a killer about a long-running series of vicious murders he'd committed, and not being able to do anything about it!'

'I accept that, but as I said earlier, a man wouldn't kill someone, confess it, and then go off and kill someone else, would he?'

'A madman might do it a year later, someone who's not in full control of themselves. We both know there are some mighty weird people in our society.'

'And they keep us in work!' he sighed.

'Mark . . .' She turned to face him now, resting her hands on his knees. 'You and I both know that in the world of crime detection, coincidence is a rare event. In this case, you heard a man confess to the murder of a female and within hours, a murdered prostitute turns up not far away. Is that a coincidence or not? Since then, other factors have come to light which suggest that the body in question is the victim of a serial killer.'

He butted in. 'It's more than a suggestion, Lorraine.'

'All right. It's a fact beyond dispute. But even so, our chief suspect, a man who admitted murder, is known to have been in the vicinity of all those crimes. Can you say that is all mere coincidence, Mark?'

He shrugged his shoulders. 'Go on.'

'Add to those coincidences the fact that only this evening we found a pair of sandals in the suspect's garage, woman's sandals which are the same colour and type as those taken from one of those eleven victims by the serial killer. Mark, tell me this – what else must we discover about Browning before you are convinced of his guilt? Hasn't the time come to write off those murders – all of them – and have them recorded as detected? And log the fact that Browning was the guilty person?'

'I am not going to do that, Lorraine, because even now we have no conclusive evidence against him.'

'And suppose we can prove those sandals *did* belong to one of the Strangler's victims? Would that convince you?'

'I would want to know where the other ten pairs were,' he said. 'And none has turned up anywhere. And I'd want to know how the sandals came to be in his possession. If we found every missing pair and could positively link them to him and link him to the scenes of the murders, then I might be convinced.' He leant forward to kiss the top of her head. 'But not until!'

'You're a stubborn Yorkshireman!' she responded. 'I just hope we can get this one sorted out before too long.'

'We usually do! We've an excellent detection record!'

'Yes, we're among the best. But come along, life's not all work and sleep. We're not supposed to be talking shop at home. It's bedtime!'

Resting her hands upon his knees, she levered herself from the floor, took his hand and led him towards the bedroom.

Detective Sergeant Tony Browne and DC Maureen Cox, the team to whom Inspector Larkin had allocated the action to trace the history of the MG Roadster, had done so without a lot of difficulty and were waiting for Pemberton as he entered the incident room at eight thirty next morning. With ample time before the conference of detectives, he led them into his office.

'So what can you tell me?' he invited.

'Browning's car, sir,' began Sergeant Browne. 'It's a 1971 MG Roadster, open top, two-seater, red colour as you know. It's always been red, no colour change is recorded. It was first registered on 27th April 1971. Between then and 1987, it had two owners, and in 1987 was purchased by a Hugh Dawlish whose address was then given as Tunbridge Wells in Kent. He sold it to James Bowman Browning in 1991, on 1st July to be precise, and the address for Browning is the one we have at Bleagill near Harlow Spa. Dawlish later moved to the Midlands where he now lives.'

'Was it a direct sale? Not through a garage or dealer?'

'No, sir, a direct sale. We have established that Dawlish is a friend of Browning's.'

'That's useful evidence,' Pemberton smiled.

'It goes back a long time. They were together at the Swangate College of Media Studies in County Durham and have kept in touch ever since. I've had discussions with Scenes of Crime at Harlow Spa about their search of the garage, and with Traffic Department. Dawlish's name is in Browning's address book, the one he kept in his flat, and it's also in several diaries and books we found in the garage.'

'Does he know of Browning's death?'

'I don't know, sir, we haven't contacted him. He was out when our officers called anyway, I believe Mr Browning senior was going to inform relatives and close friends?'

'Yes, he was. So where does Dawlish live now? You've got an address?'

'Yes, near Derby, sir, a village called Findford-on-Trent.'

'And do we know his profession or anything about him?'

'No, sir, other than to say that Browning's address book does confirm it is the Hugh Dawlish he befriended at college – it contains all the changed addresses, with appropriate amendments.'

'I want to know more about this Hugh Dawlish,' Pemberton put to his team. 'Is that something you could do as an action?'

'Yes, sir, we'd be delighted,' Browne spoke for both.

'All right, find out all you can about him, and what sort of car he runs. Like Browning, he might have two, don't forget, one of them an old MG. Tell Inspector Larkin I've asked you to look into all that but be very discreet. I don't want Dawlish to know of our interest; a lot depends upon what you discover.'

'Yes, sir, thanks,' and the two detectives disappeared to undertake their actions.

Before the morning conference of his detectives began, Pemberton wanted to know what Scenes of Crime had discovered in the garage and rang Harlow Spa CID to speak to Holroyd.

'He's left the office, sir, he's on his way to see you at Rainesbury, he should be with you any time now,' David Holroyd's secretary told him. As if in confirmation, there was a knock on Pemberton's door and his secretary showed in Detective Inspector Holroyd.

'I thought it would be better if I brought the findings with me,' he said by way of explanation for his arrival. 'It's easier than dealing with them on the phone and I thought I'd like to sit in on your conference, sir, if that's in order.'

'Seems a good idea to me,' said Pemberton. 'The more brains I get working on this, the better. Coffee before we start?'

'Thanks, sir.'

And so, over a mug of coffee, Holroyd provided Pemberton with the preliminary results of last night's search.

'The main thing,' he told Pemberton, 'is that there is no evidence of a murder or rape having occurred in the garage. It is not the scene of any crime, we're sure about that. And Forensic support us. The next point is that Browning appears to have used the garage as a place to keep everything to do with the old car and his rallies. He kept this aspect of his life quite separate from his domestic routine at the flat, but we don't know why. It was almost like two lives. Notices about events, copies of letters, repair bills for his car, lists of venues – the lot, it's all in his garage, stored and filed meticulously as we've come to expect of him. One important confirmation has arisen, sir, something we've already established – his summer holidays, until this year that is, do coincide with rallies of vintage MG cars somewhere in the country. We know he attended them, we found entries in a diary he kept in the drawer of that desk in the garage. He was not a member of a local club but was a member of the Findford-on-Trent Vintage Car Club. He had a friend down there –'

'Hugh Dawlish, a former college friend, the man who sold him the MG?'

'That's right, sir. You knew that?'

Pemberton acquainted Holroyd with a brief history of the MG. 'So we know his interest in the marque originated with Dawlish, and he sold him that car. They went rallying together?'

'Yes, sir, there were letters from Dawlish in the garage, filed away neatly. They were just to confirm the arrangements for the rallies – they used the events as a kind of reunion. It seems to have been the only such meeting they had during the year but it happened every year. From comments in some of the letters, it seems they kept in touch by telephone about major events in their lives. The diaries contain both his office and home numbers – and a mobile!'

'David, I'm going to have Dawlish investigated.'

'Good, I was going to suggest that, sir. You remember that photo in the garage? The one showing Browning with a man called Hugh?'

'I'm sure that was Dawlish,' Pemberton said.

'Right, well, I've had copies made for your teams. So what about Browning, do we drop him now?'

'I don't think so, David. I'm not convinced he's our Sandal Strangler, I'll be honest with you, but we must keep him high in the frame if we're to find out what he was up to. But I've asked DS Browne and DC Cox to target Dawlish, I want him looked at very thoroughly and most discreetly before we pull him in for interview.'

'You regard him as a serious suspect?'

'I do, either alone or acting with Browning. There's a possibility that two men might have been involved in the Sandal Stranglings. It's just a hint at this stage, nothing more. Suppose Dawlish and Browning met during their rallies? Suppose they were operating as a team? Maybe one drove the other to the scene or something. Maybe one committed the murders while the other knew nothing about it ... but it's all speculation, David. If we are to sort this one out, I don't want Dawlish alerted to our interest, not yet. Let's proceed softly, softly! If Dawlish is the serial killer, or if he has been involved in any way, he's managed to keep himself out of the frame for all these years, and that means he's no fool. Let's consider Mr Dawlish as a prime suspect while not forgetting he's a very clever one.'

'Dawlish does feature strongly in Browning's life, even if they met only once a year. There are lots of references to him in Browning's diaries, often just notes to say "Rang Hugh" every couple of weeks or so, but no one else gets that kind of treatment. In spite of their few meetings, I am sure Dawlish was Browning's best friend or even a confidant.'

'Any hint of homosexuality between them, David? Or with anyone else?'

'Not a scrap, sir, no, although in Browning's case, there's no evidence that he had regular girlfriends. I don't know about Dawlish's girlfriends. Now, the pair of blue sandals. They've gone off to Forensic to see if they can tie them in with any of the scenes. The 1991 victim – Rachel Pennock – was found in a beech wood, so if any of the earth stuck to her sandals, it can be compared with the control sample taken at the time. And there is a photo of her wearing the sandals, taken two days before she died. I don't have it, but the local force – Lincolnshire – is sending copies along to you. I said they should send them here.'

As they talked, Detective Inspector Kirkdale arrived; Pemberton motioned him to be seated as the discussion continued.

'Good, now, David, how confident are we about those sandals?'

'I'm fairly sure they belonged to Rachel Pennock, sir. If that is the case, it puts Browning at that murder scene.'

'So you think Browning is the Sandal Strangler?' Pemberton put to David Holroyd.

'Everything points that way, sir. The sandals would clinch it – they'd be damned good evidence in any trial, pretty conclusive I'd say, that's if we can prove they came from Rachel.'

Pemberton turned to Kirkdale and reiterated his theory about Dawlish, asking, 'Gregory, suppose we prove that Dawlish was the last man to see Debbie Hall alive – would that affect your opinion of Browning?'

'I would most certainly investigate the possibility of both men being involved.' He was emphatic about this. 'In Debbie's case, we know that Browning was alive at eight on the evening she disappeared, don't we? The time she was last seen alive. He was alive until the following Tuesday which means he could have killed her.'

'Right, but it wasn't him who was seen with her. It was a tall, dark man about thirty years of age. He was seen escorting Debbie on the sea-front at Rainesbury the night she disappeared. It might have been Dawlish. We need to have him identified in person by that barman, Eddie Brodie. A photo identification would be a good start.'

'But if Dawlish did escort her away for a walk or whatever, it doesn't exclude Browning, sir. He might have been waiting in the background, with the car perhaps. If both were involved, that might have been their MO. One to find the victim, the other to murder or rape her.'

'I'm having the car-park checked, the security cameras might show if Browning's MG was there.'

'Does Dawlish have an MG?' asked Holroyd. 'Has that been established?'

'That's something I've asked the team to find out,' said Pemberton. 'Although, according to Gregory, there's been no reports of any cars at or near the scenes, certainly nothing so distinctive as a red MG.'

Kirkdale nodded his agreement.

'Now I've got the prints of Dawlish,' suggested Holroyd, 'shall I show one to Brodie before the conference? I'd like to be useful while I'm here.'

'Yes, do that. He works at the Lobster on the sea-front.'

'Right, sir, I'll run down there straight away. If he's not at work yet, I can trace him. Back soon!'

And so Detective Inspector Holroyd left to go about his essential piece of work as Kirkdale returned to his own office. Pemberton decided he must see Mr Browning senior before he came to collect his son's belongings. At least Pemberton now had an excuse to seize and retain the items – Dawlish. He rang the Road Traffic Department, and asked for PC Broadbent; he had just come on duty.

'It's Pemberton here. There's been a development in the murder enquiry. It means I can't let Mr Browning have his son's belongings, not just yet, nor can I allow him access to the flat or garage at this stage. I need to talk to him. Call me when he comes in, will you?'

'He's here now, sir, in the front office.'

Pemberton groaned. 'I'll be right down,' he said.

12

Rather nervously, Pemberton invited Mr Browning into the duty inspector's office and bade him be seated. Taking a deep breath, he began. 'Mr Browning, there's been a development, not a very pleasant one from your point of view. I'm sorry to have to impart this news –'

'The brakes, you mean? Was it sabotage after all?'

'No, I'm not referring to the accident. It's about a murder enquiry which is under way in Rainesbury – you know about it?'

'Yes, I do. The prostitute. I've seen it in the papers.'

Pemberton paused, took another deep breath and continued. 'In every murder case, Mr Browning, there are lots of suspects, people whom we have to eliminate in order to track down the real killer. Innocent people, Mr Browning, people who were in the vicinity at the time, for example, personal enemies, business acquaintances, a whole range of people. They're all brought into our net and questioned. I'm sure you appreciate the need for that.'

'Yes, I think so.'

There was a puzzled frown on Mr Browning's face as he slowly began to appreciate the direction of Pemberton's statements.

'Your son's movements have brought him into focus – with others, I might add. You know that already, I'm sure. Even though he is dead, we need to eliminate him from our enquiries. I'm sure you realise that it is necessary to interview and eliminate lots of people during the process of bringing the killer to justice.'

'Yes, I can understand that.'

'In James's case, it means I must retain all his personal belongings, for the time being that is. I must also seal his flat and the garage where he kept his Roadster. We have to examine everything he owned, all that he used, to make sure nothing belonging to him was used in the crime.'

'Are you saying you think James killed the girl and then deliberately ran into that tree?'

'No, we remain confident the accident was the result of brake failure, Mr Browning.'

'I do hope so. James is – was – no killer, Mr Pemberton! I'd stake my own life on that, he's – he was – much too gentle, much too caring. You know he worked for charities? I'm sure you realise he could not have done such a thing.'

'Yes, but that's what I need to prove, Mr Browning. It's not easy for us, having to make these kinds of enquiries, because people believe we think the subjects of our enquiries are guilty. It's usually not the case. Invariably, we know they are innocent but we have to prove it. But when a man has been close to the scene of a murder at the material time, we must go through certain rather upsetting procedures in order to identify the guilty. Now, to eliminate your son, we need to talk to his friends. We have their names and addresses, thanks to the address book we found in his flat. We understand that one of his friends, his best friend perhaps, is called Hugh Dawlish. James has a photograph of himself with the man I believe is Hugh Dawlish.'

'Yes, that's true. You know him?'

'No, I don't. Now, I must stress that he is no more a suspect than anyone else. What we do know is that he and James went to vintage car rallies together, and that they've been friends since college. Does he know about James's accident?'

'Yes, I rang him yesterday. He was distraught, he'll be coming to the funeral – it's on Monday, by the way. Eleven o'clock. Requiem Mass here in Rainesbury. At Our Lady and St Hilda's, Father Flynn will officiate. I thought that would be nice, seeing he was with James when he died. James did not attend church in Harlow Spa and so I want the interment to be near my family home, where I can tend the grave. That will take place the following day. But back to Mr Dawlish. I don't like him, Mr Pemberton, there's no point in hiding my views. I don't know why but he seems creepy, I think that's the phrase people use nowadays. He befriended James at college, and I think he dominated James in some way. I got the feeling he continued to do so when they finished at college. Even so, James took great care to keep in touch with Hugh all through the years, but, well, he's not the sort of man I'd welcome as a friend. I might add he has been to our house on a couple of occasions, for weekends with James when they were students. My late wife didn't take to him either, God bless her.'

'You know more about him?'

'To be frank, no, but it's just the way he was, his behaviour . . . I don't know why really, he never harmed us in any way nor was he obnoxious or rude – in fact, I think he tried to be nice to us, but however hard he tried, I did not like the man. I'll tell you something – when I first worried about the question of sabotage, I must admit I wondered if Hugh had done it . . . perhaps that shows what I feel about him?'

'Mr Browning, can I ask a great favour of you? I don't want you to tell Hugh Dawlish about our interest in him.'

'You suspect him, don't you? It wouldn't surprise me, Mr Pemberton. I'm afraid I can't tell you whether he's been to see James recently, if that's what you want to know. I just hope he's not been leading my James into some kind of awful behaviour. James changed, you know, at college. Before he went, he was such a lovely open boy, friendly and bright, the sort any man or woman could warm to. Then, as a student, he changed, he became more remote, sullen even, and for a time afterwards, he rarely came home. People did say that sort of behaviour was normal for a student, part of the growing-up process, but in my son's case, his whole personality seemed to change. He did keep in touch, but there was none of the earlier warmth. Mind, when his mother died, he made an effort to re-establish his relationship with me – she meant a lot to him. But no, Mr Pemberton, my son is no murderer. I do hope you can prove that and so I will co-operate with you in any way I can.'

Pemberton had no intention of telling Mr Browning about his son's confession – not yet. If it did transpire that James was the serial killer, then he might tell him, but not before. He knew the priest would never reveal it.

'We will keep you informed, Mr Browning. Are you staying in the area for much longer?'

'I've decided to stay until the Requiem Mass on Monday,' he said firmly. 'There is a lot to do here. You have my hotel address and telephone number?'

'Yes, I have,' and the interview concluded in a manner which was far more friendly and affable than Pemberton could ever have dreamed.

Pemberton did wonder whether he had been rather too devious or less than honest in his discussions with Mr Browning, but decided it was all part of his overall work of detection. One outcome had been an insight, however brief, into the character of Hugh Dawlish and Pemberton felt he had made a very positive step forward. Happier than he'd been only half an hour ago, he returned to the incident room to prepare for his morning conference of detectives and then the daily news conference.

Pemberton's first task upon entering the incident room was to find Inspector Larkin. 'Paul . . .' He beckoned him into his office. 'A moment please.'

When Larkin had settled in the chair, Pemberton told him

about his conversation with Mr Browning and his views on Hugh Dawlish. 'Dawlish has told Browning senior that he's coming to the funeral Mass, which is to be at eleven o'clock on Monday here in Rainesbury. We have a team looking into his movements and background?'

'Yes, sir, DS Grant and DC Black.'

'Right. At this delicate stage, we should not visit him at his home or let our interest be known to him. Eventually, I want to speak to Dawlish myself. I can do that when he gets here. Between now and then, we need to find out everything about him. And if there's any likelihood of him not turning up at the funeral service, let me know. It might be necessary to arrest him and detain him on suspicion.'

'A top-of-the-frame suspect, sir?'

'A gut feeling, Paul. A gut feeling, nothing more at this stage.'

'I've known your gut feelings be proved right on more than one occasion. So, yes, I'll have words with the teams about Dawlish.'

'Anything back from Eddie, our barman?'

'Not yet, sir, DI Holroyd hasn't returned.'

'So what's the state of play at the moment, Paul? Anything else I need to know before I address the troops?'

'Only that we're getting replies to your fax requesting information about unsolved murders in other force areas. It's amazing how many unfortunate young women have been killed without their murderers being traced. It makes you wonder if there are several serial killers at large.'

'I've often thought so, Paul, but it would involve oceans of time to decide that. Our job's to concentrate upon the Sandal Strangler. But all incoming information is useful; detail someone to examine the reports closely, to see if there's any possible links with our murder or with the Sandal Strangler in general. Let DI Kirkdale have a look at everything when he gets in. Now, our own enquiries? What's new here?'

Inspector Larkin explained that there had been no further developments of importance overnight. Intensified house-to-house enquiries in Crayton and district had not yielded any useful information; people known to walk their dogs or to stroll through the woods or beside the river had been traced and interviewed, with no positive leads.

Night duty detectives had interviewed more prostitutes in Rainesbury, catching them as they worked the streets and clubs, but nobody could shed any light on the fate of Debbie Hall. Several of them had known Debbie, but none had seen her on Sunday night with the tall, dark man. Attempts to obtain from them a name for that man had been unsuccessful – the description was too vague to be of any general use although now that a photograph of Hugh Dawlish was available, the prostitutes and night-club hostesses would be shown copies. It was hoped someone might have seen him in town over the weekend. Similar reactions had come from those who had organised the antiques fair; they'd not recognised Dawlish. Those known to have attended would be shown a photograph of Dawlish too, in the hope he'd been noticed in and around the town. Detective Inspector Holroyd returned to the incident room moments before Pemberton addressed his detectives; already, they were assembled in readiness, but Holroyd's information was important.

'The barman, sir, Eddie Brodie. I tracked him down and showed him the photo. He says Dawlish is definitely the man he saw with Debbie Hall the night she disappeared. He got a good look at him through the bar window. He's a good witness, he'll come to look at Dawlish in the flesh if necessary.'

'Good.' Pemberton felt this was another important advance. 'So, do we wait for Dawlish to attend the funeral service on Monday or shall we lift him now for interrogation?'

'Better be safe than sorry, I'd say,' Holroyd advised. 'Let's bring him in to see what he says for himself. And while he's in custody, we can search his house.'

'Can we be sure he's never entered the frame for any of the Sandal Strangler killings?' Pemberton turned to Kirkdale who was standing nearby. 'Even in a very minor way?'

'No, sir, not even as a witness. He's a new name to us.'

'So he's never been interviewed, not even for elimination?'

'No, sir.' Kirkdale was quite certain.

'Fine, then he'll have no idea that we are beginning to associate him with any of the killings, let alone our most recent one. I would suggest that that indicates that he's not likely to do a runner. He'll take life as normal, in which case I'd like to have more background information about him and his movements before

106

we bring him in or even quiz him. I think it's important that we are fully informed about his background before we commence any interview,' said Pemberton. 'Can you get me a detailed analysis of all the murders, Gregory? As much detail as possible? Every scrap of evidence, every valuable fact that's been recorded?'

'No problem,' Kirkdale assured him. 'It's all on disc. Do you want it before you address your teams?'

'No, we've got DS Grant and DC Black checking on Dawlish's movements and background. We need to update them on recent developments. I'll speak to them before they leave after the conference. I want to see if Dawlish can be placed at any of the scenes, with or without Browning.'

'Right, I'll action that the moment the conference is over,' promised Kirkdale, who smiled as he added, 'You're holding something back, aren't you, sir? Do you know something the rest of us don't?'

'I have just the faintest flicker of a feeling about this case.' Pemberton pursed his lips. 'Maybe it's too daft even to consider or maybe it isn't, but I won't air my feelings now; let's wait until we've more information about Dawlish. Now, let's talk to the troops and get them to work, they'll be wondering what's causing the delay.'

During the conference, Pemberton updated his detectives on current progress and referred to the photograph which had been viewed by Eddie Brodie. He told them that the man's name was Hugh Dawlish and that he was a friend of James Browning. Copies were handed out to those detectives who would be working in the town for them to ask householders and witnesses if the man had been seen in Rainesbury or elsewhere, particularly during the weekend.

'What we need to do,' Pemberton exhorted them, 'is to link Dawlish with Browning in either Crayton or Rainesbury over last weekend, or to link either of them with Debbie Hall during the same period. If they were here, where were they staying? Have we a team checking hotels and boarding houses?'

A couple of detectives raised their hands, so Pemberton

continued, 'Browning lived near Harlow Spa so he was within easy commuting distance, but if his pal was staying here, then Browning might have joined him for the weekend. Ask around all the likely hotels, boarding houses and bed-and-breakfast places, but remember these guys are – or were in Browning's case – in business and would have expense accounts. You'd not expect to find them using scruffy places.'

'Dawlish never seems to have stayed with Browning at his flat,' Larkin pointed out.

'But they did use bed-and-breakfast accommodation when attending their annual rallies,' Pemberton reminded them. 'Now, this is important. I don't want you to mention Dawlish by name during these enquiries. If you show anyone the photo, pretend we want to know who he is, say he's a friend of Browning, that's all. Tell your witnesses we're trying to establish a name for him, trying to get him identified – say we want to tell him about Browning's accident, and if you're checking hotel registers, don't let the proprietors know who you're asking about. The reason for this caution is that Dawlish is on his way here and I don't want him to know we're probing his background and movements. He mustn't be alerted, not at this stage.'

Pemberton answered a few questions and then dismissed them to go about their enquiries, keeping back DS Grant and DC Black for a more detailed briefing. Prior to that, he fronted the daily news conference at which he confirmed the identity of the dead girl, Debbie Hall. He decided not to release a description of the man seen on the sea-front on Sunday night, the one who walked away with Debbie. If that description was published in the evening papers or even tomorrow's dailies, it could alert Dawlish when he arrived in town.

When the press had gone, Holroyd left to return to his own station at Harlow Spa while Pemberton asked Larkin to join Detective Sergeant John Grant and Detective Constable Ian Black in his office. Coffee was ordered and Detective Inspector Kirkdale went off to procure a detailed list of the Sandal Stranglings. Grant, in his mid-thirties and wearing rimless spectacles, looked more like a provincial solicitor than a detective while Black, thick-set and in his late twenties, had the appearance of a rugger prop forward. But they worked well together and Pemberton was not afraid to entrust them with this task. Kirkdale arrived with several copies of his analysis charts, and handed one each to the detectives, Paul Larkin and Pemberton. There was another for the noticeboard, a useful *aide-mémoire* for the teams.

After Pemberton had updated Grant and Black, Kirkdale took over. 'In all cases after the first, you'll note the bodies were found on either Monday or Tuesday although the deaths had occurred the previous weekend. That was midsummer weekend, or the weekend closest to midsummer day. The precise dates are given. Now, I'll run through the details: 1987, Josephine Crawley's body was found near Penthorne, County Durham, and this is generally regarded as the first of the Sandal Stranglings. 1988, Sophie Armitage at Oldsfield near Otterburn in Northumberland. 1989, Toni Petch at Rusthwaite near Windermere in the Lake District. 1990, Teresa Blackett at Linsby near Market Rasen in Lincolnshire and 1991 another in Lincolnshire, Rachel Pennock at Buckwold near Horncastle. In 1992, it was Gina Gibbons at Longwell near Buxton in Derbyshire, 1993 was Isa Pickford at Pontyllan near Betws-y-coed in North Wales, 1994 was Janice Gleeson at Kempley Woods in Gloucestershire and 1995 was Amy Welsh at Fulstock near Woodstock in Oxfordshire. Last year it was Kay Sinton and she was found at East Welton near Market Harborough in Leicestershire. And now, this year, it's Debbie Hall at Crayton not far from here. All were found dead in remote wooded areas, all were prostitutes from nearby towns and all had their sandals removed and taken away, as you know. Their underwear disappeared too and was never found. The girls were not known to one another and we don't think drugs or some other criminal activity was the reason for their deaths.'

'Thanks, Gregory. Now, what I want you to do,' Pemberton told Grant and Black, 'is to establish all you can about Dawlish and find out if he was anywhere near those places at the material times. We know that Browning was nearby at all the material times. If Dawlish was there, how did he travel and with whom? Has he a vintage car too? We have a team delving deeper into Browning's movements in connection with those areas. Have words with them and with the team who are going through the stuff relating to the Roadster, the papers we found in Browning's garage. I am hoping we might discover more references to Dawlish among those papers.'

'That's DS Browne and DC Cox,' Larkin told them.

'So if we can tie Dawlish with those places, and also with Browning, then perhaps we can nail Dawlish,' smiled Grant.

'At least we can be prepared to ask him a lot of searching questions.' Mark Pemberton felt a tremor of excitement. In his opinion, this was the most important development so far.

13

Shortly before lunch time that same Friday, Lorraine politely tapped on Pemberton's office door. It was standing open so he waved her in.

'Are you alone?'

'Hi!' Her appearance gave him joy as always. 'Yes, all alone, so come in and take a seat. How's it going out there?'

'The teams have all gone out, so it's calmed down, but I've been going through the papers that were brought in from Browning's garage this morning. Tony and Maureen are digging further, but I found this and had a good look at it.'

She held up a hardcover exercise book.

'What is it?' he asked.

'A diary, a diary for his MG Roadster.' She smiled. 'The journal of his car. It's an account of all the things that have happened to the car since Browning bought it. It's been completed in chronological order like a daily log would be. At first glance, it's hardly worth our interest because it records his purchase and all the trivia that's happened to the car since he bought it, such as when he got new tyres, when the water pump failed, when new plugs were fitted, when he had a scratch painted out, that sort of thing. Scenes of Crime have checked the diary for prints or whatever they look for and cleared it, but they hadn't read it.'

'And you have, and you've found something of relevance?' He could sense her excitement.

'Yes, in addition to the trivia, he's included his outings in the car and every tiny facet associated with it. The first item of interest to us is at the very beginning.' She adopted a modest attitude as she opened the book at the first page. 'It's in the paragraph where he's listing the contents of the car when he got it from Dawlish – tool box, first aid kit, spare wheel, tow rope, the canvas hood, handbook, that sort of thing. Dawlish left some of his own things behind – a torch under the driver's seat, for example, and a few coins for parking meters . . . and a pair of ladies' sandals, size 5. They were under the passenger seat.'

'Sandals?'

'Blue ones,' she said. 'Browning describes them carefully, it's the sort of thing he would do, he'd take immense pains to get things exactly right.'

'Go on, Lorraine.'

'You know how meticulous Browning was. A real belt and braces man. Well, this is a good example. He rang Dawlish two days later, that's in the diary too, to inform him of the things he'd left in the car. Listen – "Rang Hugh re personal belongings left in MG. Torch, sandals, etc. He told me I could keep torch and cash as gifts, and said he'd collect the sandals when he was next in Harlow Spa. Said they belonged to a girlfriend who wasn't worried about them. Told me not to worry, there was no panic for their return and told me not to bother to send them on by post." Then about a month later, there's a further note: "Hugh has not collected sandals. Reminded him by telephone. Told me to hang on to them, said he's not forgotten them. Girlfriend knows where they are. I told him I'd put them on a shelf in the garage, should he or she ever come looking for them." There's another entry a couple of months after that, and a further one about three months later when he wrote that Hugh did not seem interested in the sandals but that he would leave them on this shelf just in case someone turned up and wanted them. After that, he seems to have ceased to bother about them.'

'And you think those are the same sandals that you found on that shelf?'

'I don't think there's any doubt,' she said. 'They're just like the ones the prostitute was wearing in the photograph and match the description Browning gave.'

'So what's the latest on them? They've been sent off for examination, haven't they?'

'Yes, DI Kirkdale thinks they might have come from the Buckwold murder, in Lincolnshire. Rachel Pennock was the dead girl, we've got a picture of her wearing identical sandals. We've had no result yet, they're comparing soil samples found on the shoes with control samples taken from the wood where she was found. It'll take a day or two.'

'So what's your theory about the sandals?'

'First, I am sure they belonged to the dead girl, Rachel Pennock. Next, I am sure they were in the MG when Browning bought it from Dawlish. In other words, I believe what Browning wrote. He'd hardly lie in his own diaries! That means the sandals came to him via Dawlish. So did Dawlish kill Rachel or did someone else place the sandals in Dawlish's car? It has an open top, remember. Or did Dawlish pay her for sex before she died? Some time before she died? Like he probably did with Debbie Hall? One thing to remember is that Browning bought the car in July 1991: Pennock was murdered a month earlier, in June 1991. She had been murdered before the transfer of the car took place. Therefore, it suggests that that car can be linked to the murder of Rachel Pennock. It puts Dawlish very firmly in the frame, Mark. He has to be seen and made to account for his possession of those sandals. There's every reason for regarding Dawlish as a key suspect or even *the* key suspect for the Sandal Stranglings.'

'I agree with your reasoning.' Pemberton smiled at her, recalling their conversation at home and delighted at this development. It supported the idea which was forming in his mind. 'Our killer is very cunning and very clever, he must be to have avoided becoming a suspect all these years. So let's suppose Dawlish is the killer and that we interview him at this stage. All he has to do is to deny all knowledge of the sandals, or to claim they were left in his car by someone to whom he gave a lift, or thrown in, cast away by someone else. People do throw all manner of things into open-top cars, from bras to beer cans. There could be a host of explanations for the presence of those shoes. It means we must be very cautious because, at this stage, we cannot prove that Dawlish had anything to do with them. I am not going to ask him directly about them, not yet. I need to know more about him first – in fact, I want to know everything about him.'

'His fingerprints might be on the sandals, Mark, they are made of cheap plastic. Plastic is good for retaining prints.'

112

'It's a possibility, they could have survived all this time. We can try to find them – if Dawlish's prints are there as well as Browning's, it would help to establish Browning's account that the shoes were left behind in the car when he bought it. Not that I think he'd lie anyway, not in his own diary; it seems he had no idea of their importance. Remember, there's been no press coverage about the murder victims' sandals . . .'

'Those sandals are important, Mark, but I'm not saying we should arrest Dawlish immediately. I'm just saying they're a strong pointer towards his guilt, rather than Browning's.'

'And I agree. I do appreciate the difficulties in establishing the necessary chain of evidence which would satisfy a modern court of law, but we'll have a go!'

'Great – but there's more in this little book, Mark!'

'I guessed there would be.'

She said that the car's record contained, in diary form, an account of all the rallies and events to which it had been taken. Any award, however small, was listed, rosettes, cups, certificates of commendation. The car had regularly won prizes for its overall condition and appearance. Some of these had been held for one year only, others had been retained and stored in the garage. In all cases, James Browning's record-keeping had been meticulous.

'When I saw that analysis of the Sandal Stranglings on the noticeboard this morning,' Lorraine continued, 'I checked the dates against this diary. Apart from the first murder near Penthorne, and our own at Crayton, it confirms there was a vintage car rally in the vicinity at the material time. In one case – East Welton near Market Harborough in Leicestershire – the rally was actually held in the village. And, Mark, what's more important is that in his brief account of the rallies or events he attended, he says he met Hugh. He met Hugh at every one of those events. He doesn't give a surname, but Hugh Dawlish is the only Hugh in Browning's address book. What it means is that this little book puts both Dawlish and Browning very close to the scene of nine of those eleven murders. As we know, the two exceptions are the first murder and the most recent. I believe that is more than a coincidence.'

'We can't rely on coincidences. Can we prove the diary was written by Browning?'

'We can get enough samples of his handwriting to satisfy most courts,' she smiled, having anticipated that question.

'And we have reason to believe that Dawlish was the last person to see Debbie Hall alive in Rainesbury last weekend – that puts him almost at the scene of that one too,' Pemberton mused.

'And don't forget that James Browning, using the alias of Bowman, was seen by a police officer at the scene of the Penthorne murder, albeit two days after the body had been discovered. But his presence there might back up the old theory that murderers always return to the scene of the crime. I'd say his presence, for whatever reason, is another factor we can't ignore.'

'So, Lorraine, what do you read into all this?'

'There's a strong possibility they were both involved, although I have to say that Dawlish is emerging as the stronger contender in the guilt stakes. I'm not sure how they operated; perhaps Browning was a passive partner, driving Dawlish to the scene, or perhaps he was an innocent bystander or unknowing accomplice, while on the other hand he might have taken a violent and very active part. I just don't know, but we do know they were both at Swangate College at the time of the first murder. If this little book can be accepted as a true record, it shows both have been very near the scene of every other killing. Even Browning can be said to be close to the scene of Debbie Hall's murder – he lived not far away. Sadly, we've nothing yet to place either of them, or both of them, precisely at the scene of any of the killings at the material time. That is the real problem from our point of view, the one that any defence counsel would highlight. It's the one defect we must rectify. And we haven't traced Browning's precise movements over last weekend, to account for his whereabouts at the time she died, have we?'

'Not yet,' Pemberton agreed. 'But my teams are working on it and we know he lived not far away – an hour at most by car. He could have driven Dawlish and the girl out to Crayton. Whatever we discover, it is significant that Dawlish was here around the time of Debbie's murder which we know is the most recent Sandal Strangler killing. He was here the night Debbie was last seen alive . . . he was seen with her too. The coincidence is too great to ignore . . .'

'Surely you have enough circumstantial evidence to have Dawlish in for questioning straight away, Mark?'

'I told Grant and Black I'd wait until they'd done their background research. I can wait a little longer. You know he's coming to the Requiem Mass?'

'Yes, I'd heard that. Well, it's Friday now. Friday lunch time. Lots of firms close around now for the weekend, so he might already be *en route*. What's he do for a living?'

'I don't know, that's part of our enquiries. What is important is that I don't give him any reason to think we have any suspicion of his involvement. I don't want to alert him or frighten him off. When I confront him I want it to be a real shock, a complete surprise . . .'

'If he's avoided detection or even suspicion for ten years, then he's no fool, Mark. You'll need to prepare very carefully for your interview.'

'Exactly. And would you apply the same doubtful praise to Browning? That he's evaded suspicion for ten years too?'

'All right, there could be two clever killers!'

'Or,' he grinned, 'only one of them was the killer. To be precise, only one of them is the Sandal Strangler. I'm not forgetting that Browning might be a killer too, but not the killer of several women. And bearing in mind what we have just discussed, I am less convinced about Browning's involvement with the Sandal Strangler killings.'

'Are you suggesting that Dawlish is the Sandal Strangler, that he acts alone and that those deaths had nothing to do with Browning?'

'It's feasible,' he said. 'Even if both men met during their weekend rallies there'd be times when they'd not be in one another's company. One could have killed a woman without the other realising.'

'Are you suggesting we should no longer consider Browning as a suspect?'

'No, he's still in the frame but I think we should look at Dawlish in isolation, and see what he has to say, before we draw too many conclusions about Browning or any kind of criminal partnership. If we got Dawlish's local police to detain him until our teams brought him here, it would give him time to work out his answers. I think that eventuality – the fact he might be

115

questioned about the murders – is something he's been preparing for ever since his first murder. I'll warrant he's been physically and mentally covering his tracks and preparing a story in readiness for the day the police knock on his door. That means if we do detain him, he'll know why. Any serial killer would. What I am just wondering now, though, is how much he's been affected by Browning's death. The two were fairly close but I've no idea how close they were. It could have some bearing on his future behaviour.'

'He could change or act out of character, you mean?'

'It's possible. People can behave abnormally if there's a crisis in their lives, a major drama of some kind. Like the death of a close friend.'

'So you'll wait until he turns up in Rainesbury?'

'For all sorts of rather special reasons, yes.'

'I just hope he doesn't smell the proverbial rat and do a runner!'

'There are elements to this crime, or this series of crimes, which don't add up.' He wanted to be honest with her and yet found difficulty in finding the words or the justification for his anxiety. 'I can't quite put my finger on it, but I am growing increasingly unhappy about the idea of Browning being the Sandal Strangler. I must admit I wanted to prove it was him, to get a clear-up in the murder figures, but now I'm not so sure.'

'It was his own words, his own confession, which led him to become a suspect for the Sandal Strangler killings,' she reminded him.

'Yes, I know, but why did we follow that route? Because the body of a woman was found shortly after he confessed, and we had no other murders which we could attribute to him. And that still applies. No other bodies have been found in our area, we've no other unsolved murders. On top of that, there are lots of unsolved murders of women in other parts of the country – we know that from the material we're receiving even as we talk. So are we looking in the wrong place for his crime? Are we in danger of finding him guilty, without trial, of a series of crimes he did not commit, Lorraine? I can't ignore the consequences of that possibility.'

'And now you've got Dawlish in your sights?'

'Yes, but currently, Dawlish and Browning are both in the

frame. I am unable, from the information we've gathered so far, to separate one from the other. That's why I want to face this man Dawlish from cold – I want to see his face when I present him with my belief that he is the Sandal Strangler. I want to see the expression in his eyes and see how he responds. I want to watch his body language. And I don't want to give him time to prepare for a confrontation with the police, either in the Midlands where he lives, or up here in Yorkshire. Like most serial killers, the Sandal Strangler is a cold, calculating and very clever individual.'

'I respect your reasoning, Mark, your wisdom and your experience, I just hope it doesn't go wrong. If Dawlish is our man, I want you to secure sufficient evidence to lock him up for the rest of his life.'

'Which is why I think we must treat this one slightly differently from other suspects.'

'Point taken. I'll stop nattering! Now, time for a break. Lunch time.'

'We ought to tell DI Kirkdale our thoughts,' Mark Pemberton said. 'And Inspector Larkin. But,' he added, 'if we go to the police canteen, two inspectors and me, that is, we will have to be segregated from you. Constables and inspectors do not dine together! But as you are the instigator of this line of enquiry, I think you should tell them of your discoveries. I'd like you to do that. So how about it if I invite them into my office for sandwiches? I'll give you the money to get them from the canteen?'

'Highly diplomatic!' she smiled, and so it was arranged.

Over sandwiches and coffee, Lorraine explained her findings to the others, with Pemberton present. Afterwards, Kirkdale said, 'Sir, with all due respect, if Dawlish is so high in the frame, I vote we go and get him, right now.'

'Gregory, I've said it to Lorraine and I'll say it to you, I really do want to wait until he turns up here in Rainesbury.'

'I'd back my boss on this one,' added Paul Larkin. 'I've seen Mr Pemberton in action before, he does know what he's doing, and he does know his villains . . .'

'If that man gets one sniff that we're interested in him, he'll be off like a rat leaving a sinking ship.'

'Exactly, so let's plan ahead, let's provide a reception committee for him. Remember he has no idea we suspect him, so what will be his first action upon arriving here?' Pemberton put to them.

'Are we assuming he has committed murder, with or without the connivance of Browning?' asked Larkin.

'Yes, let's consider that first,' said Pemberton. 'I think he'll act as if he has not committed any of the murders. He'll shut them from his mind, that's how serial killers work. He'll come to the funeral service, he'll want to know all about the fatal accident in which his friend died, and I'll bet he'll be as chatty and as friendly as possible to us, the police. And he'll want to do what he can for the Browning family.'

'Won't he go to Browning's flat?' suggested Kirkdale. 'Ostensibly to offer comfort but in reality to see if there's any evidence against him?'

'Why should he do that? There's no one at the flat. Browning senior has told him about the funeral arrangements, so he'll come to Rainesbury. If he does, I want to talk to him and I'm going to behave as if he's a ruthless, evil and skilful killer, Gregory. You've been hunting him for years, now it's my turn.'

'But I don't want to lose the chance of nailing him for these crimes.'

'Me neither, so I suggest we play a waiting game,' said Pemberton. 'After all, time and the all-important element of surprise are on our side. After years of waiting, a few more hours won't hurt.'

With Larkin and Lorraine against him, Kirkdale capitulated, albeit with some signs of reluctance, and accepted the arguments of the others. They would wait until their suspect arrived at the funeral and, at the most suitable moment, would confront him with their suspicions. But the Requiem Mass was not until Monday – and it was only Friday afternoon now.

It was while they were deliberating these questions that Detective Sergeant Grant tapped on Pemberton's door.

'Sorry to bother you, sir, but we've been making discreet enquiries about Dawlish. We're getting some useful information about him, but more urgently, you should know he left home this morning and didn't go into his office.'

14

'Come in and tell us about it.'

Detective Sergeant John Grant entered Pemberton's office, closely followed by his colleague, DC Ian Black. There were no extra chairs in the tiny office, but Grant indicated that he and Black had no wish to be seated.

'I had no intention of interrupting your lunch break, sir,' began Grant, eyeing the sandwiches and coffee cups.

'A working lunch. Have you eaten?' Pemberton asked them.

'Yes, thanks, sir. A sandwich and a pint apiece – it works wonders after a long morning!'

'Good. Well, what can you tell us about Dawlish?'

'First, he's not at home or at work. We gave no hint of the reason for our enquiries, the lads in Derbyshire were most discreet, so I don't think we have alerted him or his office staff to our suspicions. I did wonder, though, if he could have got wind of our interest and done a runner. I thought you'd better know about his absence in case you need to issue a nationwide alert or an all-ports warning and have him picked up.'

'Thanks, but probably not at this stage. We have good reason to think he might be heading north, John, for the Requiem Mass for his friend James Browning. It's to be on Monday here in Rainesbury, but the interment will be later in the week, near his family home in Staffordshire.'

'That's a relief! It ties in with what his secretary said. He has a red MG Roadster, sir, J registered. Just like Browning's. Same year, same colour, same model. Very similar registration number too. The prefix is identical, but the numbers of Dawlish's are 868 followed by J, while Browning's were 688 J. It's easy to confuse those numbers. He's left home in that. We had a DC go to see him at the office, pretending to be a small businessman wanting advice on local advertising – Dawlish is an advertising executive, sir, with his own business in a small market town called Findford-on-Trent. HD Advertising, he calls it. Very successful too, according to local intelligence. He runs a BMW as his business vehicle – if we need to have it examined, Derbyshire police will see to it. Anyway, he wasn't at the office and his secretary said he'd rung in this morning to say a friend had died, and he was going to Rainesbury for the funeral. He said he'd be back in the office on Tuesday morning.'

'That ties in,' Pemberton agreed.

'The DC then went to his flat, pretending to be a friend, but the neighbours said he'd gone off in his MG. They said he often went off for weekends in it. He was away last weekend, they said, but they've no idea where.'

'He came here and there's every indication he's on his way here again. What sort of place does he live in?' Pemberton asked out of curiosity.

'A large detached house split into three flats, one on each floor. It's in a quiet part of Findford, backing on to the tennis courts and sports centre. Dawlish has the top floor –'

'Rented or owner-occupied?' Pemberton interrupted. He was eager to get a mental image of this man and property ownership was one pointer.

'He owns it, sir, all three flats are individually owned. The middle one's occupied by a young woman who commutes to Derby every day and the ground floor's occupied by a retired wing commander and his wife. They see everything that's going on, and keep an eye on the other flats during the absence of the occupiers. They said Dawlish was a busy but friendly man, a good neighbour who was courteous and helpful and not a scrap of trouble. No noisy parties or loud music. He was not married and lived alone, but seemed to spend a lot of time away from home, usually on business, so he led them to believe, although he did sometimes say he was going off in his MG to a rally or gathering of vintage cars. He had his own garage on the premises for the MG, by the way, according to the wing commander, and on those occasions he was at home, he seemed to spend a lot of his spare time at weekends polishing and maintaining his car. The DC left the premises after saying he was a business friend who happened to be in town and who had decided to pop in for a coffee, a long-standing invitation.'

'He'll be keeping an eye on the flat, will he? That detective? To alert us in case Dawlish returns?'

'Yes, he'll let us know if Dawlish turns up. He has no reason to think we're watching him, and there'll be no arrest or approach unless you authorise it.'

'Right, so that means we must keep our eyes open for him in this part of the world. If he's on his way now, he could be here fairly soon, unless, of course, he has some other diversion *en route*.' Pemberton then told Grant and Black of Lorraine's recent discoveries.

It all combined to produce an urgent reason for circulating a description of Dawlish and his car to all patrolling officers, with a request that they did not stop and interview him, but reported his whereabouts immediately to Inspector Larkin in the incident room, or to DI Kirkdale or Detective Superintendent Pemberton in person. Larkin said he would despatch an immediate circular to that effect – if Dawlish had left Derbyshire that morning, say ten thirty or thereabouts, he could be in the Rainesbury district by lunch time. If there were no sightings of their quarry in the town by evening, then a wider hunt might have to be instituted. Another task was to alert all the detectives currently working from the incident room; it was vital that they should know immediately so that they could take the appropriate action. Larkin said he would contact all by radio and personal telephone.

Having established that part of the procedure for tracing Dawlish, Pemberton asked Grant, 'So, John, you've something else for us?'

'Yes, sir. I had words with the local "D" Division CID in Kent – that's Tunbridge Wells by the way, where he used to live – to see if Dawlish had come to their notice. I've learned he was illegitimate, born in 1966, and his mother was a prostitute. She died in 1979 from natural causes. He never knew his father and spent his early years with foster parents. He tried to hide the fact his mother was on the game, saying she worked away from home, and he would pretend she sent him expensive presents. In fact, he often bought things himself, out of his earnings – he's always earned money, sir, newspaper rounds, window cleaning, bar work . . . but he went wrong. As a juvenile he was convicted of raping a schoolgirl – he was sixteen at the time and was placed in care with the local authority for two years. He joined the Scouts and enjoyed outdoor pursuits, doing very well by all accounts. He left local authority care when he was eighteen and seems to have kept his nose clean, then he went off to Swangate College in County Durham. That's where he met Browning. But of some importance is the fact that before he was caught for that crime – the juvenile rape – he'd been cautioned for indecent assault on girls at school – three cases as a fifteen-year-old and one as a fourteen-year-old. And he's been in the frame for a subsequent rape, sir. It occurred some years ago, in Sussex – I've got the date in my notebook – and a witness reported an old-fashioned red car parked near the scene, an open tourer. No one was ever arrested and it could not be proved that the red car was Dawlish's MG, although he was known to possess one at the time. He was interviewed and denied being responsible – it was before the days of DNA analysis and there was insufficient evidence against him to justify an arrest, let alone a prosecution.'

'So, our friend Dawlish is a convicted rapist, even if he was a juvenile at the time. Gregory – I remember you said the files contained a list of known sex offenders who might have come into the frame? Dawlish avoided that, eh?'

'Yes, there is a list, sir, but they were all known offenders who were living fairly close to one or other of the murder scenes, sir. None of the murders was in the south-east, so we didn't do a trawl of sex offenders from that area. So the answer is no, Dawlish was never listed in the files. He avoided that by the tested and tried method of not offending on his own doorstep. I might add that there are thousands of other sex offenders, known or suspected, who do not feature in the file.'

'So when did Dawlish move to the Midlands?'

'When he set up his own business. After college, he worked for an advertising agency in Eastbourne, commuting from Tunbridge Wells, and moved to Derbyshire in 1992, to set up his own agency.'

'One of the Sandal Strangler killings was in Derbyshire, wasn't it?' Pemberton asked.

'Yes, sir, at Longwell in June 1992. Gina Gibbons, a Sheffield prostitute, was the victim. Dawlish moved there, to his new business, the following September.'

'Perhaps he learned about the sale of the business while attending the vintage car rally near Buxton that year?' suggested Pemberton.

'It's quite possible. Anyway, since he moved there, he's never come to the notice of Derbyshire police. It seems he's kept his nose clean.'

'Or he's evaded their notice and ours simply because he did not live in the area of any of the crimes. In Derbyshire's case, he moved there afterwards. A true travelling criminal, a mobile villain, but is he a clever killer? A serial killer?'

'With his background, he could be, sir.'

'Well, I reckon he's motored himself right into our net – or to be more precise, I trust he's motoring north to get himself well and truly enmeshed. From this point onwards, we regard Hugh Dawlish as a high priority suspect even though we require more evidence before we can think of charging him. Paul, circulate all our teams, will you? Ask them to keep a watching brief for Dawlish and his car, but emphasise he must not be stopped or interrogated. Report his movements and his whereabouts, that's all. We've photographs if anyone needs one. And if we can ask for help from outside forces, especially those upon the routes of the M1 and A1, we might get sightings of him heading north. Anything of that kind would be useful – I want to be sure I know where to find him when I'm ready to lift him.'

'Sure, I'll fix that.'

Pemberton thanked Grant and Black, asking them to continue their investigations into the life and movements of Hugh Dawlish.

When he reported this news to his teams, some of whom were in the incident room making phone calls or checking records, it breathed new life into the enquiry. Quite suddenly, a different atmosphere prevailed – instead of having a suspect who was lying in a mortuary, they had a real live villain who was driving into their trap. But complacency was not allowed; there might be other suspects to be considered and in fact one of the teams, Detective Sergeant Whittaker and Detective Constable Aldworth, had just produced one. Their suspect was now in the interview room and the news was passed to Pemberton. He promptly went down to the operational section and located Detective Sergeant Whittaker, who was completing the record of persons brought in for questioning.

'You've a body in?' Pemberton smiled. 'Who is it?'

'A local weirdo, name of Ben Baxter, sir. Reputed flasher, peeping Tom.'

'Arrested, was he?'

'No, he volunteered to come in for questioning – at our suggestion! He has no alibi for Sunday night and we've information that he's often been seen near those woods at Crayton, spying on courting couples with binoculars.'

'He doesn't sound like a vicious rapist to me,' Pemberton said.

'He's not, sir. I don't think he'd cope with any woman, however willing she was, but we felt he might have seen something in the woods.'

'Well done, that's the kind of input we need. Thanks, I'll leave you to it.'

After intense questioning, it transpired that Ben Baxter had not been into Crayton Mill woods on Sunday – he'd been on the sand-dunes watching some nude bathing through his binoculars. The detectives discharged him with a warning. As if to complement the sudden upsurge in activity in the incident room, DS Browne and DC Cox came in early at three thirty, and they made straight for Pemberton's office. He welcomed them.

'Sir . . .' The sergeant was clearly excited by the results of their endeavours. 'We're on the Browning action, as you know, checking his car and tracing his movements.'

'And you have news?'

'We've been trying to establish closer ties between the MG rallies and Browning's holidays or his weekend movements, sir. Thanks to the book that Lorraine Cashmore found and thanks to Browning's frequent use of his credit card, we've been able to trace most of his movements – and the recent ones do tie in with the marks he made on his own road atlas.'

'And the result?'

'Without going into too much detail, sir, it puts him within five or six miles of every one of the Sandal Strangler's killings, except for the first one in County Durham. Not only that, it puts him there at the material times, i.e. the weekends before the bodies were discovered. Vintage car rallies were in the areas at the time, they were the reason for his journeys, so we are led to believe. I think we all knew that, but this book proves it – and the pattern continues. In the most recent case – our murder at Crayton – Browning bought fifteen pounds' worth of petrol for his car at a filling station on the outskirts of Rainesbury, on Crayton Road, at 5.30 p.m. on Sunday last. We've checked with the garage – the registration number of his MG Roadster is recorded, and he used a Barclaycard for the payment. We can compare signatures if we need to prove he was actually making the purchase. It puts him in Rainesbury last weekend, sir.'

'That's excellent work! It's the first time we've had Browning seen anywhere in or near Rainesbury at the material time. He was here before his accident. You'll put all this on paper, please, in great detail – we need to be absolutely sure about all these facts.'

'Of course, sir. Now, we don't have details of any routes he might have used, sir, I have no idea at this stage whether he drove straight from his home near Harlow Spa or halted *en route*. As it was a Sunday, he might have attended some other event or visited someone on the way. Nor do we know whether he stayed in town at a boarding house or hotel, or whether he travelled from home.'

'I have teams doing the rounds of boarding houses, hotels and so on, thanks, they might turn something up. But this is great news. Now, you've spoken to the filling station? Do they remember the MG? It's quite distinctive.'

'The person on cashier duty was a young girl who's not very clued up about the different types of car, sir, and she had no idea what we were talking about. I wanted to know if he'd been alone when he called, or whether he'd had a passenger, male or female, but she can't help. It seems it's a very busy filling station, being on the road out of Rainesbury, especially during a Sunday in summer. Day trippers and tourists use it a lot, so the company takes care to record all registration numbers, in case of fraud.'

'Right, then it seems beyond reasonable doubt that both Dawlish and Browning were in Rainesbury on the night of the murder and went home afterwards. That's another breakthrough – well done. Even so, we still haven't placed them actually there, at the murder scene. Not yet. But I'm sure we will! Thanks for that.'

It was Inspector Larkin's task to draw up a time-chart on a whiteboard in the incident room. Thanks to the positive information that was now flowing into the system, the gaps were now closing. He had Browning logged at 5.30 p.m. on the Sunday night, just along the road from Crayton – a mile or so from the parking area which gave access to the woods where the body of Debbie Hall was found. He had Dawlish logged at 8 p.m. the same night, the time he'd been positively identified as being in the company of the murdered Debbie. There was a gap of two and a half hours to fill. Where had each of those people been during that vital time?

The answer to that should confirm the name of the murderer – or murderers. Gregory Kirkdale came to watch Larkin as he was entering the latest information on his chart.

'I did one of those for each of the previous ten killings,' he said. 'And all I got was lots of blank spaces. Now, thanks to your teams, I can fill in some of the gaps. And the same names will appear, eh? Dawlish and Browning. Always so near, but always so far!'

'How about checking your files, Gregory, to see if we can realistically consider two men as the Sandal Strangler? A deadly duo, so to speak!'

'Sure, that seems to be an increasing possibility.'

It was then that a telephone call came from one of the teams working on the hotel and boarding house enquiries. He asked for Inspector Larkin who apologised to Kirkdale for the interruption, but Kirkdale was already heading for his own office and another examination of his files.

'DC Taylor, sir. I'm calling from a call box opposite the Royal Hotel. The red MG has arrived, sir, and a man answering the description of Hugh Dawlish has just gone inside, with a suitcase.'

'Great stuff, Andy! Stay there and keep an eye on him. I'll inform Detective Superintendent Pemberton.'

15

'This changes things,' was Pemberton's first reaction. 'I'll have to speak to all the teams, so can you fix a special conference, Paul? Call them in from whatever they're doing, tell them it's urgent.

I'll address them as soon as they're assembled. Also, I'll need extra officers brought on duty so I can put a tail on Dawlish, it'll be twenty-four hours a day surveillance until I decide to bring him in.'

It wasn't a particularly difficult task to assemble the detectives that evening prior to the end of their day's duties; several were already drifting into the incident room to complete their records. At seven o'clock, Pemberton stood before his officers. After stressing the importance of this new development he told them about the arrival of Hugh Dawlish in Rainesbury.

'He's at the Royal Hotel,' he went on. 'He was clocked arriving around 5 p.m. and he was in his red MG. The registration number is on the board, and at the moment, DC Taylor is keeping observations on him. We have every reason to believe he will remain here until the funeral Mass of his friend, James Browning, our deceased suspect; that's on Monday morning at eleven o'clock at Our Lady and St Hilda's Church here in Rainesbury. Now, the current situation is this: although there has been a shift of emphasis from Browning to Dawlish, with Dawlish emerging as our No. 1 suspect, we do not have sufficient evidence to have him arrested and interrogated, although some positive data is now being gathered. The problem is keeping him within our sights until I'm ready. I'll be compiling a file about him this evening and the moment I have sufficient evidence to detain him, I'll have him brought in for questioning. I have considered asking him to come voluntarily into the police station to be questioned for elimination purposes, but I suspect he's too experienced and too cunning to agree to that. I feel he'd say nothing if we did persuade him to visit us without any apparent good reason. Remember, he is a convicted rapist and he's been in police custody on previous occasions. He knows the procedure after arrest. My own view, after the manner in which the Sandal Stranglings have occurred and bearing in mind there's never been a named suspect until now, is that we need to have a cast-iron case against Dawlish before we even think about questioning him. So that's one of your jobs during this weekend's enquiries. I want you to bear him in mind, I want you to amass whatever evidence you can against him, and keep me informed. Make sure you know what he looks like and his background – I'm having existing photographs reproduced and we'll take a few without his knowledge over the weekend. But – and this is vital – I do not want Dawlish approached or made aware of our interest; it is very important that we maintain the element of total surprise until we arrest him.'

'He was the last person to see Debbie Hall alive, sir,' commented DC Brightman from the rear. 'That's usually sufficient justification for bringing someone in for questioning.'

'I agree. That applies to normal circumstances, but in this case, I need to tread rather more gently, rather more warily. I believe we're up against a formidable killer, a criminal with brains and cunning.' He paused for effect. 'Clearly, that barman, Eddie Brodie, will have to look at Dawlish in the flesh to confirm he was the man he saw with Debbie last Sunday evening, but we can arrange that through an identification parade when he's in custody. Now, I am sorry if I seem to be dithering on this but I'm not. I do have very good reasons for this course of action. For the tailing exercise, I need a succession of teams, experienced in covert shadowing techniques and able to take good photographs. We need to watch Dawlish until I am ready to bring him in and to report on his movements and contacts. Paul, can you see to that? Have a pair of detectives pose as guests in the hotel if you think it's necessary.'

'Sure, I'll see to that, sir.'

'The next thing to bear in mind is the precise role of James Browning. I do know that he and Dawlish were friends and there is a possibility they were both involved in the killings, although I'm not sure in what way. Maybe one drove the other to the scene and took no further part in the actual rape or murder? At this stage, no one can place either of them at the exact scene of any of the Sandal Stranglings, let alone that of our own Debbie Hall. That is something we must do; to get the killer convicted, we need to place one or other at the scene of all the crimes, and from our own point of view, at the scene of Debbie Hall's death. Don't forget that Dawlish and Browning were both in town around the time of Debbie's murder, but to date, we can't place either of them precisely at the scene. But, I have to ask this – and I would ask you to consider this during your enquiries – was Browning really involved in these killings? Are we looking at two multi-murderers with the Sandal Stranglings as just one of their lines of activity? Or is Dawlish innocent? Or Browning? Could one be committing the murders during their outings on MG rallies without the other realising? You'll begin to appreciate that this is a very complex case, ladies and gentlemen, and it needs to be most skilfully handled. Now, Detective Sergeant Browne, you're looking into Browning's movements?'

'Yes, sir,' and a hand appeared above the heads of the assembled detectives to indicate his presence.

'Any developments, Tony?'

'Just confirmation of what we thought already. Browning seems to have led a very unobtrusive private life. Apart from his trips to the vintage car rallies, he does not appear to have had a very active social life. From what I can gather, from people like his landlord, his workmates and neighbours, he seldom went out with other people. Parties, pub trips, outings to the theatre from work, none of those seemed to interest him. It means, unfortunately, that we have traced very few people who can tell us what he did in his spare time. We've quizzed the prostitutes and members of the gay scene in and around Harlow Spa, but they don't know of him. What he did at weekends and in his leisure hours is therefore something of a mystery. All we can determine is that he went home from work on a Friday evening and came back in on a Monday without regaling his workmates with tales of his weekend activities, apart from his motor rallies, that is. He did tell his office mates about those outings, going on at length about the smart cars he'd seen or how he'd won a rosette or something. He seemed to come alive when he talked about the car and his outings in it.'

'Did he ever take anyone for a ride in it?' Pemberton asked. 'Friends? People from the office?'

'No, it wasn't often he brought it to the office. Perhaps the only time he'd fetch it to work was when his official car was in for servicing or repair.'

'And none of his diaries give a hint about his other weekend activities?'

'No, sir, nothing.'

'And there's nothing in his personal papers which would suggest he and Hugh Dawlish were involved jointly in any way with those killings?'

'Not a hint, sir, no. Nothing. The only extra diary notes for those outings would be if his car won something, or had to have something done to it, like a puncture repaired or oil check. He kept very meticulous records of that kind of thing.'

'Thanks. Well, keep asking around, keep digging, Tony. Somebody, somewhere, must know where he went or what he did when he was not steaming about in his old car.'

Feeling that the enquiry had produced a new impetus, Pemberton dismissed his teams; it was not yet eight o'clock but he said those who had finished their work might leave early if they wished. Tomorrow was an important period for their enquiries; tonight, the night duty teams would update all the records in the incident room and deal with any overnight problems while Inspector Larkin went off to arrange the surveillance teams. As Pemberton was in his office, preparing to leave for home, Lorraine rapped on the door and came in. As there was no one else present, she kissed him tenderly.

'What's that for?'

'Nothing. I just felt like it. It's a been a successful day, and I thought I'd kiss you in celebration – that's if you really want me to have a reason!'

'Then I hope we can have further successes,' and he kissed her too, full on the lips.

'I came to see if you're ready to go home,' was her next comment.

'Yes, I think so.'

'So what are we doing tonight?'

'I've got to go through all the material we've gathered about Dawlish and Browning,' he said. 'I want to see if I can produce sufficient evidence to incriminate Dawlish before I interrogate him. It means a lot of reading!'

'How long will that take? To assess the evidence, I mean.'

'Dunno. A couple of hours maybe. Why are you asking?'

'I was wondering about a walk, some fresh air, before we settle down for the night. Maybe a meal in a pub somewhere?'

'Sure, so long as I can make the time for my reading.' As he spoke, Detective Inspector Kirkdale tapped on his door.

'Sir,' he said, 'do you need me for the weekend?'

'Not if you can leave your file behind, we might want access to that.'

'Sure. It's our wedding anniversary on Saturday, I thought I'd take my wife out, then return here on Monday morning. You seem to have got it almost wrapped up, Dawlish has walked right into your net, a perfect end to an enquiry, I'd say.'

'My net has a lot of holes in it, Gregory, which I hope to patch up this weekend. But yes, do as you say. You've left a contact number if there's a panic of any kind?'

'Yes, on the noticeboard. OK, see you Monday morning.'

And so the staff of the incident room began to prepare for the weekend. Being a murder enquiry, it could not and would not close until it was over; Pemberton and all his officers would be working tomorrow and Sunday, but the tempo did tend to change due to offices and factories being closed, and people taking time away from their homes. Many sources of enquiry tended to dry up. Pemberton informed Larkin that he was going home; he'd be available by telephone if he was required and would see them all tomorrow morning at eight.

Having left the incident room slightly earlier than normal, Pemberton and Lorraine had time to hurry home to get washed and changed, then decided on a walk beside the River Raine. A few minutes' drive from home, there was a convenient car-park, one exit of which led through a turnstile into the riverside walk; the path then led through picturesque woodlands before emerging at a delightful inn on the banks of the Raine.

There the river was broad and slow-moving, a mecca for rowing boats and canoes, a place of calm laced with the interest of observing people at play. Mark reckoned they'd be able to enjoy their stroll in the light of the June evening, have a meal and be back home by eleven or thereabouts – time enough to complete his brief fact-finding exercise.

At this time of year, before the holiday season began in earnest with the closing of the schools, the riverside walks and inns were moderately quiet and they had no difficulty parking their Vauxhall. By eight fifteen, therefore, they were strolling in casual clothes beside the water; a moorhen, known hereabouts as a waterhen, and her chicks swam before them, the mother bird fiercely protecting her brood against the threat presented by humans, a pair of dragonflies buzzed across the reeds like miniature helicopters and a pair of mallard swam leisurely with the flow of water as a young man and his girl, in a flimsy canoe, laughed and rowed upstream. A summer scene of gentleness and a world away from thoughts of murder and rape.

Pemberton, holding Lorraine's hand as they strolled along the wide footpath, walked in silence. Although the scene was one of pastoral calmness and gentleness, Lorraine could see he was preoccupied with other matters.

'You're thinking about Debbie Hall, aren't you?' she ventured after a time, feeling he would like to discuss his thoughts.

'Sorry,' he said. 'I should be admiring the scenery or wondering what that bird is, the one that's singing in those bushes . . .'

'A willow warbler,' she said. 'A summer visitor, perhaps the most numerous of all the birds that come to us during the warmer months.'

'You know about all sorts, don't you?' There was a hint of jealousy in his voice.

'I believe there is a big, big world beyond the boundaries of police work and crime detection.' She squeezed his hand. 'For the whole of your working life, Mark, you've been so wrapped up in your career that you've ignored other things. There is room for both, you know.'

'Yes, I know. I've tried in the past, tried to get involved in things, but work has always intruded. Crime has always dominated my off-duty moments too, interrupting my leisure time, like now. Here we are, two people in love walking beside one of the prettiest rivers in the country with interesting wildlife all about us, and all I can think about is murder and rape!'

'You wouldn't be human if you didn't think about your work,' she reassured him. 'Your work is especially demanding, you can't switch off and forget it like a factory worker on a production line is able to do. I'm sure the fellow who produces genopolators by the score on a chain belt doesn't worry about his work when he's having his well-earned pint at the working men's club. But your work is different, Mark, you can't detach yourself from it. And you shouldn't detach yourself from it, people depend on you, society needs to have its criminals caught, even if it means people like you never resting –'

'Criminals are puzzling people,' he said suddenly. 'To some extent, I can understand what motivates robbers, burglars and

132

thieves. They're greedy, they want money without having to work for it and they don't mind hurting others in order to get it, but murder? It is very difficult for me to understand how one human being can deliberately kill another, especially a weaker one, just to satisfy some urge or lust.'

'You shouldn't try to understand criminals, Mark. Your job is not to understand them, it's to enforce the law. There are others whose work is to understand criminals and decide what to do with them.'

'But police officers must understand them if they are to catch them,' he said, stooping to pick up a stick and toss it into the water.

'You're referring to Browning?' she smiled.

'Dawlish, I think, but Browning does seem to have been a strange person.' He paused to retrieve the stick which had floated into the bank and tossed it further out to stream. 'Almost a non-person in fact. If what his workmates have said is true, he was good at his job, very efficient and reliable, and yet when he was away from work, he ceased to exist – it's almost as if he was not in this world when he was away from his job – unless he was messing about in his little red car. Apart from those two aspects of his life – not forgetting his occasional trip to see his father – he was unknown. It's almost as if he didn't do anything at weekends, he never talked about his weekends when he got back on a Monday . . .'

'He worked for charity, Mark,' she reminded him. 'I seem to recall that he did work for various local charities – I'd like to bet that's what he did at weekends, quietly, unobtrusively, diligently.'

'You mean spending time in some charitable institution?'

'People who work for the Samaritans never talk about it, do they?' she reminded him. 'Or those who help out at hospices or hospitals, nursing homes and similar places. Helping the disabled or handicapped. They don't boast or gossip about it. It's something they do because they want to help others.'

'That's hardly the activity of a suspected murderer!' Pemberton said, puzzled.

'But Browning wasn't an ordinary man, Mark, we know that.'

'He's an enigma, for sure!'

'Have the various local charities been approached?' she asked him. 'There must be hundreds, ranging from Red Cross to Age Concern via Cancer Research . . .'

'I don't think any of them have been approached about the possibility of him helping out at weekends,' Pemberton admitted. 'I must admit I never gave it a thought . . .'

'If we want to know where he was at any given weekend, then surely we must ask at such places?' she stressed.

'You're right!' He now felt as if he was inefficient, allowing that to escape his attention, but she squeezed his hand.

'Come along, time to eat. Let's find a nice table overlooking the river . . .'

The Black Otter was a large seventeenth-century inn which was once the haunt of salmon fishermen and otter hunters. Now it was favoured mainly by tourists, day-trippers and sailing enthusiasts. Rich with oak furnishings, dark smoked beams and inglenooks galore, the central portion had retained its character in spite of several modernisation schemes and the addition of extra bars and a dining-room. Mark and Lorraine made for the old bar, the original with its dark interior and tiled floor. But even as he entered, he halted.

'Over there,' he said, indicating with a nod of his head the far corner. 'Don't make it obvious you're staring . . .'

'What?' She had no idea what he was trying to tell her, but the noise of the chatter from the assembled customers meant their exchange was not overheard.

'Detective Sergeant Gary Watson and Detective Constable Gillian Barber . . . assigned to tail Dawlish! That table in the far corner . . .'

'That means he must be here,' whispered Lorraine.

And so he was. Seated at another table in one of the inglenooks was a dark man with a girl; having seen the photograph recovered from Browning's garage, they knew, beyond all doubt, that this was Hugh Dawlish.

16

'Don't acknowledge Watson and Barber.' Pemberton spoke softly as he turned towards the bar, adding in a normal voice, 'What would you like to drink before we eat?'

'A dry white wine,' she smiled. 'There's a table for two near the side window. It's the only one left. Shall I go and claim it?'

'Do that, and I'll bring the menu across.'

When Pemberton joined Lorraine, he was pleased that the table offered a good view not only of Watson and Barber, but also of Dawlish and his girl companion. He noted she was about twenty-seven or eight with elfin features bearing more than a hint of freckles, and she had short, bobbed hair which was dark brown. On top, she wore a pink blouse but he could not see whether she had on a skirt or jeans, or what kind of footwear she was wearing. Dawlish was tucking into a giant plate of chicken and chips, while she appeared to be enjoying a trout salad. Having settled at his table and assimilated the surroundings, Pemberton was able to establish brief eye contact with Watson – he and his policewoman colleague had had to be content with a sandwich apiece, something they could either take with them or discard if they had to leave quickly.

After Pemberton and Lorraine had studied the menu and placed their orders, Pemberton said, 'I'm going to the loo,' and she knew Watson would follow him out of the bar.

He did. After ensuring that the Gents was deserted and that they could not be overheard, Watson said, 'It's Dawlish, sir, as I'm sure you realised.'

'I did. The photo's a good likeness. So who's he with, Gary?'

'A prostitute, sir, from the town, name of Denise Alderson. We got the tip from another tail; we picked him up on the last mile here. His MG's in the car-park. We're confident he has no idea he's being tailed.'

'I'm relieved about that! I'm here off duty, by the way, it's just by chance we picked this pub. Can you cope if he takes her off to the woods and tries to kill her?'

'Yes, sir, we've a full stake-out. We've two teams in the woods behind the Black Otter, and another in the car-park, ready to follow him if he leaves by car. I'm in radio contact with Control, a throat microphone. Control know you're here, by the way, we've reported that! You can't go anywhere . . .'

'It's part of the job!' He grimaced. 'But I'm pleased you two are with Dawlish – it would have given me something to think about if I'd found him here without any back-up troops! So where did he pick the girl up?'

'On the sea-front. His car was in a car-park not far away, he met her on the fish quay, near the telephone kiosk there, and they walked to his car then drove out here. It didn't look like a pre-arranged meeting, sir – it was a pick-up, I'm sure. Denise was touting for business, where buses hired by men's outings discharge their passengers. She's often there, the Vice Squad know her well. He came along, they chatted and soon came to an agreement. She's got a supper out of this punter. That's style!'

'He knew where to find her, you think?'

'He knew where to find a prostitute, sir, I couldn't say whether he picked this one deliberately, or whether she happened to be the first that came along.'

'It seems as if he likes to entertain prostitutes as if they're his friends,' Pemberton remarked. 'I'd have thought he would have taken her to his room at the hotel.'

'Most of the hotels know the local pros, sir, and the receptionists alert their management if they see a punter take one of the girls inside. It seems Dawlish knows the routine so far as local hotels and inns are concerned, so he makes his own arrangements.'

'Or else he favours the open air for his bit of fun! So what about his room at the hotel? Can we have that searched while he's out?'

'Yes, sir, it's being searched now, we've got access, thanks to one of our lads being well known to the manager. He'll never know we've been.'

'Good. Let's hope we can find something to link him with the scenes of the murders. If you've any problems, give me a signal. Just walk out to the Gents or take the path back to the riverside car-park, I've parked along there. I'll follow you.'

'No problem, sir. We'll be fine, you enjoy your night off. Shall I report to you when it's all over?'

'Yes, I should be home by eleven. I've some reading to do before tomorrow morning, but yes, give me a call. I'd like to know the outcome of tonight's efforts.'

And so they parted.

Their return to the bar went unnoticed by Dawlish and Denise; they were in earnest conversation over their meal and showed no interest in the activities around them. In many ways, they were like a courting couple, not in the least suspicious and not attracting the attention of the other customers. By this time, more people had arrived and the public areas were noisy and busy. Pemberton rejoined Lorraine, refilled her glass, placed his order then settled for a soft drink as he was driving.

'I don't think they want me to get involved in this observation,' he told her, knowing he'd not be overheard by Dawlish.

'I should think not, Mark Pemberton! It's their task, not yours! They're specialists. They won't want you poking your nose in, you might make a mess of things! Or you might inadvertently alert Dawlish. So leave them to it! You're off duty anyway. If we hadn't come here tonight, you'd have known nothing about this exercise until tomorrow, by which time it will be all over! So, most definitely, you are not needed here!'

'But if Dawlish has intentions of harming that young woman –'

'Your highly professional team of observers will make sure he doesn't! And if he gets close enough to try anything, they'll deal with him. But he's not due to murder anyone just now, is he? So no more about Dawlish – your supper's here!'

Later, as they tucked into their first course, Dawlish, in a loud and somewhat artificial upper-crust accent, ordered sweets and coffee for himself and Denise, then asked the waitress if he could be presented with his bill and also if he could have a VAT receipt.

And quite clearly, Pemberton heard him say, 'Dawlish. The name's Dawlish. You'll find I'm running an account – put these on it, please.'

'Yes, Mr Dawlish,' she smiled.

'Are you full-time here, or is this just an evening job?' He smiled at the pretty waitress, a girl of about nineteen with blonde hair in a pony tail. His voice was so loud that most of the customers could hear his conversation whether or not they wanted to.

'Part-time,' she said. 'I work in an office in town during the day. I'm saving up for a holiday in Crete.'

'Nice place,' he said. 'I hope you get what you want. To get what you want in this world, you've got to make a few sacrifices and work hard, so here's a tip to help you,' and he dug into his pocket, pulled out his wallet and gave her a five pound note.

'But you shouldn't, it's too much – '

'Nonsense! You've looked after us so well,' he said smoothly, 'I wish I got this kind of service where I come from. So see to our sweets and drinks, get me my receipt when we've finished and have a great time in Crete!'

'Oh, thank you, sir, thank you, yes I will,' and she trotted off to obey his orders.

'That's a bit over the top, isn't it?' Lorraine grimaced. 'I was expecting him to ask if she did modelling work, or fancied taking part in a film he's making . . .'

'*That* would have been over the top, and she'd have realised it. I'm sure she's heard every chat-up line there is, working in a place like this. But he didn't do it to please her, or to get her to agree to a date. He did it to establish his presence here tonight.' Pemberton licked his lips after tasting his medium-rare steak. 'As a result of that performance, that waitress will remember him.'

'Pardon?' Lorraine leaned forward to hear him above the buzz of conversation.

'Dawlish.' He leaned forward too, to respond. 'He's just made a great play of getting his receipt, mentioning his name and giving a large tip.'

'Lots of business people do that,' she reminded him. 'They need VAT receipts if they're here on business, and they tip lavishly.'

'Yes, but in his case, it's different. He's established an alibi, hasn't he? The waitress will remember him, and he'll have a piece of paper bearing today's date and the name of the pub. That'll support him should anyone ask where he was tonight.'

'You think he's doing this deliberately?'

'It depends upon whether he's intent on killing that girl he's with,' Pemberton said. 'He won't kill her tonight, that's for sure.

138

Too many witnesses have seen him in this pub with her, and he's made sure his visit – their joint visit – will be remembered.'

'I don't follow your reasoning, Mark.' She frowned as she enjoyed her salmon.

His voice was lost in the hubbub and indiscernible to anyone but Lorraine as he said, 'I'll give an example. Suppose he was planning to kill her tomorrow night, Saturday. Take her off in his MG, drive out into the countryside, and rape and murder her.'

'Go on,' she invited.

'And some time later, days, weeks or even months, someone comes forward to the police to say the girl was seen with him in his red MG, driving away towards the countryside . . .'

'Yes?'

'So, if the police track him down and question him about it, he'll admit he was with her. He would not deny it, he can even prove he's been to the Black Otter with her because that waitress, with her five pound tip, will remember that lovely Mr Dawlish . . . If she works Saturday and Sunday evenings too, there's a chance she might not remember which date the kind Mr Dawlish tipped her and talked about Crete. But she will remember *him* and the fact he was here; she won't remember the day or the date. If he does not produce his receipt to the police, and if the enquiry is made in three or six months' time, what's the betting Dawlish could persuade us, or his defence counsel, or a jury, that he had been in the pub at whatever time he wanted us to believe. The waitress would swear on oath that she remembered him, even if she could not remember the day or date. So, at some distant time in the future, he could admit being here with Denise, if it's in his interest to do so, and he has documentary evidence to support it, plus the waitress. And it's also evidence that the girl was alive late in the evening . . . he'll also gather evidence of the time of his return to the hotel tonight. A chat with the barman or receptionist or even a guest will help establish that. And there's the distinctive red car too. People will remember seeing that, but might not be quite certain when they saw it, especially if they're asked months or even years later. So Dawlish has laid the foundations for an alibi, should he ever want to use it, and however he wants to use it. Or if he wants a specific date, he's got the receipt.'

'So you are saying he intends to kill Denise tomorrow?'

'No. I'm not saying that. I think he sets up alibis wherever he goes – there are times he likes to cover his tracks. What I am saying is that if he did kill her tomorrow and was quizzed by the police, he could admit being with her *tonight* when she was alive. If any witnesses said they'd seen him with Denise at any other time, he could suggest they'd got their dates wrong. But she's not going to die tonight, my example is hypothetical; she'll be returned home safe and sound and she will be alive in the morning.'

'Mark,' she studied him closely now, 'are you saying this is what he might have done for all those murders? Carefully set up a false alibi?'

'At this stage, we don't know but I think it's part of his continuing routine. On the other hand, this weekend is different, he's lost a friend so he'll be in a different state of mind. His behaviour could change. No suspects have been interviewed which means that no alibis have been put forward, but it would be interesting to see what stories he does tell, if we can ever get him to talk. He's clearly arrogant and very sure of himself; if he is a killer, it will be a difficult task to prove it, particularly after the passage of so much time. There is every likelihood that he's constantly putting up smoke screens to baffle anyone who might ask about those movements he wishes to conceal.'

Just before ten o'clock, Dawlish and Denise made their move. He left his table and called in a loud, braying voice to the man behind the bar, 'Thank you so much, it was a delicious meal! I shall return!'

And he swept out with Denise, smiling.

'Is she wearing sandals?' asked Pemberton, unable to see her feet.

'Yes, golden-coloured ones,' Lorraine told him after peering through the crowds.

Such interest in the departing couple was not unusual, in view of their overtly staged departure. Gary Watson and Gillian Barber, having paid their bill a long time ago, also made their move; Pemberton could see Watson talking but could not discern his words, yet he knew he was speaking into his throat microphone. The rest of Dawlish's evening would be observed and reported upon.

'Now we can relax,' Lorraine said. 'I think I'll have another glass of wine, as you're driving!'

They returned home shortly after ten thirty, with Pemberton settling down to his reading as Lorraine prepared a nightcap apiece. And shortly after eleven, before he'd completed his work, Detective Sergeant Watson rang.

'All clear, sir,' he told Pemberton. 'They went into the woods where they attempted sex, we think, and then he took her home. He dropped her off about ten minutes ago and returned to his hotel, alone. He popped into the bar for a quick nightcap and a chat with the barman, and now he's gone to his room.'

'There is a night watch on him, isn't there?'

'Yes, sir, all through the night. He can't move an inch without us knowing.'

'And a search of his car? Can that be done?'

'We'll see to that, sir, he'll never know we've been.'

'Good, and tomorrow and Sunday we'll have to maintain our observations on him while Grant and Black dig deeper into his background. Now, has anything interesting been found in his room?'

'Apparently not, sir. He travels light. There's a dark suit, presumably for the funeral on Monday, and a few changes of clothes, hiking boots, fairly new, summer wear mainly but nothing else of interest. He carries his wallet with him, of course, containing things like his credit cards and personal effects.'

'OK, it was a good try. Now, it's time for some more reading before I turn in. Goodnight, Gary. I'll address the troops tomorrow.'

With the morning conference of detectives scheduled for ten o'clock on Saturday, Pemberton had plenty of time to marshal his thoughts before addressing them. There would be a news conference too, immediately following the detectives' briefing; the reports would need to be brought as up to date with the story as possible for the Sunday papers. Although a good deal of progress had been made, little if any of it could be transmitted to the media. Fortunately, no newspaper had picked up on the story that a serial killer might be responsible and that Debbie's savage death had parallels in other parts of Britain over a period of ten years. The problem facing Pemberton that morning, after last night's careful perusal of the data already gathered, was that there was no further evidence to implicate Dawlish.

Last night's encounter, however, had produced another possibility – that Dawlish had selected his victims in advance, had taken the trouble to establish an alibi for potential future use, and had given sufficient thought to his macabre work to convince anyone that he was not guilty. If Denise was murdered tonight, therefore, could Dawlish be considered a suspect, simply because he'd bought her a meal in the Black Otter on Friday? And paid her for sex – or attempted sex.

In addressing his officers, Pemberton began with Lorraine's hypothesis that Browning might have spent his weekends working for charities in or near his home town; one of today's actions was to determine precisely what charity work Browning did during the weekends. Pemberton asked his officers to be discreet and, if possible, not to give any hint that Browning might be a suspect for the murder of Debbie Hall. If questioned for a reason, they were to say it was part of the overall elimination process.

He then told the gathering of last night's sighting of Dawlish with Denise.

'Whichever of them is the killer, I think we have a superior and dedicated villain here, ladies and gentlemen,' he said. 'I believe he considers himself beyond our reach. I believe that after ten years, he thinks he has perfected a system of murder without the likelihood of detection. So with that in mind, please continue your enquiries. I think we need to examine in detail the events for two or three days prior to the disappearance of Debbie Hall. We still need to tie in the absences of Browning and Dawlish from their homes to establish whether one or both were at the scenes of the crimes, or had dealings with the murdered prostitutes, at some time prior to the assumed time of death. This might help us to place one or other at the scenes . . .'

He went on to say that Lorraine Cashmore would re-examine Detective Inspector Kirkdale's files on all the Sandal Stranglings with the same objectives in mind. Perhaps, hidden somewhere among the mass of detail, was a vital clue which would lead to the killer or killers.

Then there was a telephone call from Dawlish's team of watchers.

'He's leaving the hotel and heading for the town, sir, on foot.'

17

Hugh Dawlish's closely monitored trip into town turned out to be nothing more sinister than a visit to a florist to order a wreath for the funeral. Having selected the style and flowers, he wandered down to the foreshore, bought a copy of the *Guardian* and went into a sea-front café for a cup of coffee and a chocolate biscuit. Meanwhile, his car remained at his hotel as teams of detectives continued to observe and report upon his movements; that car had been searched last night, the strangler's rope being the chief objective, but no such length of rope had been found there.

Following the morning conference of detectives, Pemberton's teams had gone their separate ways, all charged with the completion of specific actions. One team was now looking into Browning's charitable activities at Harlow Spa while others were repeating their efforts to place him – and Dawlish – at the actual scenes of the murders. All had a lot of work to complete, tedious to some extent, but very necessary.

In the incident room, the morning's work was also under way but, if anything, the tempo had decreased. Now, much of the emphasis was upon the presence and motives of Hugh Dawlish; reports of his activities in town were logged in the official records of the murder investigation. Apart from a brief burst of apparent sexual activity last night, his behaviour seemed extremely ordinary and even mundane, hardly the stuff of a mass murderer. But such chores form the major proportion of any major investigation and the surveillance work had to be endured.

Pemberton knew that his officers would maintain their efficiency in spite of any lapses into boredom while he took the opportunity to reread his summary of facts about the Sandal Strangler. It was later, during a lull in the activities of the incident room, that Lorraine brewed a coffee for herself and Pemberton, and took the mugs into his room.

'Coffee, sir.' She took care to address him formally.

'Thanks. I need a break from this headwork . . . I think there's more concentrated reading to be done in a murder enquiry than there is swotting for a promotion exam! And it's about the same degree of intensity. So how's it going, Lorraine? Found any references to our suspects in Kirkdale's files?'

'I didn't come about that but funnily enough, yes, I think so. I haven't finished scanning them yet but in two cases, a long time ago, witnesses reported seeing a red-haired young man talking to the murdered prostitutes on the day they vanished. He has never been traced or identified but because each was seen alive afterwards, he was never regarded as a serious suspect. There was no report of a red car, though.'

'Maybe that was before Browning bought his MG?' Pemberton suggested. 'He didn't acquire his present car until 1991.'

'Yes, it was. One of the murders was in the Lake District at Rusthwaite in 1989 – the murder of a Lancaster prostitute called Toni Petch. She was seen by a café owner on a Friday evening around eight o'clock, talking to a red-headed man in Ambleside. Because he wasn't the last person to see her alive, though, he wasn't considered a prime suspect.'

'But it could be Browning? Was he in that part of the world at that time?'

'Yes, he was. There was a midsummer MG rally at Bowness, he went to that. It's recorded in his diary. He travelled across the Pennines on the Friday night, so it's quite possible he could have been in Ambleside around eight that same evening.'

'And Dawlish?'

'He was there too, Browning refers to him in his diary. Unfortunately, the detail is rather sketchy – Browning records, on the Saturday of that rally weekend, "Met Hugh and went to the rally. Bowness was wonderful, even if the weather was wet. A typical Lakeland summer." And that's all he says. But it does mean Dawlish was at Bowness, in the area of Rusthwaite, when Toni Petch was murdered.'

'That's all useful stuff, Lorraine. And the other occasion?'

'The previous year, 1988, at the Northumberland murder. Sophie Armitage died at Oldsfield near Otterburn. An eyewitness

144

says a similar thing – she saw a red-headed man talking to Sophie Armitage on the Friday evening; she'd been with other clients afterwards, so he was not listed as a prime suspect. The prostitutes in that area served soldiers from nearby army camps. The police thought it was probably a man from one of the camps, but he was never traced and not listed as being sought for interview. He was described as being in his twenties, well-built with noticeably red hair but no other distinguishing features. No car was mentioned – he was talking to her outside an hotel at Otterburn, one of the hotel waitresses saw them.'

'It's odd that those sightings of red-haired men have not been collated.'

'They're not in any list of suspects, sir, because there were no suspects.'

'So they got overlooked! And the diaries? Do they confirm Browning was in those places?'

'They do, he was meticulous in his diary-keeping. He went to an MG rally at Otterburn and, as on the other occasion, noted that he met Hugh during that weekend. It was their annual re-union.'

'I wonder if that Otterburn waitress is still around? If we showed her a photo of Browning, I wonder if she could identify him as the man she saw talking to the prostitute outside the hotel at Otterburn? It's a long shot, so do you think it's worth a try?'

'Well, I think it's extremely unlikely she'd recognise him after all this time, but I suppose we can try – and the café owner too.'

'Can you arrange that, Lorraine? Can we send colour photographs to the local police and ask them to trace those witnesses? Give it priority status.'

'Yes, I'll see to that. I'll use e-mail, they'll get the photos immediately.'

'Good, but I'll be honest when I say I'm rather more keen to concentrate on Dawlish. I want to put him in the frame for those killings . . .'

'Yes, I know, but if we can state the sightings were definitely James Browning, then we know, from Browning's diary, that Dawlish was with him and probably in the vicinity. That'll confirm our partnership theory.'

'It's at times like this I wish Browning was alive and able to help us,' he said.

'You've not considered another visit to Father Flynn, to try and persuade him, by fair means or foul, to inform you of the contents of Browning's confession?'

'I've considered it, but I know it would be useless. Even if I threatened him with court proceedings, he'd never break the seal of confession, even if the object of our interest is dead.'

'Shall I talk to him?'

'You can try.' He had no desire to frustrate her attempt to persuade the priest to talk. 'Is that why you came to see me?'

'No, it wasn't. Actually, a thought occurred to me and I thought I'd better check it with you first. It's about the girl we saw with Dawlish last night. Denise Alderson.'

'Go on.'

'Well, we all believe she could be at risk from Dawlish but I know it's a risk we have to take. I wondered if she ought to be warned or given closer protection? I think we've had a glimpse of the killer's MO. He selects his victim in advance, takes her out, uses her services for payment and takes her to a country setting . . . then he returns another time and does the same thing all over again with the same woman, but this time, he kills her. And she was wearing sandals last night. Maybe he's got a fetish about sandals? Isn't that how you think he's been operating?'

'Yes, that's exactly how I think he's been operating, either alone or with an accessory.'

'So you agree she does need protection?'

'I'm not sure he does intend to kill her. The killer has already despatched one victim here – to kill another would be out of sequence and, I think, out of character. It would be a break in his pattern, so I think this girl's safe. The trouble is that if we explain to her our worries and plans, she could inadvertently alert Dawlish and we might lose him altogether, we might never get the evidence we need. There's no way she could behave normally after what we would tell her. What we need is to ensure that our tails never lose him. Having said all that, we can't ignore the possibility that he *could* attempt to kill her – the loss of his close friend, James Browning, might be the catalyst to make him behave differently and kill again. But we can prevent him killing her, Lorraine. I'm confident we can ensure her safety without the risk of informing her of our suspicions.'

'There's many a slip . . .' she warned him.

'Don't I know it! But to achieve success, risks must sometimes be taken. Think of it this way, Lorraine. If Dawlish is the killer and we don't catch him this time, he'll be free to continue killing. My job is to stop him and Denise is the bait, but I daren't tell her.'

'Well, so long as you know the risk you're taking with her life.'

'It's one hell of a gamble – I hope I can crack him before he reaches that stage. Now, on another topic, we've not considered the tools of his trade, have we?'

'The rope, you mean?'

'Yes. His room at the hotel has been searched, it's not there. And last night, our teams managed to get into his car. It's not there either. So he's probably not planning another murder immediately.'

'Was the rope used on all the earlier victims from the same length? Cut off and used for that purpose, then left with the victim?'

'According to a succession of forensic experts, yes. It was the kind of rope that could be used for marine purposes or on farms or for towing cars, it's a thick strong nylon rope with a multiplicity of purposes. And it is nowhere to be found on this occasion.'

'On the other hand, if he's lost his partner in crime, he might want to show he can do it alone?' Lorraine suggested. 'Kill someone as an act of revenge.'

'Which means he will have to acquire some rope if he wants to use his well-tested and tried MO,' he said.

'And if he does, I'm sure your teams will alert you.'

'Yes, but Lorraine, think of this. He's used the same piece of rope on every previous occasion, cutting off lengths to suit his evil purpose. So where did he keep it, and where is it now?'

'Perhaps he's used it all – after all, Mark, eleven short lengths added together does make a rather substantial piece. Fifteen yards, just about the amount for a roll. Forty metres or so. I would image you could buy a coil that length in any shop. But if you're chopping a couple of feet off once a year, you'd eventually use it all.'

'So if he goes out to buy a length of rope this morning, it's more evidence against him?'

'It means he's probably going to get himself a tow rope in case his old car breaks down – that's what he'd tell you, if you asked about it.'

'There was a piece of rope in the boot of Browning's MG, it was burnt almost to a cinder, melted in fact because it was nylon, but it was definitely a piece of rope,' he told her.

'Left by Dawlish, you think?'

'Yes, I do honestly think that.'

'And cut from the coil Dawlish was using for the murders?'

'That is something only our forensic wizards could determine, but with the rope in such a burnt state, I doubt if a proper comparison is possible. The lengths of rope used on the earlier victims have been retained as exhibits by the way. But I shall ensure that any piece we find is forensically compared with the ropes used on the past victims.'

'Well, at least we know he hasn't any with him now, unless our men have overlooked it. I suppose it could be hidden, but they'd know where to look. However, it might be sensible to alert the tails, asking them to let us know if he does buy himself a piece of tow rope. Well, that's my coffee break over. Back to the files . . . seeking more red-headed men in little red cars . . .'

'You're doing a great job,' he said, meaning every word.

'I'm going to have a walk out in the fresh air, just for half an hour,' she said. 'I need a break from concentrating on the files. I'll go to see Father Flynn.'

When she left, his office seemed empty of life, devoid of any happiness and full of paper. But he was sure those piles of paper contained something he'd missed, something which would provide the enlightenment necessary to solve the riddle he had set himself. It was possible Lorraine had unlocked the puzzle by spotting the presence of the red-haired men or man. He called in Inspector Larkin to acquaint him with the discussions he'd had with Lorraine and to ask him to radio the men tailing Dawlish, alerting them to the possibility of him purchasing a length of tow rope.

'You must be psychic, sir,' Larkin grinned. 'This morning's shadows have just called in. He's been to a ship's chandler on the sea-front and has emerged with a large coil of white nylon rope.'

148

18

Dawlish had returned to his hotel bearing the coil of rope in a large plastic bag and had placed it in the boot of his car. He'd then gone to his room and visited the toilet before heading for the small public bar where he'd ordered a sandwich and a pint of beer for lunch. Pemberton's lunch had been similar, a sandwich and a glass of orange juice in the canteen, after which he had returned to the incident room. Lorraine, in the meantime, had gone to see the priest.

During the course of that afternoon, several matters were resolved. Enquiries in Harlow Spa confirmed that James Browning was an ardent and active supporter of several local charities. He spent time at weekends either with those who ran the organisations, or with the patients. He worked in the hospice, for example, tending the sick, taking them for outings in their wheelchairs or even helping with the washing-up or bed-making. At the Hospice of St Hilda, he was a very welcome supporter and liked by all, staff and patients alike. He did stints in several charity shops in town too, serving behind the counter from time to time or helping to organise fund-raising efforts; he'd been to Lourdes on several occasions with handicapped people from the town and had also taken his turn in standing in the town centre gathering funds in a collecting box and issuing sticky label badges. And without exception, everyone said how wonderful he was.

Even if he was quiet and retiring, he was a tireless worker, selfless and devoted to those in his care, and he would be sorely missed.

For many of the charitable organisations of Harlow Spa, the sudden death of James Browning was a tragedy. In gathering this information, the detectives had compared, where possible, his periods of charitable work with the times of other unsolved murders, including those which were not part of the Sandal Strangler series. It had become evident he could not have committed any of those other outstanding crimes because in most cases, the charities had kept details of their duty rosters. His name appeared on many, endorsed to show that he had actually turned up as he'd promised, thus creating an unbreakable alibi – but there were no such alibis for the Sandal Stranglings.

It had been comparatively simple, therefore, to ascertain that any absences from charitable work had been spent with his MG either at home, polishing and maintaining it, or at one or other of the rallies – and those had coincided with the Sandal Stranglings. From time to time, there were unexplained absences not mentioned in his MG diary – these, the detectives felt, were his journeys to Staffordshire to visit his parents and, later, his father only, but none had coincided with any other killing.

In presenting this information, Detective Sergeant Browne said, 'That seems to have been his world, sir. Charitable work at weekends, public relations work during the week, and not-very-frequent outings to vintage car rallies as a form of real relaxation. He was a worker, sir, a solid, dependable worker whatever he tackled, and from the enquiries we have made, he was well liked and trusted.'

'The very opposite, you'd think, of a serial killer?'

'I must admit it doesn't ring true, sir, a man like that going out and killing people. Can we be sure we're on the right track? If he was leading a really distinctly separate double life, then he's been a bloody good actor all through. But everyone speaks highly of him. Not one of his contacts hinted he was weird or distasteful in any way, even if he was on the quiet side.'

'But he did admit one murder, Sergeant. Still, thanks for all that. There was no suggestion, from any of the charities, that he took a pal along to help with the work? I'm thinking of Dawlish.'

'No, we asked. He was always alone, sir. Some of the organisers wondered if he had a girlfriend, and one – Age Concern – suggested he might like to bring a girlfriend along to help him in the shop on Saturday afternoons. But he simply said he had no time for girlfriends.'

'So apart from the rallies, Dawlish does not appear to have involved himself with Browning's world?'

'That's right, sir.'

'And during his work for the charities, Browning never gave any reason for the supervisors to be worried about his behaviour or his attitude to others, staff and patients alike?'

'Far from it, sir, he was trusted completely. Everyone said that.'

'I hope you gave no suggestion we were interested in him as a murder suspect!'

Tony Browne grinned. 'No, sir, we said it was to try and clarify a few details about his fatal accident, I said we were anxious to eliminate the question of suicide. We told them that we're satisfied it was a tragic accident, due probably to brake failure, but that we had to look at other possibilities. They were happy to talk about him once that had been established.'

'So it seems we have exhausted enquiries into Browning's background and movements?'

'I think we have, sir. So far as this enquiry in its present form is concerned, we have covered everything we can. We can sum it up by saying Browning did attend rallies close to the scene of every Sandal Strangling, at the material times – with the exception of the first and last killings. But we have been unable to place him at the scenes themselves, other than the very first when he turned up later and gave a false name. His leisure activities were geared towards helping those less fortunate than himself, and his only relaxation was his MG and the rallies.'

'Sexual orientation? You tried to determine that?'

'He was a gentle person, sir, for a man, not a rugger player or rock-climbing type. But we don't think he was a homosexual. He had several friendships with girls – one from his office for a while, but it never developed. She has been interviewed, sir, there was never any sexual relationship between them and the woman said he was too shy and reserved for her. She felt he was extremely reserved in the company of women, those were her words.'

'In that sense, he's like a lot of rapists and those who assault women, but it seems to fit his personality. A complex man, you think?'

'Not really, sir. He just seems to have devoted himself to work and caring for others, even to the exclusion of married happiness or a sexual relationship with a woman. He never seemed anxious to share his life or his home with anyone else, even in the short term. A loner, sir.'

'A sort of self-imposed penance, perhaps?'

'Penance, sir?'

151

'People who have committed a grievous sin may want to make amends in some way. That's part of Christian teaching, or religious teaching in a wider sense. I wonder if, having committed a murder, he decided to spend the rest of his life doing penance? If he had killed a woman, it would make his subsequent relationships with women very difficult – perhaps he could never trust himself when alone with one. Having listened to your account, I'm increasingly worried that we might have been chasing along the wrong track.'

'In what way, sir?'

'Think about what you have just said. You've told me about a young man who appears to have spent his life making amends for some past wrong he'd committed. Suppose it was murder, a murder for which he was never prosecuted or even suspected. From my point of view, it does look as if he's spent years trying to assuage his conscience, trying to make amends for some bygone moments of evil . . . and that suggests to me that he did not commit the Sandal Stranglings.'

'Go on, sir.'

'It suggests he committed one murder, a long long time ago, and his subsequent behaviour squares with that and with his confession. During his life he made his peace with himself, and at the point of death, he made his peace with God.'

'He took a long time to come around to the idea of admitting it to his priest.'

'Exactly. It must have been weighing on his conscience all these years. He gave up practising his faith, his father told me. Whatever he did, I think he could not bring himself to openly confess his sin to anyone, not even a priest, and that happened only when he knew he was about to die. I don't think he confessed to other murders earlier. This was his final chance to confess. His very last act of conscience.'

'All right, so far as Browning's concerned, we are no further forward and might even have come to a full stop.'

'Precisely, but in my view, it leaves the field open for Hugh Dawlish. Like Browning, he's been in the vicinity of all the Sandal Stranglings, but we don't know a lot about him. Thanks for the chat, you've helped crystalise my thoughts. You'll update our records?'

'Yes, sir, of course.'

Sitting alone in his office upon the departure of Sergeant Browne, Pemberton wondered how or why Browning had come to commit that solitary murder and then realised Dawlish might know the answer. It was increasingly necessary that Dawlish be brought in for interrogation earlier than Pemberton had intended although it was something he still resisted. But he might have to capitulate.

It was during these contemplations that Lorraine returned, shaking her head.

'Father Flynn refuses to reveal what Browning said,' she sighed as she sat at his desk. 'He was charming about it, but there is absolutely no way he will reveal anything said to him by the dying man. He asked me to express his regret at being unable to help us – I did explain about the Sandal Stranglings and said we wished to eliminate Browning from those, if we could, but not even that would make him change his mind. Sorry, sir,' and she used his formal address because Inspector Larkin was heading towards the office.

'Thanks, Lorraine, it was a good try.'

Larkin smiled at her and said, 'Don't go, Lorraine, there's been a follow-up to your efforts this morning. Both the Ambleside café owner and the waitress near Otterburn are still employed at the same places; the local constabularies showed them the e-mails of Browning in full colour and both said they can't be certain but it is possible that was the man seen with the prostitutes before they died.'

'I just don't know what to make of all this,' Pemberton said. 'Sit down, Paul, and you, Lorraine, and listen to what Sergeant Browne has just told me.'

He outlined Browning's charitable work, along with his thoughts about the feasibility of such a man committing murder and rape.

'It is possible, sir,' Lorraine said in due course. 'Wasn't there an American serial killer who worked for the Samaritans or a similar group, and did a wonderful job, even though he'd already committed countless murders?'

'Ted Bundy,' Pemberton recalled. 'He was good-looking, well educated, intelligent, well groomed, universally liked, efficient – but a ruthless killer nonetheless. I'm not sure Browning is in that league.'

153

'There's no reason why he shouldn't be,' countered Larkin.

'If it's the likes of Bundy with whom we are making comparisons, then I would guess it's Dawlish who's more like him – confident, clever, articulate, cunning . . .'

'So it's time to bring him in, sir?' suggested Larkin, not for the first time.

'I was coming around to that decision myself,' admitted Pemberton. 'But let's wait until this evening, until the teams have all reported in. If we have no further information that's useful, I'll have him in, for interrogation, stressing that it's for elimination purposes.'

By the end of that day's enquiries, no further information of relevance had been produced by the teams of detectives; as always, so much of their work had resulted in negative statements. So far as the murder of Debbie Hall was concerned, people had seen nothing, knew nothing and weren't able to help the police in any way. Pemberton felt it was due to the fact that the woman came from Rainesbury and had apparently gone for a walk with a man in a wood at Crayton, something lots of Rainesbury people did from time to time. The snag was that Debbie was fairly well known in the town, albeit among a small sector of the population, but in rural Crayton no one knew her, hence she was regarded as nothing more than another visitor going for a walk – and as such as was virtually invisible to observers.

In spite of detailed and intense enquiries, no one had come forward to say they had been in Crayton Mill Wood that weekend; no poachers had been traced, neither had any fishermen, ramblers or bird-watchers. Debbie's visit had not been observed; no red open cars had been noticed in or near the car-park and the total result of the few days' enquiries was very poor.

Journalists came for their four o'clock news conference hoping for some dramatic news that would appeal to the Sunday papers, but nothing was forthcoming. 'Is an arrest pending?' asked one journalist, the question being necessary because if an arrest had been made, or was imminent, then speculative reporting of the case could not proceed due to the laws on contempt. Pemberton assured them that, so far as he knew, no arrest was imminent, and certainly none had been made. The Sunday papers would probably produce features about the murders of prostitutes or the risks they undertook in plying their oldest profession.

By five thirty, the teams were making their way into the office to knock off at 6 p.m., an early finish because it was a Saturday. That was one of the traditions of an extended murder enquiry – early finish on Saturday and Sunday, unless something dramatic happened or an extra effort was required. The only exception, of course, were the teams currently keeping Dawlish under observation. Their work could not be abandoned and a lot depended upon the time Pemberton decided to interview him. He took Paul Larkin into his office for consultation.

'It's a question of timing, Paul. Let us suppose he has no intention of killing Denise tonight. Do we leave him in peace – remember he has no idea we have any knowledge of his part in the murders . . .'

'We've nothing to suggest he's guilty, either,' Larkin reminded his boss. 'Nothing to put him at the scene.'

'I know, but we do have a substantial amount of circumstantial evidence to link him both with Browning and with the Sandal Stranglings, however remotely. And he was the last person to see Debbie alive. Perhaps a few preliminary questions might produce something?'

'So when do you propose bringing him in?'

'I was wondering whether I should wait to see whether or not he tackles the prostitute, and have him arrested if he attempts to strangle her. We'd have grounds for detaining him then. Or have him lifted before he actually gets her into his car. I need to get under his skin, unsettle him, produce a surprise, I need to shock him, I need to give him one hell of a knock, a mental jolt just when he's least expecting it.'

'He's not expecting anything from us, is he?' countered Larkin. 'Anything we do will be a shock for him.'

'He's just bought a coil of rope, remember. Is that for his dastardly work? Or for a tow rope?'

'He might have used the last bit of his existing rope last weekend!' commented Larkin. 'So why not bring him in now? You could then have words with Denise to see what plans he's said he's made for her this evening, if any.'

Pemberton paused, then said, 'Right, let's do it. Immediately.'

19

Acting on Pemberton's decision, Inspector Larkin radioed the detectives at the Royal Hotel to ask if Hugh Dawlish had remained within the building. He was in his room, they were told. It was Room 136, and it seemed he had recently showered, an indication that he might be leaving. He had not booked dinner on the premises.

'Detective Superintendent Pemberton will be coming to the hotel within the next few minutes,' Larkin advised them. 'He wishes to interview Dawlish. If Dawlish leaves in the meantime, can you let us know immediately? And keep tabs on him?'

'Yes, sir,' was the response. 'Does that mean our surveillance duties are almost complete?'

'I doubt it. We've got to keep him within our sights until further notice. Mr Pemberton might decide not to arrest Dawlish in which case he'll probably remain at the hotel until the morning of the funeral service. We want to know his movements and contacts the whole of his time here.'

'Message understood,' came the response.

'Thanks, Paul,' Pemberton said. 'Now, Denise Alderson. I'm hesitant about making contact with her for obvious reasons, but against that, should we ask if she knows anything about the client who took her out to the Black Otter last night? In particular, I'd like to know whether he arranged to meet her again. If so, where and when.'

'She's well known to the Vice Squad in town, sir, we could arrange for one of them to have a chat with her, without making any reference to the murder. I'm sure we could discreetly find out if she'd made any further plans to meet Dawlish.'

'Yes, do it that way, but be sure to use an intelligent detective. At this stage, we don't want Denise to give Dawlish any hint that we're interested in him or that we know of his association with her . . .'

156

'No problem,' Larkin assured his boss. 'I'll be cautious. A bit of subterfuge works wonders. So you're off to the Royal. Alone?'

'I'll take two officers with me, Lorraine for one, and I need a good DS.'

'Grant's available, sir, he'd be ideal; he's been researching Dawlish.'

'Yes, he'll do nicely. I'll brief him and Lorraine during my drive to the hotel. I think I'd better be wired up too, Paul, with a throat mike and recorder. I need to get every word on record, even the drivel. So, this is what I intend to do. I want to go to Dawlish's room and surprise him; I want to see how he reacts, and then I shall begin to chat with him about Browning. I'll take it from there but I intend to make him think I'm interested in Browning rather than himself.'

'So you don't intend arresting him and bringing him in?'

'Not if I can help it, not at this stage. If he is the Strangler, he'll never admit it and I'd rather like him to think he's beaten us. I want him to drop any guard he might have planned over the years, I want him to think he's too clever for us, I want him to think we do not suspect him in any way. And, of course, we must bear in mind that he might not be a killer, that's something we must never lose sight of.'

'Meeting him face to face should tell you a lot, sir, unless he's a good actor. Right, thanks for keeping me informed. Any idea how long you'll be?'

'Who can tell? Really, I have no idea. I'll begin my chat in his room, it'll be better than here. But there's no need for you and any of the others to hang around. Let the teams go home, Paul; I can always recall anyone if it's necessary. If we do have to put Dawlish in the cells overnight, the uniformed branch will see to him.'

'Fair enough. Well, the best of British, as they say.'

John Grant and Lorraine were sent into Pemberton's office where he provided a brief outline of his plans. Lorraine would drive to the hotel while Pemberton completed his briefing in the car; furthermore, Grant would be discreetly armed as a precaution against any instability that might overcome Dawlish. Neither Grant nor Lorraine would question Dawlish or even speak to him until invited by Pemberton, who emphasised the strict limitations of this forthcoming interview.

'What I hope to establish,' Pemberton explained to them, 'is whether or not he is a positive suspect for the Sandal Stranglings. I believe he is, but we need to know more. I regard this man as a challenge, John, it will be as much a test for me as it is for him – but if he is guilty, I intend to get him!'

'You're up to date with the dates, times and places of all the Sandal Stranglings, sir?' Lorraine reminded him. 'Names of victims and so on?'

'I've spent a lot of time today ploughing through Kirkdale's files and I think I am sufficiently well briefed to hold my corner, as they say. Well, shall we go?' And he picked up his brief-case.

They descended to the ground floor and went out into the yard where an unmarked police car was parked. Meanwhile, Larkin alerted the observers at the hotel; they would keep out of sight and make no contact with Pemberton and his team during this visit, unless specifically requested. During the drive, Pemberton expanded upon his intended line of questioning but was sufficiently experienced to know that his plans could be thrown off course by any unforeseen reaction from Dawlish. From what he'd read about Dawlish, and from what he'd seen of him last night, it seemed the man would be a formidable opponent.

He reminded them that Dawlish would not be arrested and thus the constraints upon interviewing a person who was in custody would not be relevant; if Dawlish refused to co-operate, however, then he would be threatened with arrest on suspicion of murdering Debbie Hall, that suspicion arising from the fact that he had been the last person known to have seen her alive but this was to be a last resort.

'I want him to believe we suspect Browning of being the Sandal Strangler,' he emphasised. 'And remember he runs his own advertising business. This is no simpleton we're going to interview, he's a successful businessman, someone who's accustomed to getting his own way and who persuades his clients to believe what he wants them to believe. That's the power of advertising.'

After listening to Pemberton's preamble, Lorraine and Detective Sergeant Grant added a few questions of their own and so the small party drove through the busy evening streets of Rainesbury towards the Royal Hotel on the cliff top. During the ten-minute drive, the vehicle was in radio contact with the incident room, their progress being monitored by the police observers in and around the hotel. As they parked outside the front entrance, there was a final call to Pemberton to inform him that Dawlish was still in his room but seemed to be on the point of leaving.

'Good,' Pemberton muttered. 'Our arrival will get him agitated. I think we might have come at just the right time.'

Moments later, they were heading towards Room 136. There were no detectives in sight, the place seemed deserted as the other guests prepared for their evening. Room 136 was a single *en suite* room at the end of the first-floor corridor, a few doors down from the fire escape. Inside, faint music was playing. It was the theme song of an advertisement which was being shown on the television. After checking that the others were ready, Pemberton rapped loudly on the door, wondering if the sound was obscured by the noise of the TV set. Grant and Lorraine stood immediately behind him, one at each side; in circumstances of this kind, one had to be ready to place a large boot between the door and the jamb because some interviewees had an unfortunate habit of slamming the door the moment they realised their callers were police officers.

That couldn't be ruled out even here, but if Pemberton's reading of the character of Dawlish was accurate, the fellow would be much more subtle. There was no reply, so he waited for a few moments, then knocked again, louder.

'Coming!' said a voice from inside. And the door was partially opened by a tall, well-built man with dark slightly wavy hair. Pemberton recognised him as the man he'd seen in the Black Otter and in Browning's souvenir photograph. In his early thirties, he was wearing light cotton trousers of a pale tan colour, a summer shirt but no tie. His hair was wet, but combed, and there was a faint whiff of aftershave. Pemberton's immediate reaction was that, at this close range, he looked heavier than in the photograph. He'd put on some weight, he realised, the onset of middle age.

'Yes?' There was a look of apprehension on his face as he was confronted by the three strangers, one of whom carried a black briefcase.

'Mr Dawlish?' were Pemberton's opening words. 'Hugh Dawlish?' and he followed with the Findford-on-Trent address.

159

'Yes, that's me,' was the worried response, as his eyes moved from one face to another. 'Who are you? Is something wrong?'

'Can we come in?' asked Pemberton, producing his warrant card from his top pocket. 'My name is Detective Superintendent Mark Pemberton from the local police, the gentleman is Detective Sergeant John Grant and the lady is Detective Constable Lorraine Cashmore.'

'Why? What do you want? Has something happened?' was Dawlish's instinctive reaction, the door still not being fully open.

The gap was little more than two feet wide and he was standing right behind it now, half his body on view, the other half hidden by the door. It would have been easy for him to slam the door but difficult for Pemberton to force it wider for their entry.

'We'd like a word with you,' began Pemberton.

'Look, I've got a dinner engagement, I shall be going out in ten minutes or so. Can't it wait? Tomorrow perhaps? Whatever it is.' He spoke with a deep and rather pleasant voice; the public school accent was softer than last night's braying in the pub.

'How long it takes depends entirely upon you, Mr Dawlish.' There was an unaccustomed chill in Pemberton's voice. 'Ten minutes might be sufficient.'

'Can I ask what it is about?' Still he did not open the door to its full width.

'I'd rather not say, not out here in the corridor.'

Dawlish looked at them each in turn and, seeing not a glimmer of a smile upon any of their faces, eased the door wider and said, 'You'd better come in.'

As they entered the room, he closed the door behind them, first peering out to see if anyone else was waiting in the corridor.

'There's only two chairs.' He waved his hands to indicate the sparseness of the small room. 'Maybe one of you can sit on the bed? It's a tiny room, the best I could get at short notice,' and he moved across to switch off the television set. Pemberton watched him carefully.

Dawlish was playing for time; even if his actions were calm and deliberate, his mind was working at speed. His next ploy would be to ask if they wanted a drink. There was a small hospitality fridge in the corner of the room, near the wardrobe. Pemberton knew Dawlish would be trying to determine the reason

160

for this unexpected visit. If he was guilty, he'd be wondering how much the police knew.

'Can I offer you a drink? Whisky? Sherry? Wine? The room's fairly well stocked.'

'No thanks, we're on duty.' Pemberton indicated that the others should use the chairs. He would remain standing, a psychological advantage in such a case. Dawlish did likewise. Knowing better than to be seated on the bed, he stood before the window and gazed across the town below, his back to the visitors.

'So, Detective Superintendent Pemberton, what can I do for you?' Dawlish had now recovered any composure he might have lost in those first few moments and turned to face the police.

'You are – were – a friend of James Bowman Browning,' Pemberton began.

'Yes, we were at college together, in the north-east, some years ago. The Swangate College of Media Studies. We've kept in touch. I do know about the accident, by the way, which is why I am here. For the Requiem Mass, it's on Monday as I am sure you know.'

Dawlish rested his buttocks on the window sill and folded his arms. He was now in command of himself and seemed prepared to respond to their questions about James. Pemberton recognised that decision.

'We were very sorry about the accident.' Pemberton spoke sincerely. 'It's always sad when a young person dies so tragically – I witnessed the accident, by the way, DC Cashmore and I had the awful task of attending to James at the scene.'

'I had no idea . . .'

'No, of course, you couldn't be expected to know that. We were there when he died, as was Father Flynn, the local priest.'

'Oh, God, how terrible! I had no idea . . . it *was* an accident, wasn't it? I mean, you coming here like this, three of you . . .'

'Yes, we are confident it was an accident, probably due to brake failure. We're waiting for the final report on the car. It happened when he was in his MG, the open tourer, the Roadster. I believe he was a fan of MG cars, as you are.'

'He liked to drive around in one, yes. I wouldn't say he was a fanatic, not in the sense that it dominated his life, but he did enjoy owning and running a vintage MG, as indeed I do. It was a hobby for him, for me as well. I had a pair of them, you know, two very similar cars. I sold him one of mine –'

'So I understand,' Pemberton interrupted.

'You know that?' There was just a hint of surprise in Dawlish's voice.

'We traced the history of the car,' said Pemberton without explaining why and without giving any indication how he knew of Dawlish's presence in the Royal Hotel. 'We know that James liked to go on weekend rallies, to show off his car, to be with other enthusiasts. I believe that you and he had some kind of reunion, an annual get-together, at such rallies?'

There was a short interval before Dawlish responded. Although he maintained eye contact with the superintendent and a show of relaxed confidence, there was a momentary flicker of uncertainty which showed Pemberton that he was pondering the relevance and direction of this discussion. At the moment, it was not like an interrogation but Pemberton could see that Dawlish was taking infinite care in considering his responses before answering. In watching him, Pemberton was now certain that Dawlish was the Sandal Strangler and that he was putting into action the responses he'd planned over the years.

'We had a common interest,' he said slowly. 'It seemed sensible to co-operate on it, our annual get-together was part of that camaraderie. It was something provided by the rallies, a focal point, a pleasant means of keeping in touch. Attending them was always enjoyable. He and I would chat about old times, and about our current work – we did finish up working in similar fields, he with a PR firm, and me with my advertising business.'

'And what did you do on the rallies?' Pemberton asked gently.

'Do? A funny question, Superintendent. We did all the things that people usually do during such weekends. Talked about our cars, examined all the visiting models and compared them with ours, entered competitions, worried about MOTs and the effects of European laws on motoring, we touched on pollution, depletion of the world's fuel resources, the future of the motor car . . . We did a lot of serious talking, but we had fun as well.'

'And when you were not talking about cars or solving the world's problems?'

A sudden smile appeared on Dawlish's rather handsome face. 'We ate, drank and made merry! Isn't that part of the fun side too? Socialising?'

'I would hope so. You know what they say about all work and no play. So when you met James at these rallies, he was always the same? His behaviour never caused you to worry about him?'

'Behaviour? I don't follow, Mr Pemberton. What sort of worry are you talking about? He was always the perfect gentleman, if that's what you mean.'

'He never talked of death or suicide?'

'You're not suggesting his death was suicide, are you?' was the predictable response. 'James was not that kind of person. No, he was always happy and cheerful, quiet perhaps, and thoughtful, but full of life.'

'And girlfriends? Did he have any on a regular basis?'

'No, he never brought one with him. That was not the point of those events, Mr Pemberton. We didn't go as members of a club, we went as members of the public, not as part of a group outing. It was *our* reunion, you see, ours alone. For James and me. An annual get-together. We were not lovers, by the way, if that's what you are implying. There has never been a homosexual relationship between us. I like women, even if I have not yet married. But normal? What's normal, Superintendent? You tell me.'

'I would never attempt to define what is normal behaviour, Mr Dawlish,' said Pemberton. 'Police work has taught me something about human life. I know that what is outrageous for some is normal for others. Now, back to these rallies, the ones you attended. They were always in the summer, around midsummer's day, I believe?'

'Yes, there were others up and down the country at different times, but we always went to the one held on the weekend which was closest to midsummer day. It made a focus, something for us to aim for. It was midsummer when we parted after our course, it seemed sensible to arrange our reunions around that time.'

'And I believe the midsummer vintage car rallies were also held in different parts of England?'

'You have been doing your homework, Superintendent, but yes, that's quite true. It's a wonderful means of seeing something

163

of our countryside. Look, Superintendent, it's very nice knowing that the police are taking such an interest in James now that he is dead, but I really do have a dinner engagement. It is gracious of you to contact me, to clear your minds about James's death, but I must be getting along. I don't like to keep my guest waiting.'

Pemberton ignored his comments and continued, 'Did you and James attend every rally since you left college? You left in 1987, I believe?'

'More of your background research, Mr Pemberton? Am I missing something here? Is there more to this enquiry, more reason for your presence, than you have allowed me to believe?'

You know damned well there is, thought Pemberton. 'I am interested in Mr Browning's movements over the past few years.' Pemberton placed his briefcase on the bed and opened it. 'In fact, I have a list of all those rallies,' and he began to read aloud. '1988 Otterburn, Northumberland, 1989 Rusthwaite in the Lake District, 1990 Linsby near Market Rasen in Lincolnshire, 1991 another one in Lincolnshire, this time at Buckwold near Horncastle. That was the year he purchased the MG Roadster from you, I believe. Then in 1992 the rally was in Derbyshire, at Longwell near Buxton, with the next over the border in North Wales, Pontyllan near Betws-y-coed in 1993. The 1994 rally was at Kingsleadon in Gloucestershire followed in 1995 by one at Fulstock in Oxfordshire, and in 1996 it was at East Welton near Market Harborough in Leicestershire. Nine rallies, Mr Dawlish. I don't think James attended one in 1987 because that was the year you and he left college as you said, the year each of you completed your media course.'

'There is nothing criminal or sinister in two friends travelling about the country to enjoy rallies of vintage cars.' Dawlish had stopped smiling now and was frowning at Pemberton, occasionally glancing across to Grant who was saying nothing. Lorraine was also quietly seated in one of the easy chairs.

'Absolutely,' Pemberton smiled. 'Nothing criminal at all. But you and he did attend each and every one of those rallies, did you not?'

'Yes, we did. We made a point of doing so, as I've said. It was our annual reunion.'

'Mr Dawlish, I will now come to the point of my visit, and I hope you might be able to help. Very close to the venues of those rallies – a matter of five or six miles away in most cases – and upon the same weekend as each rally took place, a murder occurred.'

Dawlish merely looked at Pemberton, then said, 'Go on, Superintendent.'

'There have been nine such murders, Mr Dawlish. In fact, there was another murder in County Durham, the very weekend you and Mr Browning were celebrating the completion of your course. It was at Penthorne. That makes it ten murders, Mr Dawlish, in or near the very places you and Mr Browning have visited and, oddly enough, at the same time you were there. It is an inescapable fact that your visits and the murders coincided.'

'And there was a murder in this very town last weekend!' stated Dawlish matter-of-factly. 'When we were both here. That makes another for your total. Eleven.'

'Yes, it brings the total to eleven. Eleven that we know about, eleven that might be connected in some way, or which might not. But the most recent, here in Crayton, happened shortly before Mr Browning's accident,' added Pemberton.

'Yes, I know.' Dawlish now spoke very softly.

'Eleven murders, Mr Dawlish, and all with striking similarities. The victims were all young women, they were all prostitutes but they were all raped. And strangled. And all died when you and Mr Browning were known to be in the locality. It is that fact which has brought me here, Mr Dawlish, to talk to you.'

'Are you accusing me of murder, Mr Pemberton?' There was now a hardness in Dawlish's voice.

'No, I am not. I am gathering information, Mr Dawlish. I am endeavouring to eliminate anyone who could not have committed those crimes. As a consequence, it is important to speak to you because our enquiries show that both Mr Browning and yourself were at or near the murder scene on every occasion. That is something I cannot ignore, as I am sure you will appreciate, and I therefore need to eliminate you, both of you, even though Mr Browning is, unfortunately, no longer able to answer for himself.'

There was a long pause now and then Dawlish, in a loud and very confident voice said, 'I congratulate you, Superintendent

Pemberton, upon your detective prowess. Yes, it was James all along. I suspect you knew that. I can now confess that I suspected his involvement; I had noticed that every time we went to a rally a prostitute died. It doesn't need a genius to work out that one of us could be responsible, and I knew it wasn't me. I was fairly sure he'd committed the murders, but I had no proof – and the police never interviewed him, he was never a suspect, Mr Pemberton. So how could I betray a friend? I kept quiet about my suspicions . . . well I think you would have done the same if a friend had been involved. I mean, I never actually saw him kill those girls . . . but, well, we had been to every one of those rallies. We weren't together every minute of the weekend, of course. It all began in Penthorne, after college, when he killed a prostitute . . .'

'Are you prepared to make a statement about it?' asked Pemberton.

'Yes, I think I'd better, don't you?'

'It would help us enormously if you did,' smiled Pemberton. 'It would enable us to clear up a very worrying series of murders.'

'Yes, yes, of course. Now that he's dead, I think I can talk freely. Should I cancel my dinner date? Will it take that long?'

'Under the circumstances, I think that would be wise and your co-operation would be highly appreciated. We do need to get this matter cleared up. Can I invite you to the police station – we have all the facilities there.'

'Yes, anything to oblige. I feel free to talk now he's dead, it has been a burden, believe me. Poor old James . . . fancy him dying with all those deaths on his conscience.'

They waited as Dawlish rang a number to say, 'Look, Denise, I'm sorry, I've been called away unexpectedly on business. Very important business. Can I cancel tonight's arrangements? And I'll see you tomorrow.'

Pemberton knew the call would be checked, but it was certainly a call to the prostitute Dawlish had engaged last night. Replacing the handset, he said, 'Well, I'm ready when you are, Superintendent,' and he took a blazer from the wardrobe. 'Now, you know the Requiem Mass is on Monday, but, well, Mr Pemberton, I'm not sure how much of this will become public knowledge . . .'

166

'Where a guilty person dies before being tried for murder, we never inform the public of their guilt. Not even the coroner would announce the guilt of such a person. It seems unfair to judge a person guilty of such a serious crime when they've never had an opportunity to defend themselves in a court of law. That is our practice and I see no reason to change it on this occasion.'

'That gives me immense relief, Mr Pemberton. Mr Browning, that's James's father, is such a charming gentleman. I'd hate him to know that his son was a mass murderer.'

'There is no reason for him to know,' smiled Pemberton. 'And it will not reach the press, I assure you. But thanks for your co-operation, Mr Dawlish. I do appreciate it, particularly as you had made other arrangements for this evening. Now, the sooner we can complete your statement, the sooner you can resume your social activities.'

As they all prepared to drive Hugh Dawlish to the police station, Mark Pemberton allowed himself a smile of triumph. So far, so good.

20

'Am I under arrest?' Dawlish asked as Pemberton's car approached the police station.

'No, you are not.' Pemberton was sitting in the rear seat beside Dawlish. 'I have not arrested you on suspicion of committing anything, Mr Dawlish. I merely want you to tell me all about your friend, James Browning. You are a witness, Mr Dawlish, you are helping with our enquiries. That is your current status, it's nothing more sinister than that!'

'Yes, I think I understand. It's just that it's rather a sobering experience to be confronted by three police officers without warning and then be driven off for questioning like this . . .'

'I am sure we shall all find the experience very interesting and worthwhile,' Pemberton said as the car turned into the police station complex.

'Sir, do you want Sergeant Grant and me to remain with you?' Lorraine asked as the car drew to a halt.

'Yes, I think we should all like to hear what Mr Dawlish has to say. You've no objections if they join us, Mr Dawlish?'

'Objections? Good God, no. The sooner this is over, the happier I shall be.'

'We'll use the senior officers' lounge for this interview, it's much more comfortable,' Pemberton told Lorraine and Grant. 'Far better than the interview room. The lounge won't be required by any of them on a Saturday night! Lorraine, perhaps you could fix coffee for us all?'

Fifteen minutes later, they were all seated in comfortable armchairs in the quiet room normally reserved for senior officers. It was an odd choice; such interviews, whether they involved suspects or witnesses, invariably occurred in one or other of the station's interview rooms and so this was a noteworthy departure from the normal. But Pemberton had his reasons – he was going to continue his pretence to this man that he was not under suspicion. To prepare for his interview, Pemberton positioned Dawlish between Lorraine and Grant; he sat opposite and there was a coffee table between them bearing coffee and biscuits.

'I do appreciate your courtesy in coming here,' Pemberton began. 'It makes things so much easier, all our files are on the premises for one thing, it'll enable us to check any of the details if we have to . . .'

'Whatever you feel best, Superintendent.' Dawlish helped himself to a chocolate biscuit as he sipped his coffee. 'But I fail to see why all this is necessary when James is dead. There'll be no court case against him, will there? After all, he can't be called to account for his actions.'

'That's true, but we need to gather the evidence which is necessary to prove beyond all doubt that he was responsible. I cannot write off our files unless the evidence is conclusive. I know you have suggested he is a multiple killer, but we must investigate your allegations with all the thoroughness we can muster, as if he was still alive. You see, the country's murder statistics contain at least eleven deaths which have not been cleared up and if we can bring one or even all those investigations to a satisfactory conclusion, then it satisfies the Home Office, it shows we are doing our job and it helps us to maintain some degree of public confidence. After all, a detected murder is a great achievement, Mr Dawlish; an undetected murder is like a perpetual blemish on our record. It means the killers are still at large – and we don't like that either.'

'Well, I'll help as far as I am able. I can say things which I could not have done had James been alive and, I trust, with complete confidentiality?'

'Yes, of course. That is exactly what I hope you will do, Mr Dawlish. I want you to be completely open with us and tell us everything you know. You will do society a great public service and you can be sure we shall treat everything with the utmost confidentiality. As I said earlier, neither the press nor anyone else will learn of James's involvement. It is between us, you and ourselves. We will simply record each murder as detected; that will release lots of police officers to deal with other crimes, and the respective murder files will be closed without a court hearing.'

'So you need to take each in turn? I'm not sure if my memories are as clear as that, especially after all this time.'

'That's where our files will come to our aid,' Pemberton said. 'We have the files of every murder on hand.'

'Every one?'

'Yes, where we suspect that a series of murders is the work of the same person – or persons – then all the police forces in whose areas the crimes were committed pool their knowledge and re-sources; they collaborate during the investigations; in effect, the series of murders becomes one large investigation with a co-ordinator as the focal point.'

'Oh, I see. I had no idea things were so organised. There's been nothing in the papers, has there? About James's killings being the work of a serial killer?'

'No, happily, the press has never cottoned on to the fact the murders were linked, and we took care never to alert them. We preferred to let the killer believe we were not hunting a serial killer.'

'Can I ask how you know they are linked?'

Pemberton had to be careful here even though it was a ques-tion he had anticipated. 'Clearly, we cannot and would not re-veal all the information in our possession, but every criminal has his own method of committing a crime – his MO or *modus oper-andi*. It's like a signature, really, or a trade mark. And the same hand killed each of the women to which I have referred – we

169

know that beyond a shadow of a doubt. One clue which I can reveal is the type of victim – the girls were all prostitutes, all about the same age; they were all killed in woodland areas and their injuries were identical. In repeated cases of that kind, we can generally rule out coincidence.'

'Oh, I see.'

At this stage, Pemberton was not going to mention the sandals, the missing underwear, the rope or the nickname of Sandal Strangler which had been given to the killer. He said, 'I am sure you can appreciate that when the pooled details of the killings were studied in depth, certain similarities came to light and that told us that one person was responsible, even though the killings were in different parts of the country and many miles apart. Our duty is to find that person. Now, Mr Dawlish, thanks to you – and, sadly, thanks to James's accident – I believe we are on the verge of doing precisely that.'

'Yes, I see what you mean. But I had no idea such investigations were going on in the background, all this time . . .'

'Yes, we never give up, we never close the file on a murder enquiry. We kept our suspicions out of the papers, we did not tell them that we suspected a serial killer. That spot of secrecy was for very good reasons, Mr Dawlish, and I am sure James never thought we suspected him.' Pemberton was anxious to get this man talking while he was lulled into a false sense of security. 'Now, let us concentrate on James Browning, shall we? And I think we should start at the beginning.'

'The first murder he committed?' asked Dawlish.

'Yes, if you can help us with that, it would be of enormous value. But before that, let's go back to the time you first met,' smiled Pemberton. 'Just briefly, just to give me a flavour of your friendship. Perhaps you'd tell me how you met, how your friendship developed, what sort of a man he was, and then I'd like to discuss the first murder.'

'So this is going to take a long time?' and Dawlish smiled.

'Let's see how it progresses. If you feel you need to leave, then do so and we can resume tomorrow. You're staying in Rainesbury until the funeral service?'

'Yes, tomorrow is at my disposal but I'd like to get this thing cleared up too, Superintendent. The sooner the better so far as I'm concerned.'

Hugh Dawlish told how, when he'd joined Swangate College, he'd occupied the room next to James Browning in the accommodation block and so they'd become friends. They had never met until that time. In the second year of their course, they had opted to live in town and had shared a two-bedroomed ground-floor flat in a large terrace house. They'd remained friends, entertaining their contemporaries and taking part in a wide range of student activities as well as others outside college. James had been a perfectly normal fun-loving young man, Dawlish said; he'd had girlfriends and there'd been no hint of the quiet and unsociable character into which he later withdrew.

'Then . . .' and Dawlish paused, 'things changed.'

He took a deep breath, helping himself to another coffee from the heated flask. Pemberton did not rush him; he was sure this speech had been well planned and rehearsed over many years. Browning's untimely death would have made things easier, however; Dawlish's version could hardly be queried.

'It was the end of our course at the college. There was a party, several parties in fact. You know the sort of things. Lots of booze, food, women, music and dancing. Fun and noise, laughter. Lovely days, Mr Pemberton. Our course – thirty-six of us – went out for a meal at a pub. We'd booked in advance – nothing flashy, just a bar snack and lots to drink – then the idea was to go back to the campus where we had some music laid on in one of the assembly rooms, with dancing until the early hours. Friends and family were invited, but neither mine nor James's could attend. I don't know how it happened, but fairly early in the evening, I noticed James had vanished from the pub. I asked around but no one knew where he'd gone and then, when we were supposed to get the hired bus back to college, somebody said he'd gone off with a prostitute. He'd never done that before, not to my knowledge. It was when he didn't return that I went to look for him.'

'What day would that be?' Pemberton put to him.

'A Friday, the last day of our last week of our last term together at college. A sad time for us all, leaving friends we'd been with for three years.'

'So what time would it be when you noticed his absence?' Pemberton wondered how long it would take for a friend to begin worrying.

171

'When he went off or when we started looking?' asked Dawlish.

'Well, for starters – when he went?'

'Dunno. Eight or nine o'clock, I'd guess, although I can't be too sure. The buses were running, I think he caught a bus, with the prostitute . . .'

'And you started to look for him at what time?'

'Getting on for two in the morning,' Dawlish said. 'We were all pretty well plastered by then, but I wasn't so drunk that I didn't know what was going on. I was bothered about him, partially because they said he'd gone off with a prostitute, and partially in case he was ill. So I went to look for James.'

'Penthorne's near Durham, isn't it? It's a big area. How did you know where to begin?' Pemberton asked.

'I started with our flat. He wasn't there, and there was no sign of him having come home. Then I remembered there was a wood he loved, he and I often walked there when we were under pressure. It was a place of calmness, with a river and a small weir, fairly well into the countryside. I knew a late bus went there, I once used it to take a girl home. I knew, with some certainty, that if James had taken a girl out for a spot of romance or sex, that's where he would go.'

'So how did you get there?'

'In my MG. I kept it at the flat. My mother gave it to me, for my eighteenth birthday. I bought another later, same model, a twin-sister car almost, and sold the first one to James. I used it to drive there – perhaps I would have been over the drink/drive limit if I'd been stopped and breathalysed, but I took that risk.'

'Did the road go right into the wood?'

'No, it stopped at a small car-park. There was a gate and a sign saying there was a public footpath. We'd used it before, several times.'

'So you walked from the car-park into the wood?'

'Yes. And after a bit of searching in his favourite places, I found him.'

'Found him? So what time would that be?'

'In the early hours. After two o'clock, maybe half-past or thereabouts.'

'And what was he doing when you found him?'

'He was lying on the ground, fast asleep. In a leafy hollow, quite a way off the footpath. He was near the girl, she was dead beside him.'

Pemberton paused, trying to visualise the scene, and then, after a few minutes' silence from Dawlish, he asked, 'So what did you do, Mr Dawlish?'

Dawlish swallowed; for the first time during this interview he appeared to grow emotional, licking his lips and wiping moisture from his eyes as if trying to eradicate an awful memory.

'I tried to rouse her, she looked awful . . . there was no response, nothing.'

'Was she dressed?'

'Yes, in a summer frock. He was too, he was fully dressed, in a T-shirt and slacks. There was no sign of them having undressed. They were like the Babes in the Wood, lying there among the leaves . . .' and he brushed the hint of a tear from his right eye.

'And then?'

'I shook him, to rouse him. To wake him up.'

'And you succeeded?'

'Yes, he'd been drinking, we all had, but he wasn't incapable. I got him to his feet and asked what had happened. He had no idea, he couldn't remember anything. I had another look at the girl, she was dead, strangled with a piece of rope. Her face was swollen and blue . . . I touched her again, God it was terrible . . . but she was dead. There was no doubt about that. He'd raped her too, she was a mess, Mr Pemberton, blood all over.'

'Hmm. So what did you do then, Mr Dawlish?'

'James was dazed, I didn't know whether it was because he was half asleep or because of what he'd done or what he'd been drinking, but I made him look at her. I'm not sure whether he realised the gravity of what he'd done. I forced him to look at the girl, made him stand there and think about what he'd done, then I took his arm and walked him back to the car.'

'The buses had stopped by then?'

'Yes, the service bus which went past that point ended just after midnight. I drove him back to the flat.'

'Did you ask him what had happened?'

'Not at that stage, no. He just crashed out in bed and fell into a dead sleep, exhausted.'

'Drugs perhaps? Had he been drugged in any way? Taken anything?'

'It's hard to say. We weren't part of the drugs scene, certainly I never took anything and so far as I knew, James didn't either. I think he was just befuddled with too much alcohol, although somebody could have spiked his drink. He had no idea what he'd done or where he'd been. Anyway, next day, I told him what had happened.'

'And his response?'

'He didn't believe it. He couldn't remember anything, Mr Pemberton. Nothing at all. He couldn't even remember picking the girl up in the pub or taking her out to the wood. And when I told him about the dead girl beside him, he refused to believe me at first. I told him what I had found and how I had taken him home. He couldn't even remember me showing him her body. I was not really sure whether he thought I was telling the truth when I told him what he'd done.'

'He might not have killed her, Mr Dawlish. Some other person might have committed the crime and rendered him unconscious. It is not beyond the bounds of possibility. Prostitutes have some funny friends and contacts. You didn't actually see him kill her, did you?'

'That thought had occurred to me, Mr Pemberton, which perhaps explains the fact that I did not tell anyone about that experience. In my heart of hearts, I felt sure James was not a killer, Mr Pemberton, in spite of the circumstances in which I had found him. I gave him the benefit of the doubt.'

'So you didn't tell the police about the body? Or tell anyone else?'

'No, I'm afraid I did not. No one. I've kept quiet all these years. I must admit I was tempted to act as informer, I even thought about an anonymous telephone call to alert the police, but I failed to do so. Call it cowardice if you like, but I didn't want to get James into trouble. I reasoned that the longer the enquiry was delayed, the easier it would be for James to avoid detection. He was not a violent man, Mr Pemberton, and that was something which was totally out of character. I wanted to protect him. At that stage, I would never have dreamt he would harm a woman, let alone kill one. I wondered if the woman had not treated him very well and whether he'd lost his temper or something, so, rightly or wrongly, I did not report finding the body. I said nothing to anyone, except to James, of course. And he kept quiet about it, although for a time, we did discuss it when we were alone.'

'Is that when his personality changed?'

'Yes, from that time onwards, he became quiet and morose. He wanted me to take him back to where I had found him and the girl. He wanted me to do so the following day, so he could be sure he had done what I had said he'd done, but I refused. I felt sure the body would have been discovered and the police would have launched a murder enquiry, so I persuaded him not to visit the place. And not to say a word to anyone. I promised him I would keep quiet for the rest of my life – it was our secret, and I would never reveal what he'd done to anyone so long as we were alive. I have honoured that pledge. Now that he's dead, though, I feel I can speak.'

'If you had spoken out at the time, other lives might have been spared,' said Pemberton. 'From that start – if in fact that was his first victim – he seems to have got a taste for murder. We think he went on to kill ten more young women. It's quite an appalling record.'

'That will always be on my conscience, Mr Pemberton, but at the time, I felt I was protecting a friend. I'm sure any real friend would have done likewise . . .'

Pemberton found himself wondering what he would have done in the circumstances, but refrained from comment as he asked, 'So, Mr Dawlish, what happened next?'

'We stayed in the flat for the weekend, clearing up and packing, saying our farewells. I left on the Sunday to go home, I'd got a job, you see, and had to start on the following Monday in Tunbridge Wells. That's my home town. I got no holiday break after college . . . James said he would stay on in Durham for a week or so. He had found himself a job, but didn't start it until the first week of September.'

'So he stayed in Durham, at the flat?'

'Yes, for a few days.'

'And was there a police enquiry into the murder?'

'I never saw anything in the papers. During the short time I remained, there was no report of the murder. I went home without knowing whether or not she'd been found, or whether there had been an investigation. There was nothing in the Kent papers about it. Then James called to tell me the police had launched a murder hunt. If he hadn't rung, I would never have known the outcome.'

'And James? What did he do?'

'He got a job with a PR firm, the one he's still with – er, was with. He mentioned the murder once or twice on the phone, always to say no one had been to interview him. And gradually, he seemed to forget about it, he stopped referring to it. We met once a year as I told you – I had my MG and was involved in the vintage car scene and so I said we'd meet up at a rally or event of some kind, once a year, in the summer. I'd keep him informed and we could swap experiences. We've done so ever since.'

'James also developed an interest in vintage cars, I believe? He was driving one when he died.'

'Yes, it was a genuine interest, he was not simply emulating me. He couldn't afford to run a car of his own until his career was well established, and then, some years later, I sold him that one of mine. He was delighted with it.'

'And that first weekend reunion . . . did he ever mention the prostitute he'd killed?'

'Yes, as we were making our arrangements, he told me on the telephone that a year had gone by without him being interviewed. I think he realised he'd got away with it. I was never interviewed and neither were any of the students that I knew. I am sure the police must have traced some of them, though – through the pub we all used.'

'When the body was found,' Pemberton continued, 'the police would have sealed off the area for a couple of days or so until they had finished their work at the scene. Do you think James would have gone back there at some later date?'

'I don't know, Mr Pemberton, but it wouldn't have surprised me if he had done so. He wanted me to take him while she was still lying there, to see what he'd done and where it was, but I kept him away. So yes, it's possible. He knew exactly where she was even though he could not remember taking her there or killing her.'

'We have, in the files, a report of a red-haired man walking past the scene two days after the body had been discovered. He was stopped by the police but gave a false name and address – he said he was James Bowman, and gave the address of a Newcastle bookshop as his home address. That man was never traced.'

'That would be him. Sometimes he called himself Bowman, when he didn't want to be found out, such as when he had a one-night stand with a woman.'

'And so, over the years, he has borne the guilt of that woman's death?' said Pemberton.

'Yes, but apart from those few occasions, he rarely talked about it, Mr Pemberton. He did go into his shell, as they say, he kept away from women, in case he did something harmful to them, he once told me that, and he got himself involved in charity work, as a form of reparation.'

'And yet he continued to kill more women?'

'Yes, an odd contrast, so I'd better tell you about the others,' said Hugh Dawlish.

21

As Dawlish told his story, Pemberton realised his 'revelations' amounted to nothing more than a catalogue of supposed suspicions about his friend. He claimed to have noticed that the murders occurred when James Browning joined him for the midsummer weekend vintage car rallies, adding that he would never have considered his friend as the killer had it not been for that first murder in County Durham. That appeared to have been the catalyst for all that followed, for Dawlish had come to realise that Browning was operating to a system based on that killing. It was quite a simple system. Browning would ask that he, Dawlish, drove him from their digs – invariably bed-and-breakfast accommodation close to the vintage car rally site – to meet a prostitute he had previously chosen, not a difficult task if one knew where to look.

That meeting was always at a pre-arranged place, always in remote countryside and in woodland. Browning and the woman of his choice would be driven to the edge of a wood before being dropped off to go about their secretive business. They would then stroll into the woodland just like any courting couple, dressed like hikers or people taking an evening stroll. They merged easily with the background. Dawlish smiled as he told how the three of them would be packed into a two-seater car for the first part of those journeys and said he allowed the girl to occupy the front passenger seat while Browning squeezed himself into the tiny space at the rear. It produced a picture of happiness which was so common during the MG rallies, a sporty English summer scene.

As Dawlish explained this, Pemberton realised that such a display would not appear suspicious to a witness – an open-topped car in the summer with three laughing people on board would not register as being in any way odd, particularly when the district was full of similar cars or crews. Neither would a couple taking a walk in a wood, hand in hand, appear at all sinister to onlookers who were doing exactly the same.

'But you never actually saw him kill one of the girls, nor did you hear him admit to it?' Pemberton sought some clarification here.

'Good God, no!' Dawlish cried. 'It was the coincidences that alerted me, the coincidences which kept on occurring, year after year, every summer. Each time, James went off into the woods with a prostitute and later, I read that a prostitute had been murdered at that very place, and over the same weekend. After I dropped him off, with the woman, he always returned to our digs much later, when it was dark, so no one would see him coming out of the woods, in the gloom.'

'Did you ever learn the names of his prostitutes?' Pemberton asked.

'No, he never told me. I'm not sure whether he ever knew who they were.'

'His clothing would be bloodstained, would it not?' Pemberton continued.

'He always took several changes of clothing, Mr Pemberton, that's not a difficult thing to arrange in the summer. He was very meticulous, he always had a bath afterwards and put the stained clothing in a bin-liner and then into a dust bin.'

'You saw the bloodstained clothing then?'

Dawlish paused and frowned. 'Not as such,' he admitted. 'James would say he'd got his trousers stained from lying down on the earth or leaves of the woods when he was with the girls, he'd tell me how he'd discarded them. They were always cheap ones, he'd tell me, not worth sending to the cleaners. On one occasion, I saw the stains he referred to – dark and quite extensive but I could not swear, in a court of law, that they were blood. But always, he got rid of any stained clothes.'

'So those incidents, when you saw what you took to be bloodstains, would confirm your worst suspicions about James? That he was killing the girls?'

'They were part of the overall picture, Mr Pemberton. Like a jigsaw puzzle. If only some of the pieces are in place, you can guess at the entire picture. That's how it was with my assessment of James's activities.'

'The first girl was strangled, though, with a rope. That does not produce bloodstains,' Pemberton put to him.

'I'm sure some of his clothing was stained, Mr Pemberton but as I said, it might have been nothing more than mud.'

'Where did he get the rope he used?'

'He had a length in the car boot, a tow rope. He cut pieces off.'

'So how did he get them to the scene of the murders?'

'In his haversack, along with his spare clothes and boots. Looking back, I realise he went out specifically to commit murder, Mr Pemberton.'

'Did you ever talk to him about your suspicions, Mr Dawlish?'

'Not directly. Sometimes, though, I would refer to the murders, commenting on the coincidence that they occurred at the times and places we had visited, but James never said anything by way of a response. He'd just smile and say something like "Thank God it's nothing to do with us" or words to that effect. But it did become something of a trial for me, seeing him disappear into the woods with a young prostitute and then to learn later she had been murdered. But I must admit he kept very cool about it, he never let anything slip.'

'And still you did not tell the police?'

'I had no evidence, Mr Pemberton, not a scrap.'

'So, other than the coincidence of time and place, the timely absences of James and the occasional piece of dirty or bloodstained clothing, you had no proof that James was murdering the girls?' It was a carefully prepared question from Pemberton.

Dawlish took a long time making his reply; Pemberton wondered if he would refer to the rope or the blue sandals found in Browning's garage.

'No,' he said at length. 'That might explain why I never felt

179

confident in going to the police. There was nothing to directly link James with the murders – I wasn't sure the stains on his clothes were blood or just mud and earth, and other than the fact that he'd been with a prostitute at the time, there was no other indication he'd killed any of them. But I knew he had, Mr Pemberton. I was there, I saw his demeanour when he returned from his outings . . . he was a changed man, Mr Pemberton, ever since that first killing. And I do know he killed that woman near Penthorne . . .'

'They were all prostitutes, Mr Dawlish. Now why would James Browning kill prostitutes?'

'He was quite a prude in his own way, Mr Pemberton. He'd had a strict upbringing, church-going parents, Mass every Sunday, that sort of thing. Maybe he felt they were evil or dirty or something. But to be honest I don't know. I'm just guessing. He kept his opinions of prostitutes to himself, he never told me what he really thought about them even though he used them.'

'So why did he use prostitutes?'

'I don't know. Perhaps he found difficulty striking up a sexual relationship with his girlfriends.'

'The experience at college, at the end of course party, was that his first time with a prostitute?'

'I think it was. He'd had girlfriends prior to that, fellow students usually, but I don't think he had sexual relations with them. And I'd never known him go with a prostitute.'

'So until that time, he appears not to have had problems finding girlfriends?'

'Finding them was easy, he was a good-looking man, powerful and red-headed. Very attractive to a woman, so some of the students told me. But it was the sexual side of things – he was very shy and I'm not sure how the experience with the first prostitute affected him. But it did seem to turn him into a killer – or something did.'

'She was raped,' Pemberton told Dawlish. 'We know that the first prostitute was savagely raped. As were the others.'

'You can tell that?' Dawlish asked. 'You can distinguish it from normal sexual intercourse?'

'Yes we can, in most cases, through bruising, for example. A post-mortem conducted by a forensic pathologist will reveal a wealth of information. That is just one of the facts which have emerged – every one of those girls was raped, brutally. That is another of the coincidences that we have taken into account.'

'I never considered him a rapist.'

'It could explain the bloodstains,' Pemberton went on. 'On his clothing. The rapes were particularly brutal and savage.'

'He was always so gentle.' Dawlish spoke very quietly now. 'I can't imagine him doing anything like that.'

'The thought of exercising power over a woman can drive a man to rape,' Pemberton said. 'From our experience, a man will go with a woman for sex and if she resists, he can turn violent or even kill, then revert to being Mr Nice Guy . . . So, you are unable to provide us with any further evidence about James's activities?'

'Well, no, not really. I think I've covered everything I can remember.'

'All right. You go back to your hotel, Mr Dawlish. I'm sorry I have kept you. You might be in time for a late dinner. I will delve into our files to see if they contain anything which you might be able to confirm for us and then, if I may, and if there is any further help you are able to provide, I will ring you tomorrow and arrange a further meeting. Does that suit your programme?'

'Yes, yes, of course. Anything to help. I just want to get this cleared up and, to be honest with you, I think James would have liked the matter to be brought to a satisfactory conclusion. I think it was weighing on his mind.'

'A lot of serial killers earnestly want to be caught and hope to have their crimes stopped,' said Pemberton. 'And yet, by the very nature of their crimes, they evade detection. It's an odd sort of world they live in.'

And so the interview terminated inconclusively. Detective Sergeant Grant drove Dawlish back to the Royal Hotel and dropped him at the front door as Control alerted the observation teams. Dawlish did not contact his former dinner date; instead, he took a table in the hotel restaurant and had a long, leisurely meal helped down with a bottle of claret. Two detectives occupied a nearby table.

When Sergeant Grant returned quarter of an hour later, Pemberton said, 'Sarge, the incident room is closed and the others have all gone home. Allow me to treat you to a meal. I'm taking

Lorraine to a cosy place I know – I rang them while you were out and a table for three is available. Or does this conflict with your domestic arrangements? I'd like us to have a chat and to do so over a meal seems a good idea.'

'I'd love to sir, thanks. And it doesn't conflict with my domestic arrangements, my wife's gone to her sister's this evening.'

Half an hour later, having discarded his recording machine, Pemberton was ordering pre-dinner drinks in the Fisherman's Net, a dark bistro in the cellar of a former store.

It had been decorated with oars, fishing nets, floats, stuffed sea fish, lobster shells and sea urchins and although it specialised in fish dishes, other meals were available. They sipped their aperitifs, placed their order and prepared to enjoy it. In the background, music associated with the sea was playing while the clientele talked and laughed loudly; there was sufficient noise for Pemberton's voice not to be overheard.

'I hate talking shop on such occasions,' he began as the starters arrived. 'But I need to ask what you thought of Dawlish. John?'

Sergeant Grant shrugged his shoulders and began. 'He wasn't a great lot of help, he couldn't really say that Browning had killed the prostitutes. He really confirms all that we knew, not a lot more. Except the stained clothing. I could imagine a killer doing that, getting rid of the clothing as soon as he could.'

'Lorraine?' Pemberton turned to her.

'Apart from his description of the first murder, I found his contribution to our knowledge rather disappointing,' she said. 'As John says, he hasn't really added a great deal to what we already know about the Sandal Strangler. He says Browning was responsible, but there's an absence of real proof. You think he's guilty, don't you, Mark? Dawlish, I mean, you think he's the Strangler?' and she addressed him as Mark, knowing that Grant was well aware of the relationship.

'Yes, I do.' He was now firm in that belief. 'I think Dawlish killed all those women and I also think he's trying to place the blame entirely upon James Browning. Just think about what he's told us. He told us a good deal about the first murder – and that is understandable because he admits seeing the body – even though it was two in the morning and dark, and he never referred to having a torch. He said she'd been strangled – anyone

182

visiting the scene would know that – and the business about getting rid of the bloodstained clothing rang true, except that, in my opinion, it was Dawlish who was getting rid of it, not Browning. I think Dawlish is telling his story with the roles reversed . . . I think he got Browning to run him to the scenes and I think he did so so that Browning's car would be seen. I think he's set up Browning for these crimes; I think he's been framing Browning right from the outset, and now that he's dead, he can put the blame on his friend. I think the murders have come to an end now.'

'But what about the first murder, Mark?' Lorraine asked. 'According to Dawlish, he found Browning lying beside the strangled prostitute and took him away . . .'

'And what do you think Browning would have said about that, if he'd been alive to ask? I think he would have said he had no memory of what happened that night and, if he told the truth, he would have said he was roused by his friend, Dawlish, to find himself lying next to a murdered woman. They'd been on the booze all night, Browning was stoned out of his mind . . . and dead drunk or doped or something. How could he have committed murder and rape if he was drunk and incapable?'

'But he confessed to a murder, Mark. It would be that one, surely?'

'Yes, I think that's the one he confessed to. But I don't think he did it. I'm growing more certain that he never committed it. I think Dawlish killed and raped the Penthorne prostitute, and let Browning think he'd done so . . . as he has done ever since. I think Browning was innocent of that killing, and innocent of all the others. It could explain why he did not strike up a relationship with a woman afterwards – he daren't, in case he killed again without realising he was doing so . . . and it could explain his wish to do good works as a form of penance . . .'

'The poor man . . .' began Lorraine. 'To go through life thinking you were a murderer when you were not . . . how dreadful . . .'

'If it's true, it says a lot about the character of Dawlish, letting a friend – or to be more accurate, a stooge – carry the blame like that,' Pemberton reminded them. 'And can you imagine what a relief it would be if he could convince us that Browning had committed all the murders? It would get him off the hook completely – he'd have to stop his killings of course, but he might do

183

that, or begin a new series. He's lying too, but how can we prove that? Or prove any of my theories?'

'We haven't had the results of the DNA tests yet,' Grant reminded him. 'That should help a lot.'

'They could take a week or even two. We need corroborative evidence if we're to get this series of murders laid at the door of our Mr Dawlish,' Pemberton said.

'You have never mentioned the blue sandals,' said Lorraine.

'I think he planted those upon Browning, quite deliberately – he left them in the car he sold so that, if Browning was ever questioned, he'd have one hell of a job explaining where they had come from. And Dawlish could deny ever seeing them. And he left a piece of rope in the car he sold to his friend . . .'

'Sir,' Grant frowned, 'you're saying Dawlish has been slipping clues into Browning's possession throughout all these killings?'

'I think he has. I think he's been quietly framing his unsuspecting friend. Maybe we should take another look at Browning's belongings, but thank God he was so meticulous in his record and diary-keeping. I think he suspected Dawlish of setting him up for the first murder – and I think it was Browning who anonymously rang the police to report that body. But think, both of you. Would Browning have known about the other killings? He lived in Harlow Spa, and he always returned there on the Sunday evening following the motor rallies. We know the murders did not gain national coverage in the press, so if the bodies were not discovered until after Sunday, it's probable that Browning never knew that any other murders had been committed. So when the blue sandals were left in his possession, their significance would not have been apparent to him.'

'The people at Browning's office teased him about being near the scene of one of the murders,' Lorraine reminded him. 'A girl had seen a paper from the locality while visiting relatives.'

'So if Browning linked it to his own visit, would he think he'd committed that murder too?' Pemberton put to them. 'Would he believe he was committing murders without realising it? Or might it plant a tiny seed of suspicion in his mind about Dawlish? Or would it mean nothing, I wonder?'

'I don't think he would mention it to Dawlish,' said Lorraine.

'Or to a priest?' questioned Pemberton.

'Sir,' said Grant, 'if Browning was unaware of the continuing murders because they'd never been reported in the papers where he lived, the same would apply to Dawlish, surely? If Browning had committed them, Dawlish would not know. And yet he has described them to us – even down to the dates and places. He knew the murders had happened, he knew when, how and where. How could he know about them if they'd not been publicised nationally? In all cases, he and Browning were back home before the bodies were discovered. The only way he would know about the murders would be if he'd committed them.'

'Exactly!' smiled Pemberton. 'By pretending he knows so little, he's shown he knows far too much!'

'Shall we bring him in?'

'No, let him stew until tomorrow. He's bound to be worried about just what and how much we know, and he is being carefully watched. If he makes any attempt to leave the hotel, I've asked that he be brought in for questioning – after all, he was the last person to see Debbie Hall alive, and we haven't tackled him about that. I want to sleep on this one. He'll never admit the murders, I'm sure, unless we can trap him or disorientate him. He thinks he's fooling us, he wants us to believe Browning is guilty and to record the murders against him; I want him to continue thinking that for the time being. Anyway, those are my thoughts. Our duty is to nail him, to secure enough evidence to have him convicted, not merely enough to confirm our suspicions.'

'I am looking forward to tomorrow!' smiled Grant. 'And I hope you sleep well on it!'

'I think I shall,' said Pemberton, raising his hand to order another bottle of wine.

22

Shortly after he arrived at the incident room on that warm and bright Sunday morning, Pemberton rang the Royal Hotel and asked for Hugh Dawlish. The receptionist connected him with the room and Dawlish answered.

'Pemberton here, Mr Dawlish,' he began. 'I'd like another chat today if that's convenient.'

'Yes, of course. Shall I come to the police station?'

'If you would be so kind.' Having considered the facts overnight and devised a strategy for the introduction to this interview, Pemberton now felt in a position to go ahead.

'What's a convenient time?' asked Dawlish.

'Eleven o'clock?' Pemberton suggested.

'Yes, that would be fine.'

Pemberton next warned Lorraine and Sergeant Grant that he would like them to be present. On this occasion, the meeting would be in the interview room and it would be recorded on tape, but it would continue along the lines of the previous one: Dawlish would be told it was part of the elimination process and not the interview of a suspect.

'How are you going to tackle this one?' Lorraine asked him. 'We've no real evidence against him. Whatever we say, he's going to place the blame on Browning, isn't he? He's had more time to consider ways of doing that and Browning can't answer back. The crimes could still be attributed to Browning.'

'I'm going to abandon the head-on approach, I am not going to accuse him, not immediately. I'm going to surprise him by coming in from an oblique angle!'

'How?' she asked, interested.

'Let's wait and see,' was all he would say.

When Hugh Dawlish arrived, dressed in light slacks and a pale blue T-shirt, he was shown into the interview room where Pemberton had arranged for coffee to be available.

'Sit down,' Pemberton invited. 'It's good of you to come again. Now, you remember Detective Sergeant Grant and Detective Constable Cashmore?'

'Yes, I do. I'm pleased to be able to help, Mr Pemberton.'

'Have you any objection to this interview being recorded on tape, Mr Dawlish?'

'No, of course not. I have nothing to hide. But first, am I right in thinking this is a continuation of last night's discussion? I am not under arrest, am I?' In spite of an outward show of confidence, Dawlish did appear to be rather nervous.

Pemberton watched him fiddling with his watchstrap, something he had not done last night. A sign of nerves, tension. Clearly, he'd been worrying all night about his earlier interview and in spite of his belief that he had thrown clear suspicion on Browning, he was doubtless wondering how the police knew so much, how they knew he was in this hotel and how much they were keeping secret. That outcome was exactly what Pemberton had intended. He wanted to unsettle this man and had succeeded; it was a process which he intended to further.

'No, of course you're not under arrest. And yes, this is a continuation of our chat last night.' Pemberton went across to the recording unit in the corner and switched it on, giving his name and the name of the interviewee, along with the date and time of commencement. At Pemberton's assurance that he was not under arrest, there was an audible sigh from Dawlish and some visible relaxation as he settled into the chair and accepted a coffee from Lorraine. Pemberton took a cup too, stirred it and then commented upon the weather. It was a warm, sunny day, ideal for holidaymakers.

'The town gets very busy by lunch time on Sundays, even out of the holiday season,' he smiled. 'It's even worse in the summer, the school holidays make a huge difference to this place. July and August, they're the busiest. Kids and parents on the beach, in the amusement arcades, on the dodgems, riding on the ghost train . . . you know, I think the parents love coming here as much as the children do. I suppose it's a nice time for parents, a couple of weeks in the year when they can be kids themselves!'

'Yes, I'm sure that's true,' responded Dawlish with just a hint of puzzlement on his face.

'A good family life is very important to a growing child, don't you think, Mr Dawlish?'

'Yes, very. Very important,' and his frown deepened as he tried to understand the direction in which Pemberton's comments were heading.

'So tell me about your mother,' Pemberton invited with startling suddenness.

'My mother?' and Dawlish's face blackened. His astonishment and anger at the unexpected question was clear in the expression on his face. Of all the questions he had anticipated and the comments he had expected to hear, this was not among them.

'Yes, tell me about her,' Pemberton insisted.

'I fail to see what she has to do with this.' It was a weak response but the best he could produce at such short notice. 'She's dead, she can be no part of these enquiries, surely?'

'She was a prostitute, I believe.' Pemberton's voice was now harder, colder. 'And if my information is correct, she abandoned you as a child, you were taken into care and fostered. She died when you were – how old? Eleven? Twelve? Thirteen? Tell me.'

Dawlish did not respond; his gaze at the detective seated across the table now looked like one of hatred; the former friendliness and affability had gone. He did not reply or make any comment upon Pemberton's remarks, so Pemberton continued.

'I understand your birthday is on 24th June, midsummer day,' was Pemberton's next statement. 'We know that from James Browning's diary. It wasn't a very happy day for you, was it? Your birthday, I mean. Ever since you were a small boy. You had no parties, no real friends. Having been born to a prostitute and then reminded of it every year wasn't exactly the nicest thing to happen to a bright and intelligent child.'

Pemberton was watching his suspect now. He paused, waiting for the remarks to penetrate Dawlish's mind.

'Were you teased at school about your mother, Mr Dawlish? And when you were in care too? And what about birthday parties? Friends? I'll bet you had no real trustworthy friends, had you? How did you celebrate your birthday as a child? In your adult life, Mr Dawlish, you made sure you had somebody to share your birthday with, didn't you – James Browning. A faithful friend if ever there was one. But you never mention your birthday, do you? When you told me about the rallies and your reunions with James, they were always around your birthday, yet you did not tell me that. I would have thought a birthday celebration had some importance. And now, this very weekend, you are willing to pay for a prostitute to share a meal with you, to provide an outward show of having friends, Mr Dawlish, as you did at the Black Otter the night before last –'

'There's nothing illegal in paying someone for companionship, is there? And I never made a big thing of my birthday – well, would you?'

188

'Under those circumstances, I doubt it, Mr Dawlish. And your father? Who was he? I have no idea. Have you?'

'Look, I fail to see what any of this has to do with your investigation into James Browning and those murders –'

'You told us your mother had given you a car, for your eighteenth birthday. One of those vintage MGs. That was not true, was it?'

Dawlish paused, wondering how much this detective knew about him, and then spat, 'She never gave me anything, Mr Pemberton, nothing. No love, no warmth . . . but I had to tell people she was loving and so I said she gave me the car as a present. But I bought it for myself, Mr Pemberton. I made good, I did well, very well, considering my upbringing, or lack of it!'

'And your rape convictions, and your other offences? They happened when you were a juvenile, I admit, but nonetheless they were crimes . . .'

'Look, how much do you know about me, for God's sake?'

'Almost everything,' Pemberton told him coldly. 'I know you killed those prostitutes, Mr Dawlish, to celebrate, if that's the right word, the ignominy of your birth . . . in your mind, you were killing your mother, paying her back, every time you killed one of those girls. You used knots you'd learned in the Scouts. And every time, you kicked them in their private parts . . . kicking away your hatred. Your mother died when you were thirteen . . . and there are eleven prostitutes dead, one for every miserable year and with two more to come . . . but James's death has scuppered your plans. I think it was your way of celebrating your birthday, Mr Dawlish . . . Tell me, did she wear sandals?'

'Sandals? Who?'

'Your mother, when she was entertaining clients. You saw her, did you? When she was preparing for work?'

'Sandals? Why do you ask that?'

'Yes. Sandals, Mr Dawlish. In summer, women often wear sandals . . . prostitutes often wear sandals, Mr Dawlish . . .'

'It wasn't me . . . it was James, he took the sandals – look in his garage!'

'We have. We have found some sandals in his garage, Mr Dawlish, blue ones.'

'There you are then! He took them, he took them every time he killed a prostitute . . .'

'No, Mr Dawlish. Only the murderer knows that sandals were taken from the victims! Only the murderer, Mr Dawlish. You! The sandals were in your car, the one you sold to James. They were left there deliberately, I suggest, to frame James, to plant evidence on him should the police ever interview him. Or you. You would have pointed them towards James, wouldn't you? He told you about the sandals and you told him to keep them. Like the rope you left in the boot of the car you sold him. A length of white nylon rope. You did all that so you could frame him, Mr Dawlish, very subtly but almost effectively. And it almost worked, but not quite. He kept notes, you see, a diary, itemising every detail . . . and we have that diary. You were framing him for all those Sandal Stranglings, Mr Dawlish, just as you framed him for the first murder, in Durham. He did not kill that woman, Mr Dawlish, he was far too incapable at the time. You killed her, you killed her because of your mother, a mother you'd have been ashamed of if she'd come to the presentation of your diploma but she couldn't come because she was dead by then . . . You've hated your mother ever since you were a child, Mr Dawlish and you killed prostitutes because she was a prostitute, and you took away their sandals and underwear because she –'

'You can't prove any of this!'

'We can. We can now search your house and any property you own, Mr Dawlish. What shall we find, do you think? What do you think the forensic scientists will discover? And in addition, when you raped the girls, you didn't use a condom, Mr Dawlish. We have every one of the samples of semen you left behind. We can test them – and you – for DNA, Mr Dawlish. If the samples match, that's all the proof we need. You see, you told us all about the murders yesterday and yet they had not been publicised nationally – only the murderer could have known about them, and known some of the details you provided. James Browning did not know about them, did he? If he had, he would never have kept those sandals, Mr Dawlish, he'd have known where they had come from and he would never have telephoned you about them. He'd have got rid of them as if they were red hot . . . but James never knew you killed all those women, and he never knew you had framed him for murder all those years ago . . . How could you do such a thing to a man who thought he was your friend?'

'You said serial killers had a subconscious desire to be caught

190

and stopped, Mr Pemberton?' was his next, rather unexpected response.

'I did.'

And quite suddenly, he confessed. 'Yes, it was me. I framed James, I killed them all! You know it was me, I was going to do more as you said, another two, but James stopped me ... by dying, he stopped me. He never knew ... God, he never knew what I was doing but I couldn't stop. I wanted to ... stop, I mean. I wanted to be stopped ...' and he burst into tears, sobbing like a child as he said, 'She shouldn't have done it, Mr Pemberton, she was a dirty old cow, my mother! She would kick me out of the way, with those bloody sandals she always wore for her clients ... her trade mark ... what a bloody trade! My mother, for God's sake ... how could she?'

'Sergeant, arrest Mr Dawlish and prepare to take a statement from him,' said Pemberton. 'Then have DNA tests organised and arrange to have his premises thoroughly searched. We need to have all the evidence we can muster for this one.'

'Yes, sir,' said Sergeant Grant.

'Interview terminated at eleven twenty,' said Pemberton into the recording machine as Dawlish continued to sob with his head in his hands.

Before James Browning's Requiem Mass began on Monday, Mark Pemberton, accompanied by Lorraine, went into the vestry of the church and located Father Flynn.

'It's good of you to attend the Mass,' said Father Flynn.

'It's the least we can do,' said Pemberton. 'But before you preach your homily about James, I thought I ought to provide you with some information. It follows James's confession of murder, the part I overheard.'

'Yes, Mr Pemberton?'

'It's just that I have carried out a thorough investigation and I wanted you to know that James was not guilty of any murder. He was framed, Father, the real killer has admitted the crime and is now in custody pending a trial. For the whole of his life, James Browning truly thought he was guilty of murder.'

'Thank you, Mr Pemberton,' said Father Flynn. 'But you know I cannot comment on confessions ...'

'I know, Father.'

'If I cannot comment, perhaps Mr Browning senior would like to know what you discovered?' smiled Father Flynn. 'It would explain a lot about his son's past behaviour.'

'I'll tell him,' promised Detective Superintendent Pemberton.